"Hell's bells!"

She groaned. "What's amiss?"

Mark rubbed the sleep out of his eyes. "'Tis dawn," he began, glancing over to Belle. "You were supposed to—" He stared at her naked shoulders with growing shock. "God's teeth!" he bellowed. He leapt out of bed, the blood pounding against his temples. "Are you…naked under that?" She couldn't be! His heartbeat quickened at the speculation.

Belle lay back against her pillow, revealing a hint of the shadow between her breasts. Mark's breath came out in short gasps.

She folded her hands over her stomach. "Of course. What did you expect?" she replied.

God save me! Mark backed farther away, nearly stepping into the cooling ashes of last night's fire. *What did I do to her?* "What happened?"

Belle's pink lips puckered with annoyance. "Methought you would awake happier than this. After all, I gave you what you most desired…!"

Dear Reader,

In keeping with the season, this month's *Halloween Knight* features a bewitching heroine, a haunted castle and an inspired cat. Widow Belle Cavendish is being held by her evil brother-in-law, and it's up to a young knight and his companions to save the day. Maggie Award-winning author Tori Phillips is up to her old tricks with this delightful tale of rescue that culminates in a Halloween banquet full of surprises!

USA Today bestselling author Margaret Moore returns with her new Regency, *The Duke's Desire*—the story of reunited lovers who must suppress the flames of passion that threaten to destroy both their reputations. For Medieval fans, *Dryden's Bride* by Margo Maguire features a lively noblewoman en route to a convent who takes a detour when she falls in love with a noble knight. And for our Western readers, Liz Ireland's *Trouble in Paradise*, with a pregnant heroine and a bachelor hero, is out there waiting for you to pick up and enjoy.

Whatever your taste in historicals, look for all four Harlequin Historicals at your nearby book outlet.

Sincerely,

Tracy Farrell
Senior Editor

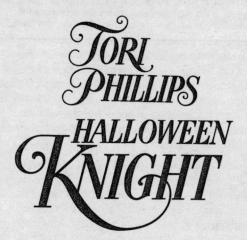

TORI PHILLIPS

HALLOWEEN KNIGHT

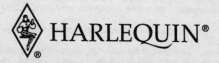

HARLEQUIN®

TORONTO • NEW YORK • LONDON
AMSTERDAM • PARIS • SYDNEY • HAMBURG
STOCKHOLM • ATHENS • TOKYO • MILAN • MADRID
PRAGUE • WARSAW • BUDAPEST • AUCKLAND

ISBN 0-373-29127-2

HALLOWEEN KNIGHT

Copyright © 2000 by Mary W. Schaller

Available from Harlequin Historicals and
TORI PHILLIPS

Fool's Paradise #307
*Silent Knight #343
*Midsummer's Knight #415
*Three Dog Knight #438
*Lady of the Knight #476
*Halloween Knight #527

*The Cavendish Chronicles

Please address questions and book requests to:
Harlequin Reader Service
U.S.: 3010 Walden Ave., P.O. Box 1325, Buffalo, NY 14269
Canadian: P.O. Box 609, Fort Erie, Ont. L2A 5X3

To five young heroines-in-training,
Rachel, Ashley & Katrina Bigelow;
Alyssia & Gillian Eiserman;
with love from
their godmother.

The time when screech owls cry, ban dogs howl and spirits walk.

—Henry VI Part 2

Chapter One

Wolf Hall, Northumberland, England
Late September 1542

"You come none too soon, Mark." The bed ropes creaked as Sir Brandon Cavendish shifted his weight. He did not bother to mask his grimace of pain from his former squire.

Sir Mark Hayward, lately returned from Ireland after a fruitless seven years seeking riches and honor in His Majesty's service, offered his arm to his bedridden mentor. "Your message smacked of urgency, my lord. I rode posthaste from London. Thank God the roads were dry." He eased Brandon nearer to the bedside table. "Am I to avenge you against the blackguard who broke your hip?" he asked with a grin.

Brandon lay back against a flock of bolsters and closed his eyes for a moment. "Belle's in trouble," he announced without a preamble. "At least, methinks she is."

Mark groaned inwardly. He had known Brandon's natural daughter ever since the little minx first appeared at Wolf Hall dressed in a ragged infant's gown. LaBelle Marie Cavendish attracted disasters like honey drew bears.

"'Tis an old tale twice-told, my lord," he muttered. He sipped his mulled cider to steady his nerves. "Methought Belle was married a few years ago. Her troubles should be her husband's now." *Poor sot!*

Opening his eyes, Brandon leveled an icy blue glare at the younger man. "She was. The boy's dead. Thereby hangs the reason for her present distress."

Mark squelched his impulse to ask if Belle had driven her late spouse into his early grave. Instead he took another drink of cider while his heart beat faster.

Brandon emptied his own mug before he continued. "Cuthbert Fletcher was never my idea of a husband for Belle. The boy was a weakling, though pretty in his features. Belle took one look at that milksop—God rest his soul—and declared that she must have him as a husband or else she would die. Nearly drove me stark mad with her artful wheedling."

Mark snorted in his cup. *Comes from spoiling her rotten since the age of two.* "But you allowed the match," he observed aloud.

When Mark had heard of Belle's nuptials four months after the event, he had toasted the health of her luckless bridegroom in Irish whiskey. He had never gotten so drunk in his life as he did on that rainy night.

Brandon gave him a meaningful look. "Because Cuthbert would take her, despite her...background." He cleared his throat. "None of the young noblemen looked twice at my Belle once they learned she was born of a French commoner on the wrong side of my blanket. Belle was the fairest maid at Great Harry's court when we took her there two years ago, yet not one of those strutting peacocks would stoop to woo her—except that whey-faced Cuthbert—the son of a wool-merchant.''

Mark tightened his grip around his mug at the thought of pretty Belle being snubbed by a gaggle of flap-mouthed galliwags dressed in satin. The lass had more spirit in her little finger than most men possessed in their bodies—and that was usually the trouble with the headstrong vixen. He massaged his forearm where it had broken eight years ago—the last time he had seen Belle.

"Most men never bother to look beyond their own noses," he remarked. A trickle of sweat rolled down the back of his neck despite the coolness of the twilight's air. "So Cuthbert died?" he prodded.

"Aye," Brandon growled. "Of a fever this past June. Belle wrote us a heartbroken letter."

Mark blinked. "She doesn't live nearby?"

Brandon attempted to pour himself more cider from the pitcher but splashed most of it on his nightshirt. After swearing under his breath, he replied, "Nay. My good Kat gave Bodiam Castle to the newlyweds as Belle's jointure estate. Belle is still in Sussex."

Mark's eyes widened. "A most generous gift from your lady wife," he murmured.

He remembered Bodiam well. Nestled in the middle of Sussex's rich farming country, the castle's honey-colored walls had mellowed since it was first built in the fourteenth century. The moated fortress had turned into a comfortable home under the loving care of Brandon's wife, Lady Katherine. Now the estate reaped a huge annual profit from its diverse crops. A dart of jealousy skewered Mark.

As the fifth son of a middling nobleman, he had inherited nothing from his father except a good family name. Nor had Mark gained any land of his own in Ireland as he had expected, despite the blood, sweat and tears he had poured into that contentious sod. No wonder Cuthbert had been eager to marry Belle! Mark himself would have married a hag witch for such a prize as Bodiam.

Brandon frowned into his half-filled mug. "Cuthbert's brother and sister were with Belle when her husband died. In July, she wrote that they were still at Bodiam to keep her company. Then…nothing. I sent her a letter in August but received no answer. Belle may have her faults, but she has always been an excellent correspondent."

Mark raised an eyebrow at this revelation. *That brat never sent me one word of contrition for nearly destroying my sword arm. Not one jot or tittle of remorse!*

Brandon continued, "Kat and I worried about her unusual silence, but we thought she was busy with the onerous tasks of managing the estate. Or that she was still overwhelmed by her grief."

Mark drained his cider. Belle—someone's wife! He vividly remembered her on the cusp of womanhood when she was thirteen. The thought of her lying…in bed…her long blond hair streaming on a burgundy coverlet…beckoning…naked…

"More?" Brandon shattered Mark's increasingly lusty daydream.

"What?"

"More cider?" Brandon waggled the pitcher.

Mark nodded and served both himself and his former master as he had so often done in days of yore.

Brandon furrowed his brow. "I intended to visit Belle as soon as the king's Michaelmas tournament was concluded. I did not dare to miss that event. Great Harry has not been himself these days after the execution of his latest wife. Poor little Catherine Howard!" Brandon shook his head, then frowned. "Indeed, the king's temper has grown as monstrous as his body."

Mark gasped. "Soft, my lord. Your words hover close to treason. These walls could harbor unfriendly ears."

The young knight had just come from Henry's court where the nobility of England cowered in Westminster's drafty galleries while they waited for the next horrific eruption from their erratic sovereign. Mark had been very thankful to receive Brandon's urgent summons away from that royal hellhole.

Brandon waved aside any disloyalty. He glowered at his lower body that was trussed in splints and miles of tight bandages. "Then this devilish thing happened. A simple jousting practice with my brother in our own tiltyard! My new charger stumbled on a pass and fell—pinioned me under him. The horse is a beauty, but marvelously heavy."

Mark eyed the bandaging and shuddered inwardly. "Your angel must have been riding on your shoulder. I've known men to die that way."

Brandon chuckled wryly. "You sound like Kat." His brief smile dissolved. "But to the point. I have lain here for nearly a month, bedridden worse than my aged father on his 'creaking' days. Then a fortnight ago, I received this." He plucked a wrinkled paper from the side table and held it out to Mark. "Tis from Montjoy. Do you remember that old badger?"

Nodding, Mark took the letter. "He still lives?" he asked, picturing the ancient steward of Bodiam, now supposedly in quiet retirement. The man must be nearly a hundred years old. Mark scanned the short note. "He writes with a cleric's hand. His letters are clear."

"What do you make of his message?" Brandon growled.

"'*A black cloud has shrouded Bodiam Castle,*'" Mark

read aloud. *"'All loyal retainers have been dismissed. Visitors are sent away. Last evening, a village lad spied Mistress Belle high in one of the towers. She begged him to send for her father. Then the boy was chased from the home park by several armed men. Come quickly, my Lord Cavendish. Methinks your daughter is in great peril. Montjoy.'"*

"I am a man on the rack, Mark," Brandon said hoarsely. "My Belle needs me and I cannot move from this dankish bed!" He slammed his fist into one of the bolsters. It exploded in a geyser of goose feathers. The two men stared at the fluttering down that filled the small bedchamber. "Kat will boil my brains for supper," Brandon mumbled morosely. "Tis the fifth pillow I have destroyed since Montjoy's letter arrived."

Mark's mouth went dry. To the best of his knowledge, Belle had never begged for anything in her life. Bargained, demanded, schemed and coerced—but never begged.

"Mayhap Montjoy exaggerates. Twas always his fashion to look on the dark side of life," Mark suggested, though a certain unease seeped through him.

Brandon curled his lip. "Aye, I know well his melancholy humors, yet this letter smacks of plain truth. The old man would not have sent it over three hundred miles simply to amuse himself. There is only one remedy for it. You must go to Bodiam in my stead."

Even though he was prepared for this request, Mark shrank from it. The old break in his arm actually ached at the thought of meeting Belle again, no matter how dire her current predicament might be.

"Surely Sir Guy would be a better choice," Mark hedged. "As your brother and a man of mature years and wisdom, he would—"

"Crows and daws, boy!" Brandon snapped, reverting

to the master Mark had served for nearly fourteen years. "Did you ride your horse blindfolded as you approached Wolf Hall? The harvest is in full swing. Guy must be here, there and everywhere at once to oversee our lands as well as his own since I am bound to this bed like a trussed hen."

Pausing, he gulped down his cider. "Nor does my good sire know a breath of this tale and twill be your hide on my wall if he does. My father still thinks of himself as a young man of four-and-twenty years when the truth of the matter is that he is nearly seventy. Daily he wages a losing battle with stiff joints and failing eyesight. Still, these infirmities would not stop him from riding south to Bodiam if he thought his beloved granddaughter was in danger." Brandon shook his head. "My lady mother would never forgive me if Papa went on that fool's errand."

Mark gave him a wry grin. "But I am just the fool you can send?"

His mentor's gaze bore into him. "Aye, there is no one else. Francis is in Paris, studying law and philosophy at the University. It appears he is more skilled with books and quill pens than with a sword and buckler."

Remembering the serious young man who was Brandon's other youthful byblow, Mark nodded. He rubbed his forearm again.

Brandon narrowed his eyes. "I know you and Belle have had your disagreements in the past," he began.

"Ha!" Mark gave him a rueful grin. "From the time she could wield a stick or fire an insult, she has used me as her personal quintain. I would much rather train wild cats to dance a galliard on their hind legs."

Brandon flexed his fingers. "She has grown into a winsome young lady since you left to fight the Irish."

Mark snorted. "And pigs fly on golden wings round yon battlement, my lord."

Brandon gave him a wintry smile. "How did you fare in Ireland? Did you make your fortune as you swore you would? After seven years, are you now the lord of a vast Irish estate?"

Avoiding Brandon's gaze, Mark stared out the narrow lancet window into the setting sun. "You know full well I am not, my lord. I was fortunate to escape the isle with a few items of clothing and my horse," he replied in a barely audible voice. "My only wealth is a peck of experience."

Brandon leaned forward. "What would you say if I gave you a goodly parcel of land east of Wolf Hall—one that was fertile ground and well-watered?"

In the face of such an offer, Mark's objections melted. He could almost smell the rich loam of those tempting fields. He wet his lips with his tongue. "And the price for this bounty is a trip to Bodiam Castle, my lord?"

Brandon flashed him a wolfish grin. "You were always a clever lad, Mark. Bring my Belle home safe and sound, and a thousand acres are yours."

Enough to buy me a wife and a manor of my own! "For such a prize, I would ride into the mouth of hell, my lord."

"You may very well do that, lad, if Montjoy's report is true."

Mark brushed aside the old steward's dire message. He was more concerned what Belle would do to him once she had learned of the outrageous price her father had paid to Mark for her return to the bosom of her family. "Have no fear for me, my lord. Jobe and I will leave tomorrow at first light. You will have the gentle LaBelle nestled in your inglenook by this time next month."

Brandon shot him a quizzical glance. "Who or what is Jobe?"

Mark chuckled. "Both my shadow and my guardian angel. You shall meet him anon."

Bodiam Castle, Sussex

As the last pale ray of the cloud-cloaked sun faded in the west, Belle heard Mortimer Fletcher's heavy key scrape the lock of her prison door. Drawing in a deep breath for strength and courage, she struggled to her feet to face her brother-in-law and jailer. A wave of giddiness assailed her. She pressed her back against the chill stone wall to steady herself until the weakness passed.

Her stomach growled for the food she knew that he carried. She could smell the succulent aroma of roasted chicken even through the thick oak panels of the door. She took another deep breath. The door swung open with a protesting squeal. A small smile of satisfaction flitted across her lips as she watched the old hinge wobble in its mooring. She had spent many days picking at the mortar with her bodkin.

Mortimer, dressed in a clean linen shirt peeking out from under a fine scarlet velvet doublet, stepped into the tower garret. He balanced a cloth-covered trencher in one hand while he gripped a lighted candle in a brass holder with the other. The key to her freedom protruded from the lock. The flickering golden light sharpened Mortimer's facial features. The man reminded Belle of a stoat.

"Good evening, mistress." He smiled in a viperish manner. "Hungry yet?" He brought the candle closer to the trencher. "Sick of bread crusts?"

Against her will, Belle's mouth watered. She knotted her hand into a fist behind her back. "I prefer to dine on toadstools and bat wings than to touch anything your cook might prepare,'' she answered as tartly as she could.

Anger flashed across Mortimer's face before he concealed it behind another false smile. "Take care what you wish for, mistress. Inside of a week you will beg me for exactly that loathsome nourishment."

He set the candle on the floor, then lifted the cloth. Belle saw not only half a juicy capon glistening in a red-currant sauce, but a small loaf of fine-milled white bread and a dish of apples stewed in precious cinnamon—cinnamon from her spice chest no doubt! The sight of the tempting supper made her feel fainter. Biting her lower lip, she turned away.

Mortimer drew a little closer to her, but she noticed that he did not make the mistake of swaggering within the range of her fingernails as he had done on the first day he had locked her in this windy eyrie. As if she still had the strength to scratch out his eyes! *He must not realize how weak I am.*

"Come, sister, let us be friends again," he coaxed in a syrupy voice that sickened her soul.

"I am not your sister, thank the good Lord!" she retorted as she backed away from him. The moldy straw of her bedding rustled underfoot.

Mortimer clicked his tongue against his teeth. "This conceit of yours does you no good, Belle. Indeed, you are pale and wan." He snickered at his own little jest. "You know Cuthbert was the dearest brother to me."

Belle knotted her fist tighter to keep from screaming. "Is that why you danced so high upon his fresh-turned grave! Ha! He often told me how his siblings plagued him during his childhood—you especially."

"Twas all in good sport, I assure you," Mortimer replied in an oily manner. "But soft, your food grows cold."

She glared at him in the gathering twilight. "My heart grows even colder at the sight of you—and your food. I know how you expect me to pay for my supper."

His black brows drew together in an angry knot. He set down the trencher near the open door and lifted a pot of ink from behind the bread. He pulled a folded paper from his doublet. "A mere dip of the pen. A few lines to scribble and all shall be joy between us as before," he said in a sing-song voice. He ventured to take a step closer to her.

Belle leaned her head back against the wall and closed her eyes. "You don't even know the meaning of those words, dull worm," she whispered under her breath. "You were born on a dunghill."

Mortimer cocked his head. "How now? I did not hear that."

She sighed. "Methinks you should bathe more often, Mortimer, for your ears are full of wax. Go away! I am not in a writing mood today or tomorrow or ever." She unleashed a torrent of her pent-up anger upon him. "I will not now, nor ever sign away Bodiam Castle to you. Come rack or ruin to us both. I will see you in hell first!"

Mortimer backed up. His hand shook as he made a sign against a witch's evil eye. "Hold your tongue, woman! Think whose dreadful name you invoke. They say the devil has his eyes and ears everywhere." He glanced over his shoulder at the black stairwell behind him as if he half-expected a satanic visitor to ascend the worn steps. "Spit on your palm and say a prayer lest you be damned."

A small laugh crackled from Belle's dry throat. "Look who calls the kettle black! Scuttle away to your beetle hole, Mortimer. Your presence offends my nostrils."

The thin man drew himself up. "I have bathed today, mistress. You, alas, have not done so in a fortnight. Tis you, not I, who offends."

Belle turned away from him. "Then begone and take your foul paper with you."

"You are a fool," he sneered. He turned on his heel and bent to pick up the trencher and candle. "God shield me!" he bleated.

Belle stared at him in the dim light and wondered if he had been bitten by a mouse. He touched the trencher with the toe of his suede slipper.

"What's amiss?" she asked.

"Bewitched!" he gibbered. "The capon has disappeared!" He pointed at the empty place on the trencher.

Belle rejoiced inwardly. *Oh, sweet, cunning Dexter!* Aloud, she remarked. "Mayhap the rats bore it away for a feast. The Bodiam rodents grow quite large, you know. Or…" She allowed a small pause while Mortimer twitched like a fish on a hook. "Mayhap twas the ghost that haunts this tower."

Mortimer turned as white as Belle's fictional specter. "What spirit? Where?"

She savored her only effective weapon against her brother-in-law. Like her late husband, both Mortimer and his puling sister were deeply superstitious.

"They say tis the ghost of the ancient knight who built this castle on the blood of innocents. Now he walks its galleries as a penance for his sins."

Mortimer shuddered.

Belle hid her smile of triumph. "And they say he guards the family who abides here in peace but woe to those strangers who break Bodiam's good cheer."

Mortimer snatched up the trencher and candle, then backed out of the chamber. "Tis you who have angered this unhappy spirit, not I!" He slammed the door behind him and rattled the key in the rusted lock. "Look to yourself, mistress!"

With another wail, he clattered down the stairs.

Belle sank to the floor. In the darkness, she listened intently for some tell-tale sound. "Dexter!" she whispered. "Dex-ter!"

A large round form filled the tiny window. Then it jumped and landed squarely on Belle's lap. She stroked the creature's sleek fur as it pawed and kneaded a bed to its liking among the folds of her bedraggled skirt.

"Have you something for me, you artful thief?" she asked, tickling its pointed ears.

In answer, Dexter dropped the capon in her open hand. He rubbed his cheek against her arm as she greedily devoured his sticky offering.

"Oh, you are a love!" she sighed afterward while Dexter industriously licked her fingers clean of the drippings. "How well you were named, for you are my only friend in this reeky place. You are truly my right-hand cat!"

Chapter Two

Jobe slowed his horse to a walk. Puzzled, Mark reined in beside the huge African. "How now, friend? We will burn precious daylight if we tarry. The road is still dry. We can make another five miles if we press on."

Jobe stared straight ahead. "We are followed, *meu amigo.*"

Mark did not glance over his shoulder but the hairs on the back of his neck stiffened. Ruffians made travel more dangerous these days, ever since King Henry had closed the monasteries and returned the beggars to England's highways. He fingered his dagger in its sheath. "Where away?" he asked under his breath.

Jobe unbuttoned his brown leather jerkin so that he could easily reach his wicked arsenal of small throwing knives. "He rides to our left but stays well back. He has been with us since midday."

Mark wet his lips. When he had sailed away from Ireland's rocky shore, he thought he had left behind such brigands as this. "Mayhap tis a traveler on a similar route. The London post road is well-used."

Jobe rumbled his disagreement in the back of his throat.

"Stop your horse and pretend to check his hoof for a stone. I wager that our shadow will halt as well."

"Done," Mark murmured, then he spoke in a louder tone. "Ho! Methinks my horse has caught a pebble!" He alighted smoothly, looking behind him as he did so. He saw someone turn off the track and disappear into a small copse of trees. He patted Artemis's neck before he remounted.

Jobe cast him a half-smile. "And so?"

Mark gathered his reins in his hand and kneed his horse into a trot. "Aye, but the knave ducked for cover before I could spy his face."

Jobe smiled, displaying startlingly white teeth against his ebony skin. "*Bem!* Tis good! I long for some good sport."

Mark frowned at his companion's enthusiasm. "Let us not act in haste, Jobe. He may have henchmen."

"More better!" the giant answered with relish.

Mark pulled his bonnet lower over his forehead. "The road turns to the left below that rise. Let us continue at our present pace. At the bend we will fly like the wind."

"And not fight?" Jobe snorted his disappointment.

Narrowing his eyes, Mark squinted at the late afternoon sun. "If our tail is still with us by nightfall, we will... persuade him to sup with us."

Jobe beamed. "More better!"

Three hours later, Mark and Jobe sought their night's shelter under the spreading boughs of an oak, its leaves decked in autumn's red and gold. Mark hoped the mysterious rider had left them.

Jobe chuckled. "He is a sly one," he said as he unsaddled his large bay.

Mark wondered why a lone robber would bother to pace

them all day. Jobe and he traveled lightly and in plain attire. The most costly things that the men owned were their weapons.

"Build up a large fire to draw his attention," he told his friend. "Meanwhile I will circle around and catch him from behind."

Jobe shook his head. "Most unwise, *meu amigo.*"

Mark frowned at him. "How so?"

The African lightly cuffed Mark's chin. "That white face of yours will shine out in the night like a second moon. Our shadow would have to be blind not to see you coming. On the other hand, I become one with the night. Besides, your life is my concern."

Mark swore under his breath. "I can fend for myself."

Jobe chuckled. "Aye, with me at your right hand." He threw off the long cape he wore. His bandoliers of knives and his copper bracelets shimmered in the faint starlight. "Build up the fire and prepare for a roast."

Mark grabbed his friend by the arm before the giant could melt into the darkness. "Do not kill the knave. England is a civilized country and twill annoy the Sheriff of Yorkshire if we leave a dead body on his highway. Bring back our guest while he still breathes."

Jobe thumped him on the shoulder. "As you say," he whispered. "Though killing is easier," he added before he disappeared.

Mark stared into the darkness and tried to follow Jobe's route, but he gave up. It seemed that the huge man had disappeared into thin air. After gathering a large armful of windfall kindling, Mark soon had a fire roaring. He unsheathed his dagger and sword, laying them close at hand while he tended the blaze.

The minutes crept by with no sound down the road. Mark stepped out of the circle of firelight, and backed up against the broad trunk of the tree. He held his sword lightly in his hand. His left forearm always ached in tense moments like this. It reminded him of Belle and the reason why he was skulking around a dark countryside instead of warming his bottom by a hearth in Wolf Hall. Gritting his teeth, he made himself think of the green pastures Brandon had promised him.

Suddenly, a yelp ripped the cool night. Mark tightened his grip on his sword and snatched up his dagger in his right hand. More yowls and snarls signaled Jobe's success. In the light of the half moon, Mark saw his friend heft a flailing body over one of his massive shoulders. The African laughed with genuine pleasure that drowned out the fearsome oaths his slim prisoner screamed in his ear.

Mark relaxed his stance. "What have you caught for supper, Jobe?" he asked in a bantering tone.

The giant dropped his burden on the ground, then held him down with a well-placed foot on his chest. "Tis nothing but a man-child, *meu amigo,* though he swears with a fearsome tongue."

The boy beat on Jobe's boot. "Let me go, you lob of the devil!"

Mark took a closer look at their prisoner, then burst out laughing. "Hoy day, Jobe! You *have* done well! Tis a worthy prize indeed!"

Jobe lifted one corner of his lip. "This little mouse? This flea?"

His taunt only incited the boy to greater oaths. "Let me up! I will show you what is a flea and what is not, you flap-eared varlet!"

Mark hunkered down beside the snarling captive. "Methinks you are a Cavendish by the look of you."

The boy went very still and turned a pair of bright blue eyes on Mark, who continued, "Indeed, Jobe, I am sure tis a member of that noble family—though he was absent from the supper table last evening. Perchance he was preparing his horse for today's outing.''

The boy said nothing but had the courage to return Mark's stare. Mark observed the boy's rapid pulse throb in his neck.

Standing, he sheathed his sword. ''Let him up, Jobe, but gently. Tis not seemly that the future Earl of Thornbury should grovel in the dust to the likes of us.''

With a rumbling chuckle, Jobe pulled the boy to his feet by the scruff of his jerkin. Then he stood behind his captive like some great bogle from a child's nightmare. He held the boy in place with a large hand on each shoulder.

Mark grinned. ''By the height that he inherits from his father and grandsire, and by the fire in his golden hair that bespeaks of his good mother, I say tis young Christopher Cavendish. By my troth, Jobe, I have not laid eyes on Lady Kat's Kitten since he was chewing on his teething coral.''

Christopher lifted his chin and shot Mark a look of disdain. ''I have not been called that puling name since I could walk. To my *friends* I am Kitt.''

The boy's inference was not lost on either of his captors. Mark gave him a warm smile. ''Then count us among your closest associates, good Kitt, for I have known your good family most of my lifetime, and Jobe is my boon companion.''

Kitt glanced up at the African. Then he ventured to touch the dark skin on the back of the man's hand. ''You are not painted?'' he asked in awe.

Laughing, Jobe shook his head. ''Only by the Lord God Almighty.''

''Tis a wonderment indeed,'' Kitt observed.

Mark crossed his arms over his chest. ''Tis even more

of a wonderment that you ride alone on the highway so
far from home.''

Before Kitt could answer, Jobe dropped to one knee and
reached for one of their saddlebags. ''Hold, *meu amigo*.
In my land, a good tale should always be accompanied by
food. Are you hungry, little warrior?''

Kitt shuffled his feet. ''I could partake of a bite or two,''
he replied with dignity.

Jobe grinned at Mark. ''Boys are the same in every
land,'' he observed.

Within the hour Kitt had consumed most of the provender that Lady Kat had packed for Mark and his companion. Relaxed by the food, some wine and the comfort-
ing warmth of the fire, the boy told a detailed story of his
preparations and escape from Wolf Hall—and his parents.

''I have come to help you save Belle,'' he concluded.

Mark searched the starry heavens for angelic guidance.
''This journey is not a social visit, Kitt. Your father thinks
there may be some danger.''

Kitt's eyes sparkled in the firelight though he managed
to maintain a serious expression. ''Good! I am prepared.''

I will throttle him! Aloud, Mark asked, ''How? You are
barely tall enough to swing a sword. Nay, tis impossible.''

Kitt swelled up like a young fighting cock. ''I can shoot
the eye out of a crow at a hundred paces with an arrow.
And I am a most marvelous horseman.''

Jobe nodded. ''In this he speaks the truth, *meu amigo*.
The boy has followed us in a most cunning manner all
day. Methinks you would not have noticed him until
now.''

Mark's vanity bristled at his friend's words. ''Why
now?'' he snapped.

The African's smile flashed in the firelight. ''Because
the young master would have told you he was hungry.''

Kitt gaped at him. "My plan to the very letter, but how did you guess?"

Jobe leaned closer and whispered, "Because I am a powerful jinn." He chuckled.

Kitt gulped and traced a hasty sign of the cross.

Mark glared at both of them. "Jobe is uncommonly wise, Kitt, but he is made of flesh and blood as we are. Now, my friend, I have need of your wise council. What are we going to do with the boy?"

Kitt gave Mark a steady look. "I am going with you to Bodiam, will you or nil you. Tis my duty as Belle's most able-bodied male relative—at the moment."

Stubborn like his father! Mark shook his head. "I applaud your courage, Kitt, but I cannot permit the deed. Your parents would hang me at the crossroads if any injury befell you." He sighed. "Blast you, boy! We shall lose three precious days to take you home and return again. Those three days might cost Belle a month of sorrow. Did you think of that?"

Kitt did not flinch as Mark had hoped he would. Instead the boy replied, "You would waste your time, my Lord Hayward. Unless Papa chains me to my cot, I will still follow after you." His expression softened. "Please, sir. Take me with you for I grow stale at Wolf Hall and I long to prove myself. My lady mother is…er… In truth, she would keep me wrapped in lambswool and placed in a strongbox if she could."

Mark tipped his wineskin to his mouth, took a long drink then asked. "How old are you now?"

"Eleven years since last March."

Mark pondered the boy's answer. He himself had been fostered to Kitt's grandfather and made Sir Brandon's page before he had turned eight. By the time Mark was Kitt's age, he had traveled to France, had lived at King Henry's court for several seasons, knew how to gamble at cards and had gotten drunk at least once. Considering Lady Kat's protective instincts toward her only chick, Mark strongly doubted that Kitt had experienced any of these adventures despite being the beloved son of such a champion as Sir Brandon Cavendish.

Jobe broke the silence. "In my land, you would have begun the rites of manhood by now, young master."

Kitt blinked. "What might those be?"

Jobe fingered one of the many knives that hung from his shoulder strap. "Once a boy has learned how to use his spear as well as his bow and arrows, and once he has learned to track game over many miles, tis time for his final test."

Kitt licked his lips like a puppy anticipating its supper. "What is this test?"

Jobe leaned closer. "His eyes are covered so that he will not know where he is taken. Then the senior warriors march him a day and a night into the wilderness."

Mark shuddered at the idea, but Kitt glowed with excitement.

Jobe continued, "Then they leave him alone with only his spear and his shield. The boy must track and kill a lion. He must skin it and drink its blood for its courage. Afterward, he must find his way back to his village with his prize. Then he is declared a man. He will keep the lion's pelt all the days of his life."

Swallowing, Mark decided that his long apprenticeship under Brandon's tutelage had not been so difficult after all.

Kitt's eyes grew larger. "And what if the lion wounds the boy or he gets lost while returning home?"

Jobe stared hard at him. "Then he dies."

Kitt licked his lips. "What of his poor mother?"

The African shrugged. "She is only a weak woman.

Women do nothing but weep or complain all the day long.
You will soon learn that for yourself.''

Kitt tossed his long hair out of his eyes. "My lady
mother was never weak.''

"Amen to that," Mark murmured under his breath. *I
would rather face a lion any day than an angry Lady Kat.*

Jobe nodded. "I see that, young master. You suckled
courage from a strong mother.''

Kitt squared his shoulders. "'Tis true. My family are the
bravest in all England." He turned again to Mark. "Do
you hear that, Lord Hayward? Even your wise counselor
says that I am ready to be a man. Let me go on this quest.
'Tis my right!'' he added pounding his fist on his knee.

Mark studied the boy's determined expression. Sighing,
he tossed away his last shred of common sense. "If we
are to ride together, I require three promises from you.''

Kitt could not contain the glee in his eyes nor in his
voice. "Anything, my lord! I will not fail you!''

Mark stood to emphasize his tenuous authority over this
half-grown lordling. "First, you will obey me and Jobe in
all matters, even if you disagree with them.''

"But what if—?" Kitt began.

Mark held up his hand for silence. "Attend to me, Kitt.
One day far in the future you will become the eleventh
Earl of Thornbury and the lord protector of England's bor-
der shire against the Scots. If you expect men to obey you
then, you must learn the virtue of obedience now. Your
noble father taught me that lesson when I was a good deal
younger than you.''

Kitt considered the point, then nodded. "Aye, my lord,
I will.''

"Second, until further notice, you will act as my squire.
Has anyone instructed you in the duties of one?''

The boy made a face. "Aye, Lord Hayward. I am not a complete fool. I agree to this condition. And your third?"

Mark stared down at him and wondered if he himself had ever looked so young and vulnerable. "Third, since we are to live together in close harmony, please call me Mark. 'Lord Hayward' sounds strange in my ear when spoken by your mouth."

Kitt grinned. "Aye, my lord…that is… Mark."

Mark resigned himself to the sure knowledge that his days were numbered when next he saw Lady Katherine Cavendish—or maybe sooner, when he met Belle. "So, my friends, to sleep. We ride hard on the morrow. Squire Kitt, prepare our beds and bank the fire."

The youngster practically fell over his feet in his haste to prove his worth.

Later, when the three lay close together under their blankets, Kitt whispered to Jobe, "Tell me about *your* lion."

The African chuckled, "Twas a leopard and my tale will make your hair stand on end. Tis best saved for the daylight hours."

"Oh!" Kitt burrowed deeper in his simple bedding.

Mark rolled onto his side and squeezed his eyes shut. *I have a very ticklish feeling about this enterprise.*

Griselda Fletcher plucked a raw pippin from the fruit bowl on the high table. She sliced and quartered it, then prized out the seeds from its core with the tip of her eating knife. She spread the pips on her empty trencher and began to count them.

"Tinker, tailor, soldier, sailor—"

Mortimer regarded her with open disgust. His sister was such a sheep! "What are you doing, wench?"

Glancing up, she frowned at him. "Seeking my future

husband since you have done nothing about finding one for me," she whined.

Mortimer clenched his teeth as his sister's high nasal voice grated on his nerves. "Hold your venom, chit," he snapped. "I am attempting to procure you a dowry or had you forgotten that one minor point?"

Griselda pulled her plain features into a sour pout. "Methinks you would have attained Belle's fortune long ago if you had just used a little more honey and less vinegar with her. Didn't I tell you—?"

Mortimer slammed his fist on the heavy table. The apple seeds jumped at the impact. "Silence! Your song grows tedious and its tune abuses my ears."

Griselda restored order among her fortune-telling pips. "Cuthbert said she was stubborn, remember? You should have let me—"

Mortimer abruptly stood. "I should have left you at home!"

The mewling woman continued, "Aye, where mayhap Father would have me wed by now. I am near six-and-twenty with no-o-o hus-husband!" She dissolved into gulping sobs.

Mortimer ignored her torrent of tears. "And you will never have a suitor if you insist upon weeping and wailing. A man does not find red eyes and a snotty nose the least bit attractive—and certainly not in his bed!"

"Oh!" Griselda shut her mouth.

Mortimer stalked over to the cheerful hearth and tossed another log on the fire. With a volley of crackles, red-orange sparks flew up the blackened chimney. He stared into the flames while he collected his thoughts. Fire had always soothed him, even from earliest childhood.

He held out his chilled fingers to the blaze. "Since the weather has turned colder, methinks Mistress Belle will soon become more. . . pliable.'' He sniggered through his nose.

Griselda furrowed her thick brows. ''But she is well enough, though sick in her mind, isn't she?'' she whimpered. ''You promised she would get better soon. You said that—''

Mortimer turned on her. ''I said that I would take the matter of Cuthbert's inheritance in hand and there's an end to it!''

His sister blew her nose in the tail of her dragging sleeve. ''By my troth, I do not know why you bothered to bring me with you, I surely do not,'' she moaned. ''All you do is rail at me the whole livelong day as if it was my fault that you cannot find that chest of jewels. You act as if it was my fault that—''

Mortimer crossed the distance between them in two quick strides. Without a word of warning, he slapped her smartly across her whining mouth. The sharp crack of the blow echoed down the length of Bodiam's empty hall.

''Take that for your faults that are beyond counting!'' he snarled at her. ''I rue the day I thought of you. Were it not for the tongue of scandal, I would have left you to snivel in your own chamber at home.''

''You s-said I was to b-be a g-good nurse for Cuthbert,'' she sobbed in her sleeve.

''Ha! What a jest! He died. Perchance twas your fault.'' He pushed his face closer to hers. ''Now heed me well, Griselda. Whisper one more word about any casket of jewels and I will flay you alive—with my bare hands!''

A dart of cunning flashed into Griselda's watery eyes. ''Not found it yet then?'' she murmured. ''Methinks that Belle was more clever than you expected. Methinks—''

Mortimer grabbed her by the shoulders and shook her until her headdress slipped off her greasy brown hair.

"Stop thinking at all!" he bellowed. "It addles your brain that, God knows, was never sound to begin with! Do nothing! Say nothing! And above all, think nothing! Now, go to your chamber and play with the rats. The sight of you makes my hand itch to strike you again!"

With a squeal of terror, Griselda scuttled toward the staircase. Mortimer swept the apple pips onto the floor and stalked out of the hall. He hated to admit that Griselda's jibe about the hidden jewels had struck too close to home. His mouth watered to think of the large ruby brooch. It lurked within some hidden spot in Bodiam just waiting for him to find it.

He clattered down the damp stairs to the underground storeroom where two of his most trusted minions systematically toiled at digging up every paving stone in the floor. *I will have my prize if I have to pull down every stone in this gorbellied castle to find it!*

Chapter Three

Early in the evening a week after the mismatched three-some had left Wolf Hall, Mark knocked on the door of a small cottage just off the village green of Hawkhurst. After a long wait, the door cracked open and Montjoy peeped around the corner. Mark gave the old man a wide grin.

"Salutations, Montjoy! Remember me?" he asked, hoping that the ancient steward had not gone soft in his wits.

Montjoy opened the door a little wider and held his glowing lantern higher so that the golden light fell upon all three of his visitors. He sniffed deeply. After a hard week of travel, Mark knew that they reeked like pigs in a wallow. He flashed Montjoy another encouraging grin.

The old man nodded with resignation as if he greeted Death on his doorstep. "Aye, Master Mark, I recall your imp's face though you have grown a bit since I last clapped an eye upon you. I presume that your beard now dents a razor on occasion?"

Mark rubbed the dark stubble on his jaw. "Aye, Montjoy. I fear I am not at my best appearance at the moment."

Montjoy raised the lantern to the highest extent of his arm and stared at Jobe. The African stood behind the other two with his muscular arms crossed over his massive chest. His copper bracelets, silver knives and a single golden hoop earring reflected the candle's light.

Before Mark could make the proper introductions, Montjoy sniffed again. "And I perceive that you now keep company with the devil. Tis no surprise. I predicted that you would dance down the road to perdition sooner or later. By the look of things, it appears to be sooner."

Kitt smothered a giggle.

Mark rolled his eyes. "Peace, old man. While tis true that Jobe comes from a hot climate, twas Africa not hell that was his birthplace. Now I call him my best friend. This..." He laid a hand on Kitt's shoulder, "...is my squire...ah...Bertrum."

At the last split second, Mark decided not to reveal the boy's true identity. Montjoy would surely fire a letter off to Wolf Hall within the hour if he realized that the precious Cavendish heir was embroiled in Belle's latest difficulty.

Kitt started to speak, but Mark squeezed the boy's shoulder to silence him. Casting him a sidelong glance, Kitt shut his mouth.

Mark cleared his throat. "We have been on horseback since dawn, Montjoy, and are weary beyond reckoning. Is Belle still in trouble or is that yesterday's news by now?"

At the mention of her name, Montjoy's expression grew even more mournful. "Tis serious business," he intoned, shaking his head. "Come in and I will impart all." He opened wide the door and ushered the three inside. He pressed himself against the wall as Jobe passed him.

Mark grinned when he saw a hot fire blazing in the hearth. The rising wind blew out of the north, bringing the sure promise of rain before midnight. "K...Bertrum, feed and water the horses. The stable is in the mews behind the house, as I recall. Then you may help with the supper preparations.''

Kitt blinked. Mark smiled inwardly. This was probably the first time the lad had ever been ordered to do a menial task for someone other than his family. High time, he thought. Kitt shot a longing glance at the fire before he ducked outside into the cold again.

Montjoy tapped the side of his nose. ''That one reminds me of someone though I cannot put my finger on it.'' Shaking his head, he shuffled to the draught chair close by the fireplace. There he eased his old body into his cushioned nest and wrapped a knitted lap rug around his spindle shanks.

''Ivy!'' he called, his voice surprisingly strong for one so frail-looking. ''A strop of ale for our guests!''

Mark unpinned his cloak and laid it over the bench by the door. Jobe followed his lead. Then the dark giant hunkered down in front of the fire's welcome warmth. A young maid, dimpling with the freshness of her youth, came into the front room carrying a platter with a jug and several mugs. Spying Jobe on the hearth, she screamed and nearly dropped the lot. Mark rescued the ale and attempted to soothe the trembling girl.

''Soft, pretty lass. Take no amiss. Jobe is as gentle as a kitten in a basket, especially to such a winsome creature as yourself.''

Ivy uttered no coherent words but merely gaped at the African. He returned her stare with a tooth-flashing smile. Burying her face in her hands, she fled into the back room.

''Hist!'' Montjoy threw Mark a look of stern disapproval. ''Ivy is a good girl and I'll not have you meddling with her virtue as you are wont to do with impressionable young things.''

Mark returned an innocent expression to the old man.

"Ah, Montjoy, you are wicked to recall my misspent youth!"

"Humph!" Montjoy poured himself a mug of ale and motioned to Jobe to help himself. "Let us attend to the business at hand. When will Sir Brandon arrive with his escort?"

In the act of swallowing the sweet Sussex brew, Mark choked at the question. He wiped the foam out of his eyes, caught his breath and replied, "My lord is not coming."

Montjoy sat up straighter. His old eyes glowed. "How now? Has Sir Brandon lost his sound wits? His own daughter is in the gravest of danger."

Sighing inwardly, Mark wondered again just how serious the matter was. Belle always had the habit of exaggerating her difficulties when things didn't proceed to her liking. "My lord is a-bed with a broken hip and every man at Wolf Hall is needed to bring in the harvest. Sir Brandon sent me in his stead."

Montjoy mumbled under his breath then asked, "How many accompanied you?"

Mark replied, "Myself, Jobe and my squire are at your service."

The steward's eyes bulged from his wrinkled face. "That is all? May the angels in heaven preserve Mistress Belle!"

"Jobe is worth ten men in any fight," Mark hastened to explain. He prayed that the old man would not suffer a seizure. "Trust me, I have seen him in the midst of a fray."

Montjoy passed a hand across his forehead as if he sought to wipe away a headache. "Fools, the lot of you! Aye, and your lord and master too."

"I am my own master now," Mark murmured into his mug. In a louder tone he asked, "Your message was most murky and full of your usual dire humor, Montjoy. Pray tell, what *exactly* has Belle done now?''

The ancient steward of Bodiam glared at him. "*She* has done nothing. Methinks the poor lass is being held prisoner against her will by that pustulous slug of a brother-in-law, Mortimer Fletcher.''

Mark lowered himself onto a three-legged stool that faced the steward's chair. The hairs on the back of his neck quivered at the sharp vehemence of Montjoy's words. "How now? Explain your tale and leave nothing out.''

Cradling his mug between his bony hands, Montjoy leaned forward. "For the first year of Mistress Belle's marriage to young Cuthbert Fletcher, all was well at Bodiam. True, she soon led the boy around by his nose but he seemed to enjoy it. The winter was hard here. Cuthbert grew pale and stayed within doors, though I saw Mistress Belle weekly when she brought me a basket of delicacies from her kitchens. She was ever kind to me and always inquired after the state of my poor health.''

Mark made a face. *She never showed me so much as a groat's worth of tender concern when I broke my arm on her account!* "Then Cuthbert died,'' he prodded.

"Aye, in June when the strawberries were at their peak. Fever—here one day and in his grave the next. Poor little Belle was grief-stricken. She loved the boy for all her willful ways.''

A twinge of jealousy wormed into Mark's heart. *What enticement did that puling milksop have to win Belle's love?* He cleared his throat. "And then? What of Mortimer?''

Montjoy sniffed deep with disgust. "Like ravens gathering over carrion, Cuthbert's brother and sister swooped down upon Bodiam a fortnight before the young husband's death. They must have packed their trunks the minute they received the news of his illness.''

Mark raised his brows. ''They came with many trunks?''

''A cartload of baggage!'' Montjoy snapped. ''Enough to last them a year and then some. Shortly after Cuthbert's untimely death things began to change.'' His voice assumed a hollow tone.

Out of the corner of his eye, Mark noticed Kitt creep into the room from the back door and slip into a dark corner. The boy stood as motionless as an alert deer. His blue eyes sparked with an indigo fire.

The old man took no notice of the squire. ''Belle came less often to visit me and when she did, she seemed quiet and withdrawn.''

Mark furrowed his brow. Belle had never been the least bit quiet except the one time she had been sick with some childish complaint. ''Had she caught Cuthbert's fever?''

She's dead! cried a banshee's voice in his brain. He felt as if he had swallowed a cold stone that now pressed against his very soul. *Please God, do not let it be that!*

''Is Belle sick?'' Kitt echoed from his corner.

Montjoy stared hard at the boy, then shook his head. ''Nay, though she would not say what was the matter except that she prayed her in-laws would soon remove themselves from her home. Then…when the wheat was ready for harvest, she stopped visiting me altogether.'' He sipped his ale then continued. ''At the same time, all the servants were dismissed.'' He snapped his fingers. ''Like that! Paid their wages and sent packing. Of course many of them came straightway to me.''

''And?'' Mark asked, keeping a wary eye on Kitt.

''They told a sorrowful tale of this Mortimer Fletcher. The man is the son of a London wool merchant! He knows nothing of administering such a large estate as Bodiam. The servants told me that he bullied Mistress Belle as well as his own sister.''

''I find that hard to believe,'' Mark countered. ''Obedience was never one of Belle's virtues.''

Montjoy allowed himself a slight shrug. ''I only report what I have heard. Once all the servants were gone, save for a lackwit potboy, Mortimer filled Bodiam with his own minions culled from the gutters and foul bogs, I warrant. Since mid-August, the castle has become a hive of scum and villains. No one goes there except to deliver supplies.''

Chills danced down Mark's spine. Belle's plight was considerably worse than he had imagined.

''And Belle?'' breathed Kitt with a tremor in his voice.

The old man cast him another appraising look before he answered. ''As I wrote to Sir Brandon: she has been seen in one of the towers.''

''Which one?'' Mark asked. Having lived at Bodiam for six years, he knew every nook and cranny in the castle.

''The northwest corner,'' Montjoy replied. ''One of the village boys spied her while he was fishing. She was in the garret chamber.''

Mark whistled. ''He had good eyesight to recognize her through that narrow window.''

The old steward nodded. ''She waved and called to him. He could only catch the words *my father* but twas enough, especially when Mortimer set a pack of varlets after the boy.''

Jobe suddenly came to life. ''Methinks twill be most excellent sport.'' He chuckled.

Montjoy gaped at him with open horror. ''Tis no afternoon's pleasure that I speak of but the life of a dear, sweet child. This Mortimer is sly and cunning.''

The African grunted. ''More better!''

The old steward drew himself up. "Attend to me, son of Satan! The man is a very snake. I myself ventured to knock at the gates. I demanded to see Mistress Belle. Do you know that he laughed in my face and threatened to have his minions toss me into the moat? I feel infinitely sorry for his wretched sister."

Mark cocked his head. Where there was a wench, there was a way. A plan began to form in his mind. "Tell me about Mistress Fletcher."

"Ivy!" Montjoy called. The girl appeared at the doorway but refused to cross the threshold.

"Aye, sir?" she asked. She did not take her eyes off Jobe.

"Ivy was a chambermaid at Bodiam in happier times," Montjoy explained to Mark. "Tell them about Griselda, child."

Ivy made a face. "She is like a sour dishcloth. Limp and always complaining."

Mark crossed to her side. Gently he put his arm around the maid and lifted her chin so that she was forced to look into his eyes. "Tell me, pretty Ivy," he said in his most seductive tone. "Is Mistress Griselda comely?"

Ivy relaxed in his loose embrace and smiled at him. "I would not venture to say so, my lord," she said with a giggle. "She is thin like an eel, has the voice of a jay and the face of a horse."

Mark caressed Ivy's little chin. "And is this paragon of beauty betrothed to some fortunate suitor?"

Ivy giggled again. "Her? Nay, my lord, and there is the nut and core of her unhappiness. She is desperate for a husband. At night, she shuts herself up in her chamber and whispers spells to conjure up one. Twas enough to give me the shakes."

Mark drew the maid a little closer to him. "Fear not, sweet soul," he murmured.

Montjoy rapped his knuckles on the arm of his chair. "Hear now, Mark! None of that! Release the child. She is not for your pleasure. Ivy! Fetch supper at once!"

With a chuckle, Mark stepped away from the smitten creature. His vanity enjoyed the momentary conquest. Though Ivy was far too young and innocent for his taste, she reminded his body that he had not been with a woman since he had left the king's court. "Peace, Montjoy! Your girl is safe from me."

The old man sniffed with disapproval. "I have never known any maid who was safe from your devilish charms."

Except Belle. Mark rounded on Kitt who plainly was much taken with the winsome Ivy. "You! Squire! Do not stand there like a dead tree. Help serve our food for we are famished. And mind you—do not practice your lecherous wiles upon little Ivy."

"But . . .but I never intended—" Kitt stammered.

Mark waved him out of the room. "Begone!" Then he smiled at Montjoy and Jobe. "I have thought of a most rare plan. LaBelle Cavendish will be free from her tower within the next twenty-four hours."

And those thousand acres are practically mine.

The turning of the key in the rusty lock awoke Belle from her light sleep. She pulled herself upright and rubbed the last bit of drowsiness from her eyes. Since the day was overcast she could not tell the hour. A dull headache drummed against her temples.

The person on the far side of her prison door fumbled with the lock. Belle relaxed against the wall. "'Tis only poor Will," she told Dexter.

The black-and-white cat sat at her feet with his tail wrapped over his front paws. He stared at the door as if he expected a mouse to crawl under it. At long last, the bolt slid back and Will stepped inside. A gust of cold wind sailed through the lancet window, lifted some of Belle's loose bedding straw in its path and carried them through the open portal. She shivered inside her filthy gown. The material was a light wool and it offered scant protection against the cold blasts from the north that whistled outside the walls. In the space of one short day, autumn had arrived in full force. Tonight would be bone-chilling.

"Goo'day, mistress," said Will as he set down his full bucket with a hard thump. Clean water sloshed over the top and splashed Dexter. The cat jumped sideways then leapt to the comparative safety of the window's narrow ledge.

Belle gave a wan smile at the bumbling young man. Will had been a potboy and turnspit at Bodiam ever since she had moved into the castle when her father had married her stepmother. Though Will had grown tall and brawny, his mind was still that of an amiable eight-year-old child. She was glad that Mortimer had not tossed him out with the rest of her loyal servants. Not that Mortimer had a compassionate bone in his body. It was merely a practical matter of finance. Will worked for nothing but food and a place to sleep. Since his wits were poor, the boy would give no trouble to the current despot who ruled Bodiam. Thank heavens for Will's gentle soul and sweet nature! Belle suspected she would have died of starvation by now if it were not for his kindness and Dexter's cunning skills.

"Good day, Will." She flashed the boy as bright a smile as she could muster. "What's the news today?"

Will squatted down beside her. "I wager you will never guess—not in a month o' Sundays!" He giggled.

Though her stomach rumbled with hunger, Belle bided her time. Will would take deep offense if he thought she was just interested in the morsels of food he brought instead of his news. She knew no one ever spoke to him except to hurl curses. She took his large hand in hers.

"Let's see. Did the cook fall into the soup, perchance?" Giggling again, Will shook his head.

"What a pity!" Belle kept her tone light and teasing. "Hmm. Did Mortimer dig up something of interest in the storeroom?"

Will wrinkled his nose. "You are colder and colder. Come, guess again!" He wriggled all over with suppressed excitement.

Belle pretended to think. "Can you give me a hint? Just a wee one?"

Will's grin broadened. "Tis something to do with Mistress Griselda."

Belle furrowed her brow and pondered in earnest. Will loathed her sister-in-law. What could have sparked his interest in her? "Is she going back to her father's home?" Belle asked, half afraid of the answer. If Griselda left Bodiam, there was no telling what evil Mortimer might do.

The potboy made a face. "Tis not *that* wondrous but the next best thing."

Belle's patience with Will's game wore very thin. All she could think about was food. "I have made three guesses," she pointed out.

Will gave her a very superior look. "And all of them were wrong."

Belle squeezed his hand by way of encouragement. "Then you must make it all right, Will. Please tell me, what is your great news?"

The boy puffed out his broad chest. "Mistress Griselda has got herself a suitor."

Ignoring the gnawing pain in her stomach, Belle gaped at him. "Surely you jest with me."

He shook his head. A light brown curl fell into his eyes. "Not so, never! He came this morning on a great horse."

She furrowed her brows. "How on earth did he gain admittance? Is he a friend of Mortimer's?"

The lad made a face. "Nay, the master gives many sour looks at him but says nothing. One of the guards told me that this nobleman stood on the moat's bank opposite Mistress Griselda's chamber window and he sang to her—for near half an hour, they say. Then the mistress commanded that the gates be opened. Since then she has done nothing but smile and smile and smile."

Belle sat up a little straighter. "Tell me, is this poor swain deaf, dumb and blind?"

Will considered the question carefully before he replied, "Methinks not. He looks fair in his parts, though I would not swear to it. After dinner he sang again to Mistress Griselda. I heard him myself. He has a pleasing voice. And she turned red like an apple when he kissed her hand. But his squire is a right lackwit," he added with a note of satisfaction.

Belle perked up at this intelligence. She wondered if the new squire might possibly be malleable enough to help her escape. So far, Will had been singularly stubborn in that particular area. The poor boy had been thoroughly cowed by a vicious beating. Aloud, she asked in a casual manner, "How now? What does this squire do?"

Will rolled his eyes. "'Tis what he doesn't know *how* to do. A right stumblebum—even worse than me. He has already angered both the cook and the steward by his poor service at dinnertime. Cook boxed his ears. But the lad's nice to me all the same. His name is Bertrum."

"I shall remember him in my prayers," murmured

Belle. *And in my thoughts. Mayhap this Bertrum will be the angel of my freedom.*

Will rose, then picked up yesterday's empty water bucket and prepared to leave. Belle uttered an anxious bleat.

"Oh, Will!" She reached out to him. "Haven't you forgotten to give me something?" she asked, praying that Bertrum's sudden arrival had not addled Will's memory. She pointed to the basket still hooked over his arm.

Stopping short, he grinned sheepishly at her. "Aye, ye are right, Mistress Belle! My mind mistook—almost."

He pulled out the usual stale bread, then added a generous wedge of cheese that he had stolen from the kitchen. He dropped his precious gifts into her lap. Dexter hopped down from his perch and trotted across the floor to investigate the source of the delicious aroma. Belle covered the food with the hem of her skirt, then blew Will her customary kiss.

"May all the angels protect you," she whispered to him.

He touch his fingers to his forehead. "And with you, Mistress." Then he slammed the heavy door behind him.

Belle bit into the cheese, savoring its sharp tang on her tongue. Dexter sat beside her and watched as she devoured her meal. His pink underlip quivered. After she swallowed the last morsel, she sighed then cocked an indulgent eye at her loyal companion.

"How now, Dexter! Do not reproach me with those great golden eyes of yours. You know *you* dine very well and at your leisure, while I must wait for the crumbs to fall my way." She patted her lap. Dexter hopped onto the proffered spot, circled once to find a position to his liking, then lay down with his front paws tucked under his chest.

Belle stroked him as she thought aloud. "What do you think of Will's news? A moonstruck suitor for Griselda, accompanied by a bumbling squire? Tis a rich jest indeed. It almost makes me want to laugh—if I could remember how to do it. Oh, Dexter, will I ever laugh again?''

But the faithful cat had gone to sleep.

Chapter Four

The midnight watch on Bodiam's parapets had trod their appointed rounds for over an hour before Mark stole up the spiral stone staircase in the northwest tower. Although he carried a lantern, it was not yet lit for fear of attracting unwanted attention from a score of Mortimer Fletcher's evil-looking minions. Mark needed no light to guide his way. In his green salad days, he had often roamed Bodiam's galleries and stairways in the dark searching for one or another of Lady Cavendish's adorable maidservants.

As he passed one of the arrow slits, he pulled his thick wool cloak tighter around his shoulders to ward off the keen draft that knifed through the opening. Pausing at the top of the steps, he pressed his ear against the stout door in front of him. He heard nothing but the whine of the wind. He backed against the far wall and stood stock still until the watch called out the next quarter hour.

Satisfied that he had not been observed, Mark knelt and lit the lantern candle with a spark from his tinderbox. In the flickering flame, his elongated shadow danced across the wall's rough stones. Mark held the light close to the door then he whistled with surprise. A large iron key protruded from the lock. Mortimer was a fool to have complete confidence that no traitor lurked among his vile servants. After casting a final glance down the steep stairwell, Mark gently turned the key. The bolt protested with a teeth-gritting squeal. The noise was enough to wake the dead. The short hairs on the back of Mark's neck stiffened.

He lifted the handle and gave a little push. The door creaked open like the lid of a coffin. All the old tales of goblins and ghosties that Mistress Sondra Owens used to spin around Bodiam's kitchen hearth flooded back into Mark's memory. Lady Kat's wise woman often sent the young maids into flights of hysteria with her bloodcurdling stories. Mark had taken those opportunities to soothe the girls' fears with many a stolen kiss and cuddle. He grinned at the memory. Like a shadow, he slipped through the narrow opening, then closed the door behind him.

A bundle of rags stirred in the corner of the privy alcove farthest from the open window. Mark gripped the lantern's ring tighter. "Belle?" he whispered.

Two golden eyes pierced the darkness like no earthly creature. Mark loosened his dagger. "In the name of Saint Michael, I command you to be gone, hobgoblin!"

A wraith-like figure pulled herself into a sitting position on an untidy heap of foul straw. "How now, Mortimer?" she croaked in a mocking tone. "Methinks tis long past your bedtime. What churlish intent prompts this visit at such a late hour?"

Mark could barely believe his eyes or ears. Twas Belle's voice, exactly the same as the one that often taunted his dreams, but the creature before him looked more like her spirit than the merry gremlin who had made his last year at Bodiam such a misery. "Belle?" he whispered again. Drawing nearer, he held up the lantern.

Her eyes blinked in the bright light. Beside her, a dark object disappeared under the straw. "Sweet Saint Anne!"

she murmured, passing a hand across her forehead. "My hunger has conjured a nightmare."

Mark's apprehension changed to exasperation. "My gracious thanks for your sterling opinion of me, Belle Cavendish. Methinks after such a long time the very least you could say would be 'How nice to see you again, Mark' especially since I have traveled many miles to rescue you."

Shielding her eyes from the lantern's glare, she stared at him. "Mark Hayward?" she breathed at last.

He executed a curt bow. "In the flesh and at your service—at least for the present time."

For one dazzling instant her face lit up with a radiant smile that banished every sensible thought in Mark's head. The chill room grew perceptibly warmer. Then she shuttered her expression and replaced it with her more familiar one of amused contempt.

"Ah ha! I see that you still crawl between heaven and earth," Belle remarked.

Her tart tongue made him itch to shake her but the sight of her wan face broke his heart instead. He knelt down beside her. "What has happened to you, *chou-chou?*" he asked, reverting to the pet name he had called her since she had been a toddler.

Belle's eyes narrowed. "Surely tis obvious even to you, Marcus," she replied, not looking at him. "I have been lying about on goose down quilts all the livelong day and pleasuring myself with sweetmeats while singing roundelays." Her lower lip trembled before she bit it.

Mark stroked her sunken cheek. Her skin was dry and cold to his touch. "God's teeth! I will kill Mortimer Fletcher by inches. Tis a good thing that your father cannot see you in this wretched state."

At the mention of Brandon, she attempted to rise. "Papa? Oh, where is he?"

Mark caught her before she fell to the hard floor. Belle weighed nothing in his arms. With his free hand, he fumbled with the clasp that held his cloak around his neck. "Soft, Belle. Your father is still at Wolf Hall."

A faint sheen of tears filled her eyes, but she dashed them away with the back of her hand. "He did not come for me?" she whispered.

Mark wrapped the cloak around her and held her close to his chest willing his warmth into her thin bones. "Tush, *chou-chou.* Do not think ill of him. He lies abed with a broken hip."

She gasped.

"He will mend in time and with Lady Kat's gentle care," Mark soothed. "'Tis fear for *your* safety that pains him more than his injury. He has sent me in his stead."

Belle arched one of her delicate eyebrows. "Then I suppose you will have to do. Beggars cannot be choosers. Where are your men-at-arms?"

Mark smoothed a lock of her golden hair. "I fear I have none, only—"

She bolted upright in his arms. "What!" she wailed. "Oh, Mark! I see your brains are still as thick as Tewksbury mustard!"

He fumed in silence for a moment. His brilliant plan for Belle's escape was not working as he had expected. Though she was as weak as a milksop, the chit showed no inclination to express her admiration or gratitude for all the trouble—not to mention the personal sacrifice—he had already endured on her behalf.

"Do you take me for a fool, Belle?" he growled.

She snapped her fingers. "Nay, sir! If I could, I would not take you at all!"

Mark was torn between the urge to kiss her or to shake her. "You ungrateful little wretch! I have half a mind to leave you as I found you." He attempted to gather her back into his embrace. He had liked that part of the rescue very much.

Belle glowered at him. "Begone then! Methinks I have given you enough amusement for one night."

Mark glowered back. Their cold noses practically touched. "You will note that I am not laughing, Belle."

Her mouth, faintly pink, enticed him. Her lips hovered near to his—just as they had done at their last meeting. Just before Belle had pushed him out of the apple tree.

She wrinkled her nose. "Cudgel your lusty thought, Mark. These lips are not yours for kissing and the time is out of joint. By my troth, I had rather be wooed by a snail than to be rescued by one."

"A snail?" he snarled. The minx had not changed one jot in the last eight years. She was still as impossible as ever. "So be it!" He rose, carrying her with him. "We have dallied here too long as it is."

Belle beat against his chest with her fists. Though her blows had none of their former strength, Mark was hurt by her lack of cooperation.

She grimaced. "Unhand me, you purple-headed malt-worm!"

He tucked the cloak under her chin. "Tut, tut. There is no need to thank me now, Belle. Later on, of course, you may shower me with your proper gratitude."

She bit his thumb.

He almost dropped her.

"Belle!" He shook her to gain her full attention. "As much as I have enjoyed this pleasant chitchat with you, do you not think it wise that we quit this dank cell and make a swift exit into yonder woods?"

She wriggled out of his arms. "Nay!" She sank down onto her reeky pallet.

Mark thought of a number of dastardly things he could do to speed along this frustrating enterprise but he rejected all of them. If Belle didn't kill him afterward, Brandon would. Then it would be good-bye forever to Mark's future estate. He dropped down beside her.

"In plain words and simple sentences, pray explain to me *why* leaving Bodiam is not to your liking?" he asked stretching his patience to the limit

Belle shook her hair out of her face. "Because this castle is *mine*. Is that simple enough for your understanding?"

Mark failed to comprehend her obtuse logic.

She sighed. "Oh, why am I infected with *you?*"

He attempted a dash of levity. "Because I am the most wonderful man you have ever known?"

She jabbed him several times with her finger. "Don't you dare give yourself airs with me, you gull-catcher! I am not one of your hot wenches dressed in flame-colored taffeta."

A warm flush of embarrassment crept up Mark's neck. Belle knew him far too well for comfort. "I never thought—" he began.

"Ha!" she cut him off. "Of course not! Tis why men like you fill this poor world with ill-favored children!"

Mark counted to ten before he trusted himself to reply. "Let us forget my past sins for the moment, Belle. Instead, let us attend to the matter at hand before daylight takes us by surprise. If you refuse to leave here because Bodiam is your home, then *exactly* how do you expect me to rescue you?"

For once she allowed her defenses to drop. "Papa was supposed to come with an army," she replied in a voice filled with despair.

She took his hand in hers and held it close to her heart. Her gentle touch sent hot blood rushing through his veins. Mark took several deep breaths to steady himself. His nose tickled.

"You have no idea what it is like to be a bastard, even one that is as well-loved as Papa loves me," she said softly. "There is nothing in this world that is mine by right—not my name, nor a title, nor acceptance in society, not even the motley rags I wear. I have nothing—except Bodiam. My sweet stepmother deeded her castle to me for my lifetime." She lifted her chin a notch. "And I will never relinquish it, especially not to that double-dealing sot of a brother-in-law who seeks to wrest it from me."

She leaned closer to Mark. "If I steal out of my own home like a thief in the night, Mortimer will claim that I abandoned my property and that he, as the brother of my late husband, could take possession according to the law. By God in His heaven, Mark, I swear I will *never* leave Bodiam."

He squeezed her hand. "Even if you die for it, *chouchou?*" he asked in a gentle voice.

"Aye," she answered.

Mark put his arm around her and drew her against his side. Again he was struck by how thin she had become. He could feel each one of her ribs. His anger at Mortimer increased a hundredfold. Killing was too good for the scullion.

"Methinks you are going to cause me a heap of trouble—again," he remarked in a rueful voice.

She snorted. "You once told me that I excel in trouble-making."

Mark chose to ignore that jibe. "Then if you will not leave the castle, we must find a way to make Mortimer go," he reasoned aloud though he did not know how he could effect this miracle before Belle died from the cur's maltreatment.

Instead of pushing him away, she snuggled inside the crook of his arm and rested her head on his shoulder. "How many men did you say accompanied you?"

He swallowed. "Only one—though he fights like ten...and my squire," Mark added as an afterthought. Belle would kill him if she knew that Kitt slept within Bodiam's unhappy walls.

Her lips curled into a weak smile. "Is your squire's name Bertrum by any chance?"

He blinked at her. "How the devil did you—?" He rubbed his itching nose.

For the first time, Belle actually laughed. The music of her mirth filled his ears like a summer's song.

"Don't tell me *you* are Griselda's unfortunate suitor?"

Mark shrugged. "Twas not a bad idea for gaining entry into the castle though I must confess I was not prepared for the woman herself. Zounds! Mother Nature did not fashion Mistress Fletcher well. And may the good Lord amend her voice or render it silent altogether. She squeals like a stuck pig!"

Belle gave him an arch look. "My spy tells me that you sang to her, paid her loving compliments and kissed her hand."

"Twas all in counterfeit, chuck. I swear!" Why did he feel like an impaled worm on a fish hook? "Trust me, sweet Belle. Twas all for you."

Belle rapped him on the chest with her knuckle. "Ha! I have heard you whisper that watery vow in a trusting maiden's ear too many times."

Mark rubbed his nose again. "Do you think I *enjoy* playing Griselda's swain?"

A mischievous smile curled her lovely lips. "After all

these years of chasing skirts, methinks tis a just punishment for you, Marcus.''

He pulled his handkerchief out of his sleeve and blew his nose before giving her an answer to her cruel observation. ''I had only intended to enact the role one day before I carried you out of this den. The mere thought of Griselda's company is enough to curdle any man's ardor—even mine.''

Belle chuckled. ''Poor Marcus! I fear you must continue to act the love-struck fool for a while longer.''

He swore into the depths of his handkerchief. Either the dust or the moldy straw made his nose run and his eyes water. ''Until when?'' he asked groaning inwardly.

''Until I can devise a plan to send Mortimer and his illfavored sister fleeing from Bodiam forever.''

Mark sneezed. ''Forsooth, you are a wicked lass to wish this fate on me, Belle. By the book, what plagues my nose?''

In answer, Belle lifted a corner of her blanket. An overweight feline regarded Mark with large amber eyes. ''I had forgotten that you cannot endure the company of a cat. Tis Dexter, my best friend.''

Mark sneezed again by way of salutation. ''Does he reside with you here?''

She nodded. Then she lifted the great hairy brute out of his nest and plopped him on her lap. ''Aye, he keeps me warm at night and brings me bits of food now and then—also the occasional rat, quite dead, of course.'' The creature purred in a loud, bragging manner.

Mark shuddered. ''How delightful!'' He regarded the cat with open disgust. ''Belle, forget this foolish whim. You should not sleep another night in this hole with a ratbearing cat!'' *I would make you a far better bedfellow if I could.* Taken aback by this thought, Mark hurried on.

"Once in the safety of Wolf Hall we will plot against Mortimer and his ungodly sister."

Belle hugged the cat closer to her. "Never! You may as well go home, Mark, and leave me in mine."

With a muttered oath, he stood and brushed bits of straw from his dark blue hose. As a child, Belle had been as stubborn as a jackass. Why did he think she had changed now? "Very well! I am a fool of all fools but I will do what you ask of me, though the cost is high. That shameless jade tried to lead me to her bedchamber after supper this evening. Aye, and we had only met a few hours earlier!"

Belle whispered into one of the cat's pointed black ears. "Poor Griselda must be *very* desperate indeed!"

"She breaks looking glasses with her toothy smiles," Mark muttered.

Belle waved him away. "Begone, Marcus. Get your beauty sleep so that you may be even more enticing to the fair Griselda on the morrow."

"This is not what I had bargained for," he grumbled. He sneezed again.

Belle peeled off his cloak and held it up to him.

He shook his head. "Keep it. The night is cold. Twill warm you better than that ball of fur."

"Nay, I cannot," she insisted. "Mortimer visits me daily. He would spy it at once and guess your true intentions. The knave may look like a toad, but he has a quick mind. Be warned. He hides a thousand daggers in his thoughts."

Mark retrieved his cloak with great reluctance. "Sleep well, *chou-chou,*" he said with forced cheer. "I will come again tomorrow night."

"May your angel protect you till then," she replied.

He put his hand to the latch, then paused and glanced

over his shoulder at her. In spite of her miserable condition, she tossed him a challenging look, the very same expression she had worn just before she had pushed him off the tree branch. The memory of that last encounter simmered in his mind. *Why not?*

He put down his lantern, crossed the space between them in three long strides, then bent over her. Before she could utter a startled objection, he kissed her full on her lips.

His broken arm and the eight years' wait had been well worth it. Belle tasted of paradise. He ducked her flailing fists.

"Where," she sputtered with delectable anger, "in your great heap of knowledge, did you locate *that* idea?"

He winked at her. "Been thinking about that for a long time, *ma petite chou-chou.*"

Humming a bawdy tune under his breath, he let himself out of the little chamber. Once on the other side of the door, he sobered. With great reluctance, he relocked Belle's cheerless prison.

Dexter mewed in Belle's ear then patted her face with one of his forepaws. Slowly she awoke to a gray day. Fat raindrops plopped on the stone ledge of the open window.

"Go find a rat, Dexter," she groaned as she snuggled deeper in the delicious warmth of her blankets.

Blankets? Belle shook the cobwebs of sleep from her mind. Dexter sat down and stared fixedly at her. His long white whiskers quivered. Barely believing her sudden good fortune, Belle counted three blankets where last evening there had been only one. The topmost was her familiar filthy covering that had kept the winds at bay. It hid two plain brown blankets made of thick wool—clean and free of rents.

"Oh, Dexter! What kindly spirit visited us last night?"

Mark's kiss still tingled on her lips. She banished the disturbing memory. Nay! He had left her long before she fell asleep.

"Besides he hates me," she explained to the cat. "He nearly lost the use of his sword arm because of my childish prank. That kiss of his was merely...unfinished business."

Dexter got up, stretched then pawed at a loose pile of straw. He mewed once or twice for Belle's attention. His claws scraped against something unfamiliar.

Belle investigated. Dexter had unearthed a covered crock that was still very warm to the touch. When she raised its lid, the aroma of stewed meat and seasoned vegetables wafted in the chill breeze.

"Oh most blessed spirit!" Belle cried with joy. Lifting the pot to her mouth, she drank greedily. "Kat would chide my lack of proper manners if she saw me now, but tis a goodly broth! Heaven-sent to be sure!'

Dexter licked his lips with a long pink tongue by way of reminding Belle to share her wealth as he had shared his with her. She poured a little gravy into the lid.

"Someday, Dexter, you will overeat and explode," she observed with a smile. Then something red in the straw caught her eye. "More wonders?" she asked the cat.

She picked up one of her stepmother's precious roses, its stem plucked free of thorns. The last bloom of this year, Belle surmised as she inhaled its rich perfume. This gift, more than the blankets or the stew, brought rare tears to her eyes.

No one had ever given her a flower before, not even Cuthbert.

Belle brushed the velvet petals against her cheek. "I wonder, Dexter, if Sondra's tales are true. Does the ghostly knight of Bodiam really exist?"

Not for a moment would she allow herself to believe that Mark Hayward, the bane of her childhood, was her mysterious benefactor. She must put that lunatic idea out of her mind at once before it had a chance to take root there.

"Tis not Mark's style at all," she told the purring cat.

Chapter Five

Mark overslept the next morning and the rain-plagued day only went downhill from there. When Kitt appeared with his shaving water, it was merely tepid instead of steaming hot the way Mark liked it. He opened his mouth to chastise the boy but held his tongue when he saw a fresh bruise under his eye.

Mark touched the injury. "More of that beslubbering cook's opinion?" he asked.

Kitt turned away. "I fell over my own feet," he replied. "Indeed, I have been informed that they would make a fine pair of shovels," he added in an undertone.

Mark stropped his razor while his anger grew warmer. "What pignut told you this witticism?"

Kitt shrugged his shoulder then turned his attention to his bedmaking. "Tis none of your concern, Mark. Jobe says that a man must fight his own battles."

Mark considered this bit of wisdom as he lathered up his face with cold soapsuds. "You are still in the schoolroom, Kitt." he remarked. While he shaved, he observed his apprentice squire in the looking glass.

Kitt tossed his head. "Not now. I am on the road to a new beginning, Jobe says."

Methinks Jobe says far too much in this stripling's innocent ear!

Kitt shook out Mark's hose, then laid his other clean shirt across the lumpy bed covering. "How fares my sister?" he asked in an off-hand manner.

In the mirror, Mark saw that the boy cast him a penetrating look. "As well as can be expected," he answered, rinsing his razor. "Belle was never fond of small dark places." He chose not to reveal her true sad state to her brother. Being blessed with a strong dose of the Cavendish temperament, the lad would no doubt hurl himself headlong into some rash deed.

Kitt polished one of Mark's boots with his sleeve. "Then why do we tarry in this fetid place? You told me that we would be in Hawkhurst by now. Let us grab Belle and be gone."

Mark dried his face with a scrap of hucktoweling. Mortimer Fletcher was a parsimonious host. "There are complications. Your sister refuses to leave Bodiam and thereby hangs the tale."

Kitt's jaw dropped. "She's addlepated!"

"Agreed," Mark growled under his breath.

"I will shake some sense into her woolly head," Kitt announced. "Lead me to her!"

"Nay." Mark pulled his shirt over his head, then held out his arms to the boy. Kitt stared at them. Mark pointed to the bandstrings that hung down from each cuff. "A good squire ties up his master's laces."

With a snort, Kitt attended to his new task. "Belle is my sister," he continued in a low tone. "As her brother, tis my sworn duty to—"

Mark grabbed a handful of Kitt's collar and backed the boy against the wall. "Listen to me well, my little minnow. I am caught between two people who are hell-bent to destroy each other: your sister and Mortimer Fletcher. We must tread our way carefully between them if we expect to quit this place with the minimum of bloodshed. Tis no schoolboy game that we play here, but one in deadly earnest. You will do exactly as I say. For the time being, Belle is not to know you are at Bodiam. Have I made myself clear, pudding-head?"

"Marvelously much," Kitt snarled. Then he nodded. "I will obey you—for now. But I like it not!" With that bit of defiance, he banged out of the chamber with the basin of soapy water.

Mark shook his head at his reflection. Why did God make the Cavendish family so stubborn?

Mark planned to snatch a quick breakfast, then ride into the forest where he would meet Jobe. Instead, Griselda pounced on him like a cat at a mouse hole.

"Good morrow, Sir Mark," she squealed in that ear-piercing voice of hers. "You slept well?"

He fixed a painted smile on his lips. "All the night through, sweet dumpling." He forced himself not to choke on his words. Of all the many maids he had wooed in the past thirteen years, Griselda was the most unappealing and perversely the one wench most anxious to invite him between her sheets.

"I would have warmed your dreams," she simpered through her nose as she latched onto his arm like an apothecary's leech.

"I fear I did not dream at all," he murmured. His stomach gnawed for food.

Griselda caressed his cold fingers. "Then I shall make it my duty and my pleasure to give you sweet dreams every night, my dearest love."

Twould be nightmares! Mark widened his smile. "I look forward to that happy time, my dainty duck."

Griselda pulled him back from the stairway where he could smell the aroma of roasted meats and baked breads in the hall.

"Why wait?" she whined. "We have already agreed to the match. Tis nothing but a few words in front of the church door between us and our bliss."

Mark dug his heels against the paving stones. "Nay, my sportful honeycomb! Twould be a most unseemly haste. I have not yet spoken with your brother, nor signed a betrothal agreement." *Nor given you a kiss to seal the bargain,* he added to himself with a shudder. *Nor will I ever! I would rather dance a galliard in hell first!*

Griselda stuck out her thin lower lip in a ghastly pout. She reminded Mark of a well-dressed gargoyle. A man should not have to face such sights on an empty stomach.

"Then find Mortimer!" she shrieked as she practically threw him down the stairs. "For by my troth, sweet Mark, I shall not go cold to my bed again this night! Seek him in one of the storerooms for he spends much time down there in the dark."

Like a mushroom or some other bit of fungus, Mark thought as he fled from the panting shrew. He paused at the laden sideboard in the hall to fortify himself for his interview with Fletcher. While washing down an onion and parsley omelet with some ale out of the pitcher, Mark was accosted by one of the potboys.

"Here now! Tis for dinner, that!" the dull-eyed oaf said, pointing to the ravaged dish. "And tis not dinnertime yet."

Mark swallowed his food before speaking. "But I have not broken my fast until now."

"Oh," said the overgrown boy. He scratched his head. "But still, tis for *dinner* and cook will be full of wrath if he knows that ye have made a great hole in his omelet."

Mark beckoned the servant to lean closer. He whispered

in the boy's ear, "Then we shall not tell him, shall we? Besides, tis a passing good bit of victual. Try some. I shall not betray you," he added.

The lackwit grinned, looked over his shoulder, then scooped out a portion twice as large as Mark's. He nodded at Mark while he ate.

Mark returned his smile. "A word to the wise, my friend. Wipe your mouth free from crumbs or else twill be *you* and not I that the cook will cudgel." Then he left the lad to his fate.

Mark hoped to catch Mortimer unawares at his mysterious business in the depths of Bodiam's large storerooms but the man met him on the stairs.

"How now, my lord? Methinks you have lost your way." Mortimer blocked further progress with a dissembling smile on his face.

"Indeed so?" Mark replied, knowing exactly where he was within Bodiam's walls. "I had thought these steps might lead to the flower garden that I spied from my casement."

"A walk outside on such a foul day?" Mortimer ascended a step closer, forcing his guest to turn around and retrace his journey. Mortimer ushered him into his small office off the hall. He offered the nobleman the better of two straight-back wooden chairs that flanked a worn oaken table.

Once they were seated, Mortimer opened the conversation. "My sister is much taken by you, my lord." He rubbed his hands together as if to warm them. "Methinks you will make her a fine husband."

Mark swallowed a knot in his throat. He had never intended for his deceit to run this far, but thanks to Belle's obstinacy, he now found himself in a most ticklish predicament. Bedding maids was one thing, but marrying one was quite another—and matrimony with the loathsome Griselda was past all imagination.

Mark leveled his gaze at Belle's tormentor. "You are kind to say so, good sir," he replied with a false smile. If he had to keep grinning like a painted poppet his face would soon crack in two.

Mortimer regarded him with the calculating eye of a merchant about to begin sharp negotiations for a sack of wool. If Mark did not play his part to perfection, he suspected that he would soon find himself on the far side of the moat—or worse, bobbing head down in its green waters.

Leaning forward, he put his elbows on the table. "You and I are men of the world, so let us not fritter away the forenoon with dull prattle. What dowry are you prepared to offer me to relieve you of the fair wench?"

Mortimer nodded with satisfaction. "You are a man after my own heart," he replied.

You speak the exact truth in that, you puking moldwarp. Mark continued to smile. "You have a goodly castle here. Is the holding large?" he asked.

Fletcher inclined his head. "A middling sort. You know, a few farms, some grazing lands and a small wood for hunting."

Jack-sauce! Bodiam is half of Sussex and worth a prince's ransom! "Is the property entailed or claimed by creditors? I do not intend to incur any debts if I take your sister to wife."

For the first time, Mortimer looked uncomfortable. He drummed the tabletop with his fingers as if he played an imaginary virginal. "No creditors have a claim to it, but..."

Mark lifted one brow. "The estate is not *yours?*"

The man turned a mottled reddish color. "I am the legal

guardian of Bodiam and can assure you that what I offer
will be yours free and clear.''

Now we arrive at the meat of this poxy feast. Mark
skewered his host with a penetrating look. "Exactly who
owns this fair castle?" he asked softly. *Let us see how
close he cuts to the bone of truth.*

Mortimer released a deep mournful sigh. "Tis a sad tale,
my lord.''

"Tell me," Mark prodded. "I enjoy a story well-told.''
How clever a liar are you?

Mortimer affected to look somber. "Griselda and I had
a brother named Cuthbert. A sweet lad but often sickly.
Two years ago, he married into the Cavendish family.
Have you heard of them?''

Mark nodded. "Aye, they are a right noble clan from
the north. Most fortunate for your brother.''

Mortimer curled his lip in a sneer. "Only half right. The
chit in question is a Cavendish bastard. Twas she who was
fortunate to find any decent husband at all.''

Mark clenched his fists under the cover of his sleeves.
How dare this churl speak of Belle as if she were nothing
but a tavern strumpet! He longed to leap over the table
and throttle Mortimer. "And so?" he asked, keeping his
voice steady.

Mortimer did not notice the fire in Mark's eyes for he
warmed to his sniveling tale. "My father warned Cuthbert
that he would drag down the family's good name with this
union, but the boy was besotted with the wench and would
not listen to common sense. They married. A year later..."
Mortimer lowered his voice. "He fell ill of a strange fever.
Griselda and I rushed to his side, but . . . he died.''

Mark fought the urge to make the sign of the cross that
had formerly been a habit when one spoke of the dead.
Ever since Great Harry had broken with the Church in

Rome all such popish displays of piety were forbidden. Instead, he murmured, "God bless his soul."

"Amen," Mortimer answered, then hurried on. "Between you and I, methinks she *killed* my poor brother."

Anger throbbed in Mark's brain. *You will surely sup in hell!* "Tell me more," he growled. *Dig your grave a little deeper.*

"Aye!" Looking satisfied, Mortimer sat back in his chair. "You would only have to see her to know how cruel and cunning she is."

"Then show her to me," whispered Mark. "I have never gazed upon a murderess before."

Mortimer gulped then shook his head. "Alas, I cannot. Since her husband's untimely death, she has been taken ill herself. No doubt her great sin weighs her down with righteous guilt. Trust me. I have her—and her estate—in my safekeeping."

"How safe?" Mark snapped. *Safekeeping indeed! The knave was more two-faced than Janus.*

Mortimer surprised him by suddenly laughing. "Ah ha! I knew you to be a rogue the instant I clapped my eye on you!"

These words and Mortimer's sudden levity made Mark uneasy. "Are you a conjurer who knows the secrets of men's hearts?" he asked lightly.

"Nay, take no offense, friend. I am no wizard. We two are alike in our thoughts, and so I know yours as well as my own."

Bile rose in Mark's throat. *Be thankful you do not read my mind this very instant.* "And what thoughts of mine are the twins of yours?"

Leaning across the table, Mortimer whispered, "To see the Cavendish wench dead and these estates back in the hands of upright men such as ourselves."

Mark's breath caught in his throat. An icy chill ran down his spine. This devil couldn't mean he would kill sweet Belle! "Is she near death?" he forced himself to ask.

Mortimer chuckled. The sound was far from mirthful. "Who knows?"

God shield us, Belle! I hope you have thought of a clever plan or else we'll both be crow's meat ere the week is out.

Mark fiddled through the onerous dinner with little appetite. On the other hand, Mortimer and his vile sister enjoyed the various courses with gluttonous delight. Griselda's table manners alone were enough to turn Mark's stomach, while thoughts of poor Belle starving in a cold garret tore his heart. Tonight he would bring her a real feast—and hopefully talk some sense into that pretty head of hers. As soon as the last of the stewed apples had been removed, Mark rose from his seat. Griselda clamped herself to his side.

"Would you care to hear me sing, my lord?" She giggled. "Or do you have other pleasures in mind to while away such a gloomy afternoon?"

She is bold as burnished brass and terrifying as a witch met at the crossroads. After years of pursuing the weaker sex, Mark discovered that he did not enjoy the role of the prey. *Alas, turnabout is fair play.* "I fear I am prone to headaches when confined indoors."

Her claws reached for him. "Then I will soothe your brow."

He ducked away from her. "Nay, saucy puddleduck. My thanks for your concern but a ride in the fresh air will clear my malady."

Griselda glanced at the arched window that dominated the hall. Wind-driven rain lashed at the glass panes. "'Tis near to drowning out there, my lord. You will catch your death in this weather.''

Tis far safer in the midst of the storm than inside this charnel house. He pried her hands from his arm. ''Bertrum!'' he shouted down the length of the hall. ''Quit lollygagging! Saddle our horses at once!''

Kitt's blue eyes widened. ''*Now*, my lord?'' he ventured.

Mark sidestepped another one of Griselda's amorous attacks. ''This instant or twill be your hide nailed to the door!''

Kitt muttered something under his breath as he scuttled down the wide stairway toward the courtyard. Mark all but ran after him.

Within the half-hour, the two were riding through the familiar woods that surrounded Bodiam Castle. Though the rain pelted his face and chilled him through his sodden cloak, Mark felt alive and free for the first time in twenty-four hours. If it was not for that hard-headed minx in the northwest tower, he would keep riding all the way to London.

Thinking of Belle curbed his enjoyment. She hated confinement. Mark recalled the time years ago when she had been locked in the buttery for some household transgression. She had screamed and kicked the stout door for several soul-wrenching hours. When Kat finally released her, she was horrified by the sight of Belle's bleeding hands and feet, but the child had not shed one tear of pain or remorse. With her head held high, she limped up the stairway to her secret refuge in the dovecote. There she had stayed until long past nightfall. Afterward, no one ever mentioned the incident, nor had Belle ever again been confined against her will—until now. Like an exotic wild bird, she wasted away inside the cold damp walls of her cage, yet she refused the freedom he offered her.

Mark tightened his grip on the reins. While he had ridden south on Brandon's errand the rich estate that Belle's father had promised the land-poor nobleman had filled his mind. Now that he had seen Belle's piteous condition and met her jailer, Mark's thoughts turned to revenge. He longed to strike Mortimer dead and lay Bodiam and all its possessions once again at the feet of their rightful owner. Patience, he counseled himself as he ducked under a dripping bough. *We are too few for a frontal attack but there are alternatives to a fight. We must use all our cunning—and soon before Mortimer plays his end game.*

Mark expected to find Jobe cold, wet and in a foul mood in his hideaway. Instead, the delicious aroma of roasting meat greeted Mark and Kitt when they dismounted in front of the old woodcutter's croft. Inside, Jobe had a small but cheerful fire crackling in the cobblestone hearth. Several fat rabbits, skinned and skewered, cooked over the flames. Jobe's immense presence filled the small room.

"Welcome, *meus amigos!*" he roared when Mark pushed open the rough-planked door. "Your dinner is ready."

Kitt shook the raindrops from his cap. "How did you know we were coming?" he asked in surprise.

Jobe only chuckled, laid a finger against the side of his nose and winked in reply.

Mark unpinned his cloak. "Jobe has the gift of second sight, Kitt. I do not know how he does it; I only know that he can sense the future."

"Aye," the man agreed, "Just as I knew that the lady would not accompany you this day—though why she won't, I do *not* know."

Kitt regarded the African with increased respect. "Most

marvelous wonderful! Can you teach me how to do that, Jobe?''

He chuckled again. ''You must be born the seventh son of a sorcerer in the dark of the moon as I was.''

''Oh.'' The boy sighed. ''My father is only a knight.''

Mark warmed himself in front of the fire. ''Tell me, wise friend, do you see a happy ending to this mad enterprise of ours?''

Jobe did not answer at once. He removed the rabbits from the fire and deftly jointed them on a large wooden board. He passed the succulent portions first to Mark then to Kitt before he replied. ''I see devil darkness and brilliant stars falling from the skies,'' he intoned in a deep-timbered voice. ''I see misery, greed, yet laughter and...'' Pausing, he stared at Mark.

The hairs on the back of Mark's neck quivered a warning. ''What?'' He said a quick prayer that Jobe had not foreseen his death.

The African's smile split his broad face. ''*Amor, meu amigo!*'' His laughter rolled up from deep within his chest. ''The goddess of love will enfold you in her silver snares!''

Mark shook his head firmly. ''Nay, your prophecy has gone awry this time. I am not the marrying kind. There are still too many flowers in the garden for me to savor.''

Jobe only laughed again, then addressed Kitt. ''You will see anon, little one. Mark my words.''

Kitt looked from one man to the other then swallowed. ''Can you...? I mean, do you see into my future, Jobe?''

The giant placed a large hand on Kitt's golden head and looked deeply into the boy's bright eyes. At length he nodded. ''I see a strong heart and many adventures. You will drink life to the dregs.''

Kitt blinked with confusion but dared not question Jobe

any further. With a grin, Mark passed his wineskin to the boy. "Do not pretend to understand what Jobe says. I never do, yet somehow things seem to happen as he says." He narrowed his eyes. "But not falling in love, Jobe. I flatly refuse to do that."

The African only shook his head. "Tis too late, *meu amigo*. You have already done so."

Chapter Six

The long hours since dusk crept by like tardy schoolboys. Belle wrapped her precious blankets tighter around her shivering body. Dexter snuggled closer against her side before he resumed his dreams of fat silver fish. The girl stroked his sleek body.

"Ah, sweet cat, how I wish I could be like you these days! Full of food, a warm coat and without a care for tomorrow." She sighed. "Tomorrow is all I have to live for now." How swiftly her happiness had disappeared since Cuthbert's death! Only her anger at his feckless brother fueled her weakening body. Her stomach growled. Will had forgotten to bring her fresh water today. Nor had she heard from Mark.

"Where is that flap-mouthed coxcomb?" she asked aloud in the enveloping blackness of her prison. She curled her lip. "Playing the ardent suitor, methinks. Aye, and enjoying his easy conquest. No doubt Griselda's calf-eyed looks flatter that jolthead's vanity." She curled herself around Dexter's ample body and shut her eyes. "Mark Hayward is a pig's bladder," she murmured as she allowed herself to drift into the comfortable oblivion of sleep.

The grating sound of the key in the door's lock awoke

Belle with a start. By the time she had pulled herself into a sitting position, Mark had slipped inside.

He hunkered down beside her and flashed her one of his cocky grins. "Good evening, Mistress of the Manor."

Belle's heart fluttered again, as the treacherous thing had done the previous night when Mark had first reappeared in her life. The impish wiry boy whom she remembered from her childhood had turned into one of the most handsome men she had ever seen. His devilish brown eyes that had so often goaded her to tantrums in those distant sunny days now shimmered in the lantern light with sensual promise. Her mouth went dry when she looked into their bottomless depths. No maid had resisted Mark's honeyed wooing when he was her father's squire. Surveying the man that he had become, Belle knew that he must have left a wide swath of broken hearts in Ireland. She yawned to prove to herself that she didn't give one fig for Mark's lusty odyssey.

"I have a plan," she told him without bothering to wish him a good evening nor to inquire the state of his health. He looked far too virile.

Mark cocked one of his dark brows in the most beguiling manner. "How now, Belladonna? No kind word to greet me?"

She blew a stray hair out of her eyes. "In case your sight has failed you, Mark, we are not seated amid civilized company. All my kind words have dried up in this hellhole."

Mark's unnerving grin only widened. He put down the sack that he carried. When he untied it, a delicate warm aroma of fresh bread tickled her nostrils. Dexter crawled out from under the blankets and sauntered over to inspect the latest offering.

Mark cast the cat a wary glance. "Not for you, kitty,"

he muttered as he rummaged in the bag. "Here." He handed Belle something wrapped in a well-used napkin. "Tis a chicken pie, not rat poison, *chou-chou*," he added. "And I suggest that you eat it before your beast does."

Belle almost thanked him but decided that she shouldn't encourage him. The memory of last night's surprise kiss still unnerved her. Instead, she stuffed her mouth full of the delicious meat and vegetables. Dexter pounced on stray crumbs. Before she had finished the last of the pie, Mark handed her a thick slice of bread slathered with fresh butter and garnished with pickled relish. She sighed with contentment. Mortimer might be a spare man in many areas, but he certainly did not stint when it came to his cook.

Mark sat down on the filthy straw and stretched out his legs. His blue hose tightened over taut calf and thigh muscles. His presence was so utterly male, so bracing. Belle sucked in her breath, though she affected a sneer.

"Mind your pretty clothes, Marcus," she taunted. "You are not sitting on perfumed sheets in some lady's bower."

He chuckled. "I have sat in worse bogs in Ireland, *chou-chou*. Drink this." He handed her a covered cup.

"What is it?" she asked lifting the top. She recognized the sweet aroma. "Warm milk? I am well past my infancy, Mark."

He shook his head. "Nay, tis a posset with sackwine, egg yolks and spices, prepared by my very own hands. Burned my thumb in the bargain. Drink it up, *chou-chou*. Tis good for you."

He watched her like a hovering nurse while she drained the cup. Though she relished every drop of his delicious surprise, she refused to give him the satisfaction of knowing how much she enjoyed this unexpected treat. If she let her guard down just once he would never let her forget it.

He crossed his ankles. "Now that you have finished

your snack, pray tell me the details of your plotting. I am sure twill be vastly entertaining.''

Ignoring Dexter's soft mews of protest, she licked her fingers clean of the chicken sauce and pastry flakes. "Tis more entertaining than Griselda singing love songs to you, I'll warrant,'' Belle remarked in a snide tone. She wondered why she took exception to Mark's counterfeit courtship of her sister-in-law.

He grimaced at Griselda's name. "God mend her voice—and soon, I pray. She murders both the melody and the rhyme. Speak to me of happier thoughts—like leaving this godforsaken place.''

Rubbing the side of her nose, Belle ignored Mark's broad hint. "Have you noticed how superstitious the Fletchers are?'' she asked.

He nodded. "At dinner, when Griselda knocked over the salt, I thought both brother and sister would jump out of their skins. They tossed some over their left shoulders and enjoined me to follow suit. I felt like twice a fool.''

Belle allowed a small smile. "Just so. Tell me, do you know today's date? I have lost all track of time since Mortimer locked me in here.''

A dark shadow fluttered across Mark's face before he erased it with a shrug. "I did not think I needed to travel with an almanac but tis a Thursday and Mortimer mentioned something about the approach of All Hallows Eve within the fortnight.''

"Excellent!'' Despite her pleasure at this news, she shivered as a brisk wind blew through the open window.

Mark unfolded his arms and shook out the folds of his thick cloak. "Come sit beside me, Belle. I will keep you warm.''

The seductive tone of his voice and the glint in his merry eyes whispered a wealth of meanings with his invitation—all of them dangerous. Her heart skittered inside her breast. She pursed her lips. "A pretty speech, indeed, Master Cupid. I am sure you have had hundreds of wenches tumbling to that lewd offer."

Mark snorted with exasperation though he still held out his cloak. "Cease your chiding, Belle. Your hallowed virtue is safe with me. I offer only the warmth of my cape for I see that my blankets cannot keep out all the chill of this cell."

His blankets! Though Belle had suspected that her morning's bounty had been his, she loathed the very idea. Mark had rarely done a kind thing for her in his life—and then only when her father was watching. His gift of the rose made her especially uneasy. *He's up to something.*

Aloud, she replied. "My thanks for the blankets and the food. Methought Will had brought them. The potboy's kindness has kept me alive these past few weeks."

Mark nodded again. "Then I shall be kind to Will, even though he is a great stumbling clod. Now, be not so stubborn, Belle. Come sit close to me and tell me what madcap scheme dances in your head."

Belle shivered again, partially with cold and partially from some emotion she did not care to investigate. Ruing her unkempt appearance, she settled herself within the hollow he had created for her. Mark draped his cloak around her and tucked its ends securely under her feet. Then he slipped his arm about her shoulders and pulled her closer against him.

"Zounds, *chou-chou*," he said in an odd, hoarse voice. "You are as skinny as a bird in midwinter."

"I see you save all your sugared words for Griselda," Belle snapped.

Mark's heat seeped through her like a blacksmith's furnace, leaving her light-headed with the unexpected sensation of protection. She drank in the comfort of his nearness. Instinctively she rested her head on his broad shoulder and allowed herself to relax.

He tapped her nose. "So, *chou-chou*, what masterpiece of mischief have you concocted?"

Belle willed herself not to sink into the delicious sleep that beckoned to her. "Tis simple, Marcus. We frighten the Fletchers out of their wits so that they will flee from Bodiam as from the plague. Then all will be well again."

"Hmm," he rumbled. "Tis a gladsome thought, but how? Why would they leave so cozy a nest?"

Belle suppressed a desire to yawn. "Do you remember those tales of the Black Knight of Bodiam?"

He chuckled. "Aye, Mistress Sondra had a deft way with her words. She even made the hairs on the back of *my* neck quiver. She sent many of Lady Kat's little maids into hysterics." He laughed again.

Belle jabbed him in the ribs with her elbow, putting a stop to his lecherous memories. "Aye, you rogue, and I saw how you spent many an hour in the hayloft calming their fears." She furrowed her brow as she remembered spying on Mark and his conquests. How those silly chits had giggled under his caresses. Belle had hated Mark yet yearned for his gentle touch.

"You should have been minding your own business, Belle," he replied in a slightly hurt tone. "Besides, I was not a slobbering debaucher as you like to think. The girls were virgins—for the most part. A little kissing and a few cuddles were all that we did. No harm in that."

Belle ignored his defense. The churl would say anything if it had an advantage to him. She jabbed him again. "Pay attention, ratsbane! The hour runs apace. When Mortimer next comes to visit me, I will plant the story of the ghostly knight in his fallow brain. I will say that the knight will ride forth on All Hallows Eve and that death will stalk anyone who angers him.''

Mark nodded. ''Good so far. I will play upon Griselda's fears with stories of this knight so that her teeth will rattle. But then what?''

She cast him a mischievous grin. ''You must effect a haunting. You were always good at mummery and sly tricks, Marcus. I trust you have not lost that talent with old age.''

He squeezed her gently. ''A few ideas come to mind,'' he murmured in a far too seductive tone.

No wonder weak-kneed maids fell into his arms at first sight! Belle felt herself falling under his spell. An unexpected excitement surged through her. She kicked him. ''Exactly *what* sort of ideas, Mark?''

Swearing softly under his breath, he rubbed his ankle. ''You are a thankless vixen, Belle. I offer only to rescue you and you act as if I were leading you down the primrose path to perdition.''

She made a face. ''Tis all one to me,'' she retorted, though she lied through her teeth.

Griselda pulled her dressing gown closer around her and listened to the wind howl through the courtyard—or was that the moaning of tortured souls that cried out in the midwatch of the night? Lifting her candle a little higher, she whispered a quick prayer to her guardian angel and hoped he was paying attention. She glanced over her shoulder, but the corridor was silent. Mortimer's chamber door was shut fast. No light gleamed from within. Griselda tiptoed past it.

Her brother would beat her black and blue if he knew what she had in mind. The Fletchers might not be a noble family, but their father had instilled in his children a burn-

ing pride in their reputation. None had learned that lesson
better than Mortimer. Griselda was a shameless harlot to
even consider stealing into a man's bed and seducing him.

Nevertheless, she scurried on.

Sir Mark was not just any man, she reasoned as she
negotiated the narrow stairs up to the second floor of the
postern tower. He was handsome far beyond all of her
wildest dreams. He dressed with a subtle flair that accen-
tuated his manly parts and when he spoke, pure poetry
poured from his lips. Such kissable lips! Griselda got
goosebumps at the mere thought of them caressing her
hand. Best of all, he was hers—almost.

Fate that had been so unkind to her in the past had
finally smiled upon Griselda when she least expected it.
Out of the blue, her dream suitor had come riding across
Bodiam's drawbridge and straightway into her heart. Mortimer might grumble and play the suspicious protector, but
she knew her brother realized what a lucky catch Sir Mark
Hayward was. His very demeanor, his fine clothes, his
well-groomed horse all spoke of a wealthy man—and a
noble one as well!

She stopped before Sir Mark's door. Her heart beat in
her throat and waves of giddiness threatened to overwhelm
her. Her hand trembled when it touched the latch. *He'll be
asleep and won't know what has happened until I am lying
naked beside him—then his raging male lusts will drown
out any qualms.* She swallowed a hard knot in her throat.

Naked—in his bed! Griselda had never done such a daring, wanton act in her life. The prospect excited her past
all common sense. She turned the handle slowly and
slipped into his chamber. The large poster bed was
shrouded in its heavy velvet curtains to keep out the night
drafts. Lifting the hem of her gown, she advanced slowly

lest she trip over a discarded boot or wayward stocking. Holding her breath, she drew back one of the drapes.

His bed yawned empty. Not even the imprint of his head marred the plumped pillow.

Griselda frowned. Surely she had come to the right room. Indeed, the bed had fresh sheets and was turned back, waiting for its absent occupant. Then she remembered that Sir Mark had said something about being wakeful at odd times of the night.

He has gone for a stroll to clear the fumes of the wine. When he returns, I'll be waiting for him. What a surprise! Griselda blew out her candle, shed her clothing and slithered in between the bedcovers.

The wind outside the diamond-paned glass window increased its howl. Then she heard a noise like a mouse skittering across the floor—or mayhap twas Sir Mark returning from his nocturnal ramble. Unable to lie still and wait, Griselda parted the curtain to take a reassuring peek.

Instead of the tall form of her heart's desire, she saw a slim, pale wraith with silvered hair. It stood in the middle of the room and stared at her. With a squeal of terror, Griselda dove deep under the goose-down quilt. A roaring sound filled her ears. Her heart beat faster. Her hands grew ice cold. The bed seemed to spin on an invisible axis.

With a low moan, Griselda fainted dead away.

Mark laid Belle's sleeping form back on her poor straw pallet. He tucked the blankets snug around her. Dawn's pale light already painted the sky outside her narrow window. Mark stroked her wan cheek. In sleep, she looked so young and vulnerable. If he possessed two ounces of common sense, he would carry her out of here right now and run to Jobe. By mid-morning, they all could be safe inside Montjoy's cottage. By this time next week, Belle would be back at Wolf Hall and Mark would be the master of his own estate.

Yet he knew she would waken before he could get her out the door and would scream the very stones down on his head. Stubborn chit! He leaned over and brushed his lips across her forehead. She sighed in her sleep.

Surprised at the tenderness she had evoked within him, Mark drew back. Then he pulled another napkin-wrapped packet from his sack and placed it under her hand. Dexter watched every move with unblinking golden eyes.

Mark gave the cat a hard look. ''Tis a morsel for your mistress and not for your belly, you glutton. Touch it and I'll turn you into a muff.''

Dexter continued to stare at him. Mark adjusted his cloak, gathered up the cup and napkin, then dropped another kiss on the top of Belle's head. He rose and strode toward the door. He took one last look before departing. How tiny she looked! How helpless he felt!

''Guard her well, cat!'' Then he swirled out the door and locked it behind him. He muffled a sneeze in the folds of his cape before he descended the spiral steps like the ghost he planned to portray. While he had cradled Belle throughout the cold night, he had formed several ideas for the haunting of Bodiam. He smiled to himself as he slunk through the shadowed courtyard. Mistress Sondra Owens's Black Knight would soon ride again.

Mark returned to his room without any of Mortimer's inattentive guards noticing him. Just as he started to open his door, someone hissed behind him. Pulling his dagger from its sheath, he whirled around to face a tousled and shivering Kitt.

''How now, boy!'' he muttered. ''Tis too early for tricks.''

Kitt put his finger to his lips, nodded toward the door

then motioned down the stairway. Puzzled, Mark descended after his fledgling squire. They slipped into the small alcove outside the postern gateway. Clad only in his nightshirt, Kitt shivered in the cold. Mark draped his cloak over the boy's shoulders before asking him, "What is it? Why are you not asleep?"

Kitt tossed a hank of hair out of his eyes. "Mistress Griselda is in your bed and as naked as the day she was born—or so it looked to me, though by my troth, I did not linger to examine her closely."

Mark grinned. "So that is the way the world turns, is it?"

Kitt blinked. "I do not understand."

Mark ruffled the boy's hair. "Mistress Griselda seeks to entrap me into a hasty marriage in case I might have second thoughts."

"But you do not intend to marry that harpy, do you?" Kitt asked.

Mark shook his head. "Twould be a fate worse than death. The question is what am I to do now? If I try to carry her back to her room, she will surely waken and scream for all the household to witness how I have debauched her."

Kitt grimaced. "But you have not touched her!"

Mark clapped him on the shoulder. "Lesson number one, Kitt. Women have wily minds that often work at cross-purpose with men's superior wit. Your bloody-minded sister is a good example."

"Tis not fair, Mark," he protested.

Mark smiled, wondering if he himself had ever been that innocent. "Aye, that is God's own truth, but we poor males are often the worse for it."

"And Mistress Griselda?"

Mark leaned back against the rough wall and considered

his narrow options. "We will go immediately to the stables where we will bed down near our horses. Lord knows we both could use a bit more sleep. When the grooms find us, we will say that we have spent the whole night there be-cause…because the wind made our good mounts restless. After that, we will make a great show of washing at the trough, chatting with the potboys and in general letting all and sundry know that we were nowhere near my chamber last night. Mistress Griselda will slink back to her own room with nary a word against me."

He chuckled. "Methinks this is the first time I have ever run *from* a naked lady in my bed." Then he glanced down at Kitt. "Where are your nether clothes?"

The boy gave him a wry look. "In the room with Mis-tress Griselda. I was in the privy attending to personal business when she came in. Upon seeing her, I ran without thinking."

Mark swore under his breath. "We'll have to borrow something from one of the stable lads. You cannot go rid-ing bare-bottomed over hill and dale."

Kitt brightened. "We go home today? Have you con-vinced Belle to leave?"

Mark frowned. "Nay, your sister is as wooden-headed as before. But we have thought of a plan whereby Morti-mer Fletcher and his ill-favored sister will wish they had never set foot in Bodiam."

Kitt quivered with excitement. "Good! Let us start now!"

Mark pinned the cloak under Kitt's chin. "Let us find you a pair of breeches first."

Chapter Seven

For the first time since her imprisonment, Belle looked forward to Mortimer's daily visit. She and Mark had no time to lose if they were to ply the Fletcher siblings's superstitious fears by All Hallows Eve, when the spirits of the dead were reputed to stalk the land. If anything could frighten Mortimer enough to abandon Bodiam it would have to coincide with the ancient festival of the dead. Leaning against the wall by her window, Belle drew in deep breaths of the morning's brisk air while she pondered her plan of attack.

She hated to admit, even to herself, that she was growing weaker despite Mark's fortifying meals and warm attention. The deprivations of the past month could hardly be erased by a few mouthfuls of meat and an extra blanket or two. Perhaps she should bow to Mark's wish. They could steal away tonight. Thoughts of Wolf Hall filled with warmth, food and her loving family brought tears to her eyes. She dashed them away.

Bodiam was hers. She had meant it when she had told Mark that she would die for it. Its honey-colored stones and graceful arched windows claimed her heart and soul.

"Oh, Papa," she whispered to the wind, "I wish you were here!" She knew that Brandon would understand.

The sound of hoofbeats on the wooden drawbridge broke her melancholy mood. Pressing herself against the wall, she craned her neck to see who was leaving Mortimer's lair.

"That knavish pignut!" she uttered aloud when she recognized the larger of the two riders. "Griselda's charms must have been too much for him to bear! That pigeon-livered maltworm is abandoning me, Dexter." *I should not have acted so haughty nor treated him so unkindly.*

She chewed her lower lip. "Look you, Dexter! See how he flees! Mark was always a coward. He broke promises at the turn of every hour. Oh! There is not one good quality that he can claim. I should never have put my trust in that pernicious snipe!"

Just before the pair reached the edge of the surrounding forest, Mark reined in his horse and looked toward her tower. Belle stepped in front of her window to show him that she witnessed his cowardly retreat. Mark kneed his silver-gray mount and the horse responded by rearing on its hind legs. Horse and rider danced in place for a few seconds.

Show-off! You will never grow up, Marcus.

Then he put his fingers to his lips and gave the piercing whistle that Belle recognized as her grandfather's call to summon his beloved dogs home for the day. *Home!* Her heart lightened.

Belle grinned at her cat. "Mark has finally come to his senses, Dexter. Methinks he is going for more help." Knowing that the guards on the battlements could not see her, Belle waved her hand out the window. Mark doffed his burgundy cap in return and his young squire blew her a kiss. *Cheeky lad!* She chuckled in spite of herself. *Little*

Bertrum will learn all of Mark's bad habits inside of a year.

She watched the man and boy disappear into the depths of Bodiam's forest. In her mind's eye she followed their progress down the familiar track toward the town of Hawkhurst.

The key rattled in the rusty lock. Belle hastened to her usual place at the far end of the small chamber before Mortimer opened the heavy door. Once again he bore a covered trencher. His smile looked particularly reptilian.

Belle pulled the cat into her lap. "Behold who comes to visit us, Dexter," she remarked. "A double-tongued snake!"

Mortimer arched his brow. "At one time I had hoped that we two could become the best of friends, LaBelle," he replied. His eyes glared coldly at her. "I could have made you a fine husband."

Belle snorted. "The very idea makes me shudder, Mortimer. In faith, I do earnestly desire that we become better strangers." *Now to drop the first pebble into his pool of superstition.* "In fact, I advise you to leave me alone before you anger the protective spirit within these walls with your perfidious speech."

Mortimer's hand shook a little. "What spirit is this, wench?"

Belle hid her elation behind a mask of indifference. "Why, the Black Knight of Bodiam, of course. I am sure that I have told you of him. Methinks you should choose your words to me with more care, Mortimer. All Hallows Eve draws apace, you know."

He turned slightly paler. "What has that to do with me?"

Belle stroked Dexter's long body. "Folks hereabouts do say that the Knight awakes from his yearly slumber and rides through the castle walls. They say he visits each nook and cranny of Bodiam on that night and showers his blessings upon all his family who sleep within his protection.'' Lowering her voice, she continued, ''But woe to any person who wishes evil on his descendants for death comes swiftly.''

Mortimer gulped. ''Tis but an old wives' tale.''

Belle shrugged. ''Perchance, but if I were you, I would be on my guard just the same. You will know if he is coming by the signs.''

The poltroon wet his thin lips. ''What sort of signs?''

Belle pretended to think. ''The usual things, I suppose— candles blowing out on themselves, curtains fluttering, strange sounds and lights in the night....''

Mortimer made a strangled noise in his throat. ''My men swore they saw a light coming from *your* window last night,'' he whispered.

Hogspit! I didn't think they could see Mark's lantern! And yet, this mistake may turn in our favor. Widening her eyes, she pretended to look startled. ''Last night you say? But I slept heavily all through the dark hours. I saw no light. And I have no candle to cheer me, thanks to your tender mercies. Methinks your minions were woolgathering.''

Mortimer shook his head. ''They swore they saw a golden light gleam from your window for several hours.''

Belle feigned shock. ''Tis true? Then perchance the Knight is already awake and roams his old home. Of course he would visit me, Mortimer. After all, I *am* the only family member in residence.''

Mortimer frowned. ''Griselda and I are your family as well,'' he said.

Tis working! Belle shot him a sneer. ''By marriage only, *not* at all by the bonds of blood or love. If you have a guilty heart, Mortimer, then mend your ways at once or you will suffer for it.''

His face hardened. Belle realized that she had overplayed her hand.

''Dissembling harlot! You are false in all you say!'' he snapped. He turned on his heel to go, but stopped before he reached the door.

''Your prattling nearly caused me to forget. Here.'' He placed the trencher on the floor and inched it toward her with the toe of his boot.

Belle could not mask her surprise at his sudden generosity. ''How now, brother-in-law? What jest is this?''

''Your dinner, my dear,'' he replied in a cool voice.

Despite its enticing aromas, Belle turned away from the tempting dish. ''Take it, Mortimer. I will not sign my home away for a mere mouthful of stew.''

He chuckled. It was not a cheerful sound. ''Tis nothing of the sort. Consider this meal as a gift. I am feeling particularly bountiful today.''

Belle eyed him as she would a snake in the grass. ''There must be a reason.''

''Indeed.'' He rubbed his hands together. ''Good fortune has sent Griselda a rich young lord to woo her.''

Ha! Mark is rich in pretty words and false promises but not in gold or lands. Aloud, Belle replied, ''Give Griselda my heartiest congratulations.''

Mortimer strode out onto the landing. ''Mayhap I will if I can recall your words.'' He closed the door slowly. ''Enjoy your dinner,'' he added before he slammed it shut. He laughed as he turned the key.

Belle dismissed the churl from her mind. She lifted the cloth. The tender breast of a succulent duckling swam in a honey-glazed orange sauce. A fresh loaf of bread, still warm from the oven, lay next to it, ready to sop up the delicious drippings. Belle's mouth watered. Before she could reach for the bird, Dexter pounced upon it.

"Away, you beast!" she screamed at the cat.

As quickly as he had leapt onto the dish, he backed away, spitting and shaking his head. Puzzled by Dexter's unusual behavior, Belle watched him as he once again approached the food. He tried to bat the napkin over the dish in an effort to hide it from sight. Then he shot Belle a look of pure disgust.

She wrinkled her nose. "Do not glare at me, Dexter. I did not cook it." She regarded the trencher. The glistening duck peeked from under the corner of the cloth and beckoned her ravenous hunger. Yet a bell of caution chimed in her head. Dexter was not the only one who acted in a strange manner. Mortimer's behavior had also gone against the grain. She pulled off a small piece of the well-cooked flesh and held it out to the cat.

"Is it not to your liking, my friend?" she asked.

Dexter approached the morsel cautiously, sniffed it then batted it out of her fingers. He shook his head several times. His long white whiskers bristled. Once again he stared at her with his large golden eyes.

"Is there something rotten in this fair offering, I wonder?" she mused. She sniffed at the sauce. Though the orange and honey smelled sweet, she noticed a less pleasing odor as well.

Summoning up her courage, Belle dipped her finger into the sauce then gingerly tasted it with the tip of her tongue. Mewing, Dexter paced back and forth.

Belle detected a bitter undertaste. She spat out the droplet then rinsed her mouth several times with clean water from her bucket.

"God shield us, Dexter! Tis some vile trick of Mortimer's to sicken me with his rotten fowl." Belle covered her hand with the napkin then carried the foul trencher to the window. She tossed the entire thing down into the moat. "Heaven help the fish," she murmured as she watched the tainted food disappear below the surface of the leaf-green water.

The shock of her brush with treachery left her feeling weak. Trembling all over, Belle sank to her pallet and wrapped herself in her blankets. Dexter snuggled next to her. His rough tongue rasped against the cold skin of her hand. She gathered him into her arms and buried her face in his thick coat of black-and-white fur.

"You are the very best of all friends." She shivered again. "If I am ever freed from this doleful place, I promise you the largest platter of the most succulent herring."

Dexter purred in reply.

Mark and Kitt collected Jobe from the exile of his little hut. Together the three rode into Hawkhurst and proceeded by a roundabout route to Montjoy's cottage. The old man opened the door before Mark could knock.

"Tis high time you've returned, my Lord Hayward!" Montjoy croaked, ushering them into his home. "Greetings, son of Satan," he added to Jobe.

The African merely laughed. "And good health to you, Father Fox," he replied.

Montjoy looked faintly surprised by the salutation. Then he permitted a tiny smile to cross his face. When he turned to Kitt, he lifted one white brow. "And methinks I have the honor to address young Master Christopher Cavendish, do I not?"

Kitt shot a quick glance at Mark, who rolled his eyes. The old man's memory was more keen than Mark had expected. It had been five years or more since Brandon and Kat had moved their family north to Wolf Hall.

He sighed. "Aye, Montjoy, you are correct, but I pray you, do not bandy the news about the town. Kitt is with me...under sufferance."

Montjoy hooded his eyes like an elderly owl in midday. "As I suspected." He settled himself in his accustomed seat by the fire. "As soon as I remembered who this sprig was, I wrote straightway to his parents."

With a groan, Kitt sank down on the hearthstones. "I will be in serious trouble when my lady mother next lays an eye upon me."

"Nay, lad," Mark muttered. "She will spare you and kill me instead—by inches." So much for his hopes of a prize piece of the Cavendish land. "When did you send this dire message to Wolf Hall, Montjoy?"

He folded his bony hands over his spare stomach. "The day before yesterday. Twill take Lady Kat at least two weeks before she arrives, methinks. Plenty of time to complete your task. By the way, where is Mistress Belle?"

Mark eased himself on the stool across from his host. "Still in her prison. There have been...complications."

Without looking the least surprised, Montjoy nodded. "There are often complications with the Cavendish family. Headstrong, the lot of them." He stared at Kitt who wriggled under his piercing scrutiny.

Mark growled his agreement. "Belle refuses to leave. Says she won't abandon her home. Says she'd die first." He gave Montjoy a steady look. "By my troth, methinks she means it."

The old man released a sigh that came from deep inside him. "I was afraid twould be the case. Mistress LaBelle took Bodiam into her heart from the first day she crossed over the drawbridge." A whisper of a smile flitted across his face. "She nearly fell into the moat trying to catch one of the swans."

Kitt whistled through his teeth. "She had more courage than I. I have a hearty respect for those birds myself."

Mark smiled at his squire's candor. While still a toddler in leading strings Kitt had tried to ride one of the arrogant creatures and had been chased up the front stairs of the castle by the outraged bird.

Montjoy flickered an eyebrow. "I recall the incident, Master Christopher."

Kitt turned red and stared into the fire. Sitting beside him, Jobe smiled but said nothing. Mark snapped himself back to the present. "Belle and I have hit upon a plan to force the Fletchers to leave her home—permanently."

"Might I suggest the application of prodigious amounts of gunpowder under their beds?" Montjoy remarked.

Mark nodded. "You have come closer to the bull's-eye than you suspect, Montjoy." He whispered, "We intend a haunting."

The former castle steward wet his lips. "I trust that Mistress Owens's ghost stories figure in this plan?"

Before Mark could reply, Jobe burst into rich laughter. "See, Kitt? I told you that this grandfather was as crafty as a fox. Much wisdom lies within his head. Now you see why we honor our elders in my own land."

Montjoy inclined his white head to the giant. "I am gratified to know that there is at least *one* intelligent man among this gathering. Prithee, Mark, explain to me this haunting."

Mark rubbed his chin. "The exact details have not yet been worked out but you will soon hear tales of strange sounds and sights in the night upon the castle walls."

"A good start," Montjoy agreed. "And what is my part in this tomfoolery—for I suspect that is why you have favored me with your company here today?"

Mark nodded. "Indeed, Montjoy, but first I crave a

piece of paper, pen and ink for I must send an urgent message to Sir Andrew Ford in Warwickshire.''

Kitt brightened. ''Uncle Andrew? But methinks he is too old to come haring down here even to help Belle.''

Montjoy cleared his throat. ''I am considerably older than my Lord Ford yet this mischievous jester intends to drag *me* into his piece of mummery.'' He skewered Kitt with his sharp gaze. ''Attend to this bit of philosophy, young Christopher. Age is merely a state of mind.''

Kitt opened his mouth, saw Mark shake his head and promptly withdrew his unvoiced objection.

Jobe grinned. ''I like you more and more, good Father Fox.''

Montjoy pointed to the top drawer in his cupboard where Mark found the writing materials he required. He hurriedly penned a terse letter to the Cavendish family friend who had once been the old Earl's squire. His companions kept their peace; only the scratching of the quill across the thick paper broke the silence in the small room. With a final flourish, Mark signed his name, then blew on the wet ink.

''There now, my friends. Let us hope that Sir Andrew will send all that I need by return messenger.''

Kitt's blue eyes gleamed. ''Fireworks!'' he breathed. ''My notable uncle is a master in the art of devising the most wondrous display of fireworks you ever saw,'' he explained to Jobe. ''Each year at Twelfth Night, Andrew amazes my family with his clever work. Truly, tis this side of magic.''

Jobe grinned with a great display of white teeth. ''Most excellent! Tis a sight I would like to behold.''

Mark folded his letter and dropped a hot blob of red wax on the flap to seal it. ''You will, my friend, if Sir Andrew Ford proves true.''

* * *

Mortimer enjoyed his midday dinner with particular relish, though Griselda hardly noticed his unusual appetite. She was utterly besotted with her admirer. Mortimer practically laughed aloud when Sir Mark's inept squire served the roasted duckling that swam in its delicious honey and orange sauce. He licked the rich drippings from his fingers while he wondered how much of the meat his sister-in-law had managed to swallow before sleep overpowered her. An everlasting sleep—and the end to all his problems. Just as he had done with Cuthbert. What a pickle-brain fool he had been to have allowed Belle's beauty beguile him into dreams of marriage! Ah well, better late than never.

Mortimer toasted himself with a second large goblet of unwatered wine. Griselda failed to remark on his good cheer. Mortimer usually watered his drinks liberally. Sir Mark noticed nothing at all save to praise Griselda's green gown—a ghastly color on her; her slim waist—bone thin in truth; and her dainty fingers—that Mortimer knew squeezed her suitor's knee under the table at every opportunity. Such drivel was enough to put a man off his dinner.

In the midafternoon, Mortimer resisted his desire to investigate Belle's garret. Even the smitten Griselda might notice the change in his routine. And Sir Mark Hayward? A wild card in the pack to be sure. There was something about the nobleman that tickled his memory but he could not catch it. Mortimer shrugged away his doubts. Though he suspected that Sir Mark was as much a cad as himself, prudence must be the watchword. He must not offer too much food for thought to the lovesick lord.

When Mortimer spied Will on his way to Belle's tower with her bread and the bucket of clean water, he stopped him. "Mistress Belle is sick and methinks the disease is contagious,'' he told the gaping lackwit. ''I will tend to her myself. Be off with you!''

Scratching his shaggy hair, Will ambled back to the kitchen. Mortimer relaxed. He did not want to run the risk that Belle still lived. He had no idea how long the poison would take to do its deadly work. Belle must be cold and rigid when she was discovered. Twenty-four hours should do the trick.

Mortimer rubbed his hands together. Bodiam was his now—every stone and lintel of the great rambling place. He stuffed his knuckles into his mouth to keep from shouting his glee to the cloudy heavens. Tomorrow, he would sorrowfully inform the pastor of Hawkhurst's parish church that the beloved Belle Cavendish Fletcher had wasted away from her widow's grief. She had joined her dear departed husband in paradise. There would be a funeral. Mortimer flinched at the thought of the expense, but good form must be followed to banish all doubts. Lord Hayward and that overwhelming Cavendish family must never suspect foul play—or was that fowl play? He chortled when he thought of the deadly duck.

There would be much weeping and wailing during the next few weeks. Mortimer realized that he would have to display a proper respect for the sorrow of the Cavendishes though he heartily loathed Belle's entire family. But once the last clod of earth filled her grave, the blessed law of England would hand to Belle's surviving brother-in-law the keys to this castle—especially everything in it.

Including a large ruby brooch with its dangling pearl— *that* was the real prize of Bodiam. Though he had only seen the fabulous jewel on Cuthbert's wedding day, Mortimer remembered it in every sparkling detail. Rubbing his hands together, he descended into the gloom of the cellars under the withdrawing chamber to inspect the slug-like progress of his treasure hunters. Once the castle was legally his, he would dispense with this slow stealth. He would raze Bodiam to the ground within a month.

Chapter Eight

When Mark learned of Mortimer's grim trick, he sweep Belle into his arms and held her tightly against his pounding chest. But for the grace of God and the cleverness of the cat, he could have been clasping her lifeless body. Belle thought that Mortimer only meant to sicken her into signing the deed, but Mark suspected that murder was Fletcher's true intention. That stark realization turned his initial white-hot anger into cold fury.

So that is why the blackguard was so cheerful at dinner! He thought she was dead!

Instead of protesting his embrace, Belle laid her head on his shoulder. In the silence of the friendly darkness, they clung to each other for a few breathless moments. Then Mark stepped back and cupped her face in his hands. How fragile she looked in the pale beams of the moon!

"Tis settled then," he told her. "You will not stay here a moment longer."

"But—" she began.

He laid a finger across her lips. "*Listen* to me for once, Belle. If you insist upon remaining in this garret you will have no second chance, I assure you. Methinks Mortimer would strangle you with his bare hands if necessary."

She swallowed. "I will never give up my home to him!"

Mark stroked her cheek. Soft like the petal of a rose. "Nor do you have to. Tis time for Belle Cavendish to become another wraith of Bodiam Castle."

Her cornflower blue eyes flashed with her old fire. A mischievous smile curled her lips. "Tell me more!"

He tapped her nose. "Nay, *chou-chou.* I will show you." With that he lifted her in his arms and started for the door.

Belle squeaked with surprise. "Mark, what are you doing?"

"What I should have done in the first place, Belle. I'm taking matters into my own hands. Now transform into a ghost and be silent!" He slipped out the door with Dexter at his heels. Mark turned the lock behind them, then adjusted his dark cape over her.

"Where are you taking me?" she whispered from under the concealing cloth.

He chuckled. "To the land of shadows, my sweet."

"I can walk!" she protested.

"But I can run faster if it comes to that." *Pray God twill not come to that.* "Now close your pretty mouth, *chou-chou.* This next part of our journey will make or mar us."

She muttered a French oath but lay still in his arms. Once again, Mark marveled at how feather-light she was. Mortimer would pay and pay for this, he vowed.

Earlier that day, Mark and Kitt had investigated the lesser-used sections of the castle, searching for a suitable base for their supernatural operations. In his idle conversations with Mortimer, Mark had learned that the new lord of the manor was unfamiliar with much of the retainers' old quarters, particularly in the west wing. Since the general dismissal of the loyal castle staff, many of the chambers now lay vacant.

Holding his tender burden closer to his heart, Mark crept among the deepest shadows at the outer edges of the central courtyard. Though the buttery door was locked for the night, he remembered from his earlier days at Bodiam how to pry open the hatch.

"Hold tight," he murmured as he swung his legs through the opening.

"Do I have a choice?" she asked.

He landed on the balls of his feet. "Nay," he whispered. *Too bad this midnight lark couldn't have taken place in a happier time.* At thirteen, Belle's figure had budded with sweet promise of the beauty she would become. Her newly acquired charms had not been lost on her father's lusty twenty-year-old squire. Mark's arm ached when he recalled the disastrous end to his wooing.

Dexter, despite his ponderous size, easily followed Mark over the hatchway's sill. Mark elbowed the hatch back into place, then hurried down the gloomy passageway to the narrow stairs that led to the gallery above the huge kitchen. On the landing, Mark paused and listened. The cook and the four potboys shared two adjoining chambers at the far end of the passage. Their loud snores echoed off the stone walls.

Satisfied that none of the servants were awake, Mark turned down a narrower passage that ran at right angles to the first. A large dusty tapestry hung down to the floor at the far end. Without pausing, Mark slipped behind it.

The dust tickled his nose as he fumbled for the latch of the door concealed there. With a small squeak, the door swung open on its rusty hinges. *Must grease that.* Bounding between Mark's feet, Dexter led the way into the cozy room that had once been the private preserve of Montjoy when he had ruled over Bodiam's daily life.

Mark set Belle on her feet. "You are home," he whispered. He shut the door as quietly as he could. "Forgive me for not preparing your bower properly, but I had not expected you to arrive here so soon."

Belle blinked her eyes and looked around. She grinned when she recognized the chamber. "Perfect!" she murmured.

"Indeed!" Mark felt very pleased with his choice of a hideaway. No one now living at Bodiam, with the possible exception of dim-witted Will, knew of this room's existence. "I fear the bed sags a little and the mattress is moldy, but—"

Belle shook her head. "'Tis heaven, Mark! I have slept on a cold floor for over a month." She whirled on him and gave him a hug that heated his blood and sent it racing through his veins. "You are a wonder! Oh, thank you!"

Then she spun out of his arms before he had the chance to pursue the depth of her gratitude. She ran her fingertips along the armchair that stood next to the empty fireplace. A threadbare cushion was all that remained of Montjoy's bolsters that had comforted his aching joints on his "misery days." She tapped lightly on the thick window glass that kept out the night's frosty gusts.

"Thank heavens for Montjoy's aching bones!" Belle laughed. Built next to the kitchen flue, his snuggery was the warmest spot in the castle.

Mark nodded. "Remind me to thank Lady Kat for hanging that tapestry. It may have kept out the drafts and noise then, but 'twill keep out your enemies now."

He drew closer to Belle. In the moonglow that shone through the tiny square window, she resembled too closely the ghost she would soon portray. "The dawn comes on

winged feet and the cook will soon awake. There is much
I must do before then. Give me your gown."

Belle narrowed her eyes. "If you think for one moment
that I will lie with you in gratitude, you are—"

Mark stopped her mouth with a hard kiss. He had only
meant to silence her, but the fires that he had banked for
so long suddenly roared into flames. He teased her lips
with his tongue. Belle made small mewing noises in her
throat, then to his surprise parted her lips under his. Mark
wound her in his embrace and deepened his kiss. He drank
from her sweet spring as if he had been parched for many
years—eight to be exact.

With great reluctance, he released her mouth. "Ah, *ma
petite chou-chou,* you were always a tease."

She bristled. "I didn't ask for—"

He covered her lips once more with his. "Hush!" he
whispered between his urgent kisses. "Did anyone ever
tell you that you talk too much?"

She gripped his arms and shook him. "Methinks I
would rather kiss your horse!" She licked her love-swollen
lips.

He chuckled. "That could be arranged, though you will
have to wait a few more days for the pleasure. Now, *chou-
chou,* we have bantered long enough. Give me your
gown."

"You pig!" she snarled.

He held up his hands in front of his face in case she
took it into her head to use her claws. "Peace, Belle! I
have no carnal desires for you." *My tongue will surely
shrivel for that lie!* "I intend to use your garment to effect
the first of our hauntings."

She cast him a hard stare. "Truly? On the shreds of
honor that you still possess?"

In reply, Mark spread his cloak on the lumpy mattress.

"Go to sleep, *chou-chou,* while I work my magic elsewhere."

Belle turned her back to him, then wriggled out of the filthy garment. Clad only in her tattered shift, she scurried to the bed and wrapped herself up in his cape. "I shall keep watch for your return," she murmured. Her eyelids fluttered shut.

Dexter leapt onto the bed beside her and wiggled his thick body under a corner of the cloak.

Snatching up the gown, Mark rubbed his itchy nose. "Mark me, cat, some day soon you and I will trade places. In the meantime, guard her well." Then he stole out of the room, leaving Belle to sleep in true peace.

Back safely in his own room, Mark shook Kitt awake.

"How now?" the boy muttered. "Tis morning so soon?"

"Nay," Mark replied as he hunkered down by the cool fireplace. "Tis the witching hour. Get up and dress in your darkest clothing."

The boy stopped yawning. "Are we to play at goblins now?"

Mark scooped up two large handfuls of the ashes and bundled them in Belle's pitiful remnant of clothing. "Aye, foot it, boy! We must be back in our beds before the cock crows."

Something intruded into Mortimer's sleep. Through a muffled mist of blackness, a man shouted "Who goes there?"

Another called, "Tis here!"

A third bellowed, "Tis there!"

"Tis gone!" cried a fourth.

Mortimer slowly opened his eyes. The glass panes of his chamber window reflected dancing red-orange flames.

The castle burns! He threw back his thick down coverlet and swung his legs to the floor. More cries of alarm brought him to full wakefulness. Without bothering to search for his fleece-lined slippers, he dashed across the rug and pushed open his window that overlooked the courtyard.

A dozen men-at-arms, each one holding a blazing torch, crisscrossed the open quadrangle of the castle. Sleepy-eyed servants stumbled from various doorways in various states of undress.

"You!" Mortimer shouted at the nearest guard. "What's amiss at this unholy hour?"

The man did not hear him but continued to thrust his torch into the darkened nooks behind doors, inside rain barrels and under the low roofs of the woodsheds. More shouts, more frenzied searching convinced Mortimer that some order must be brought into this chaos before those sheep-witted dolts truly set Bodiam afire. He lit his bedside candle, grabbed his dressing gown and located his slippers. Knotting his sash with one hand while he held his candle aloft with the other, he hurried down the gallery.

Griselda poked her head out of her door. "What is it?" she screeched.

"Stay in your room!" he shouted over his shoulder. "I need none of your hysterics now!" Mortimer clattered down the main staircase.

His sergeant-at-arms met him in the hall. The gruff man's skin looked bloodless in the eerie light of his torch.

Mortimer shook his finger in the man's face. "Fowler! What is the cause of this hellish din?"

Fowler rubbed his rough beard. "Damme, Master Fletcher, I know not. A half hour ago the men on the gatehouse battlements heard hoofbeats."

Mortimer furrowed his brow. "At this time of night?"

"Aye," the sergeant replied tersely. "The men reported that it sounded as if the rider crossed the causeway then rode over the drawbridge into the keep."

Mortimer's heartbeat quickened. "I left strict orders that the bridge should be raised at night, you clodpate!"

"Aye," the man snarled in reply. "It was—still is. The gate is still double-locked and barred, yet the men swear that the hoofbeats came into the courtyard and circled around."

Mortimer's mouth went dry. "And then?"

Fowler licked his lips. "Then wee lights blinked on and off." He lowered his voice. "Like the will o'wisps that haunt the swamplands and moors."

Mortimer's neck hairs prickled. "The devil take it, man! You have all been hoodwinked by someone who drank too much ale at supper!"

Fowler slowly shook his head. "Though I did not hear the phantom horse, Master Fletcher, I swear upon my mother's soul that I saw the lights."

Mortimer gripped his candlestick until the carving on the stem bit into the palm of his hand. "Where away?" he asked in a hoarse whisper.

Fowler pointed to the northwest tower. "Several winked at the arrow slits ascending the stairs, then they disappeared. Then once again they winked at the bottom and began the ascent again."

Mortimer's blood pounded in his temples. "And what did you see when you investigated?"

Fowler looked away. "No one dared draw near the tower, Master Fletcher."

Mortimer's anger overcame his fears. "What? I pay you maggots to defend my home. Your bravery costs me a pretty penny, yet a few lights turn you into a gaggle of geese?"

Fowler stood his ground. "I'll fight any man who casts a shadow upon my courage," he growled. "Any man of *flesh and blood*. But I will have nothing to do with spirits and demons, nor should anyone with half a wit," he added with a glare.

Before Mortimer could spew more of his nervous anger, another one of the guards ran up to them. "Tis there again!" he babbled. "The light in the highest tower window. It shines like a beacon."

Belle's chamber! Mortimer felt light-headed.

"Hoy day, what is going on?" drawled the voice of his guest from behind him.

Mortimer spun on his heel. Sir Mark, dressed only in his nightshirt, yawned in his face. "Is there some sport at play here?" the nobleman asked with a grin.

Blast the knave! Mortimer plastered a reassuring smile across his mouth. "Tis nothing but a false alarm, my lord. A few of my men have drunk more than they should. Pray forgive the disturbance. Return to your slumber. I will attend to their chastisement."

Lord Hayward yawned again and scratched his head. "Aye me, Master Fletcher. Twas the first good night's sleep I have enjoyed since I came under your roof. Hell's bells, twill take me hours to return to the land of Morpheus." He leaned closer to Mortimer and flashed him a leer. "Mayhap I will soothe myself with that sweet young wench I passed in the hall."

A roaring filled Mortimer's ears. "What wench?" he asked in a faint voice. Save for Griselda there were no other women in Bodiam—now that Belle was…gone.

The tall lord chuckled. "A toothsome creature by the quick look I had of her. Long blond hair flowing down her back and slim as a willow. Shame on you, my good host! You should have told me of her sooner."

Mortimer almost gagged. The bitter iron taste of bile filled his mouth. "Pray ex...excuse me, my l...lord," he stammered. "The air gr...grows colder and I m...must see to my m...men. Get you to bed!" With that, he practically ran down the wide steps into the courtyard. Fowler followed a short distance behind.

Mortimer's thoughts tumbled against each other in confusion as he crossed the quadrangle. When he passed by his terrified retainers, they grew silent and fell in behind him. At the door to the tower he paused. All the narrow windows facing inside the castle were dark as pitch.

He pointed to the lowest one. "You saw lights there?" he asked the sergeant.

A chorus of "Ayes" answered him from the assembled guards.

"And a light still glows from the top floor, Master Fletcher," one of them added in a small voice. "If you lean over the portcullis you can see its beams dance on the moat. Twas there not five minutes ago."

Several of the hardened men muttered prayers and made signs against the evil eye. Not one of the sheep offered to go up the tower's winding stairs. Mortimer gritted his teeth. Only he knew who lay behind the locked door at the top. No one save that witless fool Will had ventured up there since Mortimer had imprisoned Belle over five weeks ago. He took a deep breath.

"Very well! Since none of you have any real blood in your veins, I will see this wonder for myself."

Mortimer kicked open the door. No one behind him moved an inch. Flinging an oath over his shoulder, he began the steep ascent alone. Under his breath, he whispered charms to ward off whatever evil lurked above him. Nothing moved in the shadows as he passed from the first to the second floor. In the surrounding silence, he heard his heart pound within its ribbed cage.

A thin sliver of light gleamed under the door on the topmost floor. The key stuck out from its lock with mocking invitation. Mortimer was glad that no one could see his trembling hand. He now regretted that he had not asked Sir Mark to accompany him. He gripped the candleholder.

The door was still locked. Mortimer's sweating fingers fumbled with the key. Cursing, he wiped his slick hands on his dressing gown, then tried again. When the door swung open, Mortimer nearly dropped his candle with fright.

A lighted taper affixed by its own wax atop the whitened skull of some horned beast greeted him. The gruesome thing's lower jaw was completely gone. The night wind that blew through the unprotected window caused the flame to dance upon its wick. Mortimer inched his way inside the cold chamber.

The ice-cold, *empty* chamber.

Every nerve in his body screamed at him to flee. He forced himself to stand still and look again. Against the far wall lay the small heap of dirty straw that had been Belle's pallet. The ragged brown blanket lay there—neatly folded. Beside it was the small pitcher for her water—now broken in half.

In the exact center of the chamber lay Belle's ragged gown, pooled on the floor as if she had just stepped out of it. Some grayish matter lay within its ring. Mortimer's curiosity overcame his fears. He advanced with mincing steps. What he saw made him drop the candlestick.

A heap of fine ashes lay amid the gown's folds and protruding from them were a few white sticks. Mortimer touched one and discovered to his horror that it was the brittle bone of—a duck.

"Holy Mother of God!" he cried aloud as he backed away from the terrifying sight.

Instead of Belle's dead body, only her dust remained sprinkled with the mute evidence of her demise. Jesu! How could he explain this ghastly occurrence to anyone? What was he going to tell the Cavendish family? And what infernal fire had consumed Belle's body so quickly yet left her ashes so cold?

Just then a gust of wind blew out the candle on the skull, plunging the chamber into total darkness.

With a howl, Mortimer fled the room. He slammed the door shut against the unbelievable sight within, then plunged down the winding stairs. Between the second and first floors, he heard a low chuckle behind him. Blinded by his panic, he ran faster, nearly pitching headfirst against the round wall. The laughter behind him increased in volume—a mirth deeper, richer, more demonic than anything he had ever heard before.

Mortimer had no idea when or if the terrifying sound ceased. At the base of the stairs, he fainted.

Jobe heard Mortimer's collapse on the stone floor below him. With a self-satisfied grin, the huge African slipped back into the west wing's gallery that joined the drum tower on the second-floor level. There he retrieved his bundle of bedding, food and other necessities. When he heard the door at the base of the tower slam shut, he quietly ascended the spiral stairs to Belle's abandoned prison as Mark had directed him. Jobe locked himself into the garret chamber—the very last place Mortimer would think to look for any mysterious guest who planned to haunt the castle during the coming days.

Working by the wan light of the half-moon, Jobe tossed the filthy straw and ash-strewn gown out the window. The broken pitcher followed immediately afterward. The shards made two small "plops" into the moat like the sounds of leaping fish. Then he covered the open window with several layers of black woolen curtains that Kitt had located from some unknown source. Jobe lit the candle on the cow's skull. Mark's master stroke, he thought. Mark had remembered the bleached head from the days of his youth when the moat had been drained and cleaned. He told Jobe that Mistress Belle, at the age of nine, had latched onto the grisly thing and had squirreled it away in her special hiding place. Sure enough, after twelve years, it had still lain in the dovecote as Mark had remembered.

Jobe shook out the feather bed and his thick wool blanket. After enjoying a late-night snack purloined from the kitchen, he blew out the candle, then rolled himself up in his bedding. Before settling down to catch a few hours of sleep, Jobe sent a prayer of thanksgiving to his ancestors in the starry heavens above him.

"Most excellent sport," he whispered to the ancient ones. "There is very strong ju-ju here. I feel it all about me. But one thing I beg, O Fathers," he added with a small frown. "Help me protect my good friend's life and so satisfy my debt to him. Mark Hayward is too reckless by half."

Chapter Nine

Belle groaned and batted at the hand that shook her shoulder. She half-opened her eyes. "Go away, Kitt! Tis too early to get up."

Her little brother chuckled. "Nay, Belle. Tis nearly noon."

His familiar voice jolted her. Kitt! Why wasn't he at Wolf Hall studying his Latin verbs? Belle bolted upright on Montjoy's sagging bed. "Sweet Saint Anne! What are you doing here? Oh, no! You're Bertrum, Mark's squire, aren't you?"

Kitt puffed out his chest. The boy had grown since she had last seen him. A wide smile so like Papa's wreathed his face. "You have hit the target dead center. I have come to rescue you." he announced proudly. He placed a small tray of food on her lap. "Zounds, you are as bony as a plucked chicken."

Despite her joy at seeing him, she bristled at his candor. "I perceive that you have learned how to flatter a girl, Kitten."

He squared his shoulders. "I am not a kitten any longer, Belle," he told her with a surprising note of maturity in his treble voice. "Tis time I became a young lion, Jobe says."

Belle bit into the still-warm pigeon pie. "Very well," she replied between mouthfuls. "But how did you convince Papa and Kat to send you on this misguided errand?" She swallowed and stared at her handsome brother. "My God, Kitt! You have no idea what a hornet's nest you have blundered into."

He sat down on the bed beside her. "But I do, Belle." His expression turned grim. "Mark told me what that pernicious base-born callet tried to do to you. By the rood, I swear I will avenge you."

Taken aback by mild-mannered Kitt's expanded vocabulary, Belle gaped at him. "And just who has taught you such pretty speeches? Mark? I will claw out his tongue at the first opportunity. Did *he* urge you to this mad romp? You should be home where tis safe."

Kitt eyed her. "So should you, sister. Do not chide Mark. This adventure is my own doing and none of his. He was as unhappy as you when he learned that I had followed them." He grinned at her. "Though they did not discover me for over a day," he added with pride. "Jobe says that I would make an excellent tracker."

Belle sopped up the gravy with a hunk of bread. "And who, pray tell, is this Jobe that you admire so much?"

Kitt chuckled. "He is like no one whom you have ever seen, I warrant. He is the greatest warrior in all of England—except for Papa and Uncle Guy, of course."

"He had better be," Belle remarked more to herself than to her brother, "or I will flay him by inches for encouraging you in this mad enterprise."

Kitt had not only brought her breakfast but also firewood for her little hearth, fresh linens for her bed and warmed water for washing her face and hair. He had even remembered soap. "I…er…borrowed some from Mistress Griselda," he explained, turning a little pink.

"Oh?" asked Belle as she worked the thick lather through her oily locks. The sensation felt delicious! "Is stealing something else Mark has taught you?"

"Nay," he replied as he poured the rinse water over her head into a clay basin. "Jobe did. He says that I have a natural talent for slipping in and out of a woman's bower."

"I cannot *wait* to meet this paragon of virtue," she muttered, squeezing out the excess water from her hair.

Despite her disapproval of Kitt's latest skill, Belle gratefully donned the clean shift and a plain gown that her brother had liberated from Griselda's wardrobe. The feel of fresh clothing on her body almost made her weep. She blinked away the moist drops from her eyelids before Kitt could spy them.

In the meantime, her little brother bustled about the tiny chamber in a most business-like manner. After tightening the bedropes, he built her a fire in the small hearth and emptied the dirty water down the privy located in an alcove. Belle marveled at his efficiency. The Kitt she remembered had never done a single chore in his pampered life. Was Mark actually teaching the boy something useful?

She cleared her throat. "So where is Mark this fine morning? Still asleep?"

Kitt made a face. "He would pray for such a boon. Instead, at this very moment he woos Mistress Griselda in the garden."

Belle exchanged a grin with her brother. "Good! Twill serve to puncture his vanity a bit. I almost feel sorry for him."

Kitt arched an eyebrow exactly as their father often did. "You should, Belle. Griselda is bound and determined to seduce him lest he escape her bondage of matrimony. Why only the other night, she slipped into his bed.''

A hot flush of jealousy washed over Belle. ''And exactly *what* did Mark do?'' she spat out the question.

Kitt gave her a decidedly wicked grin. ''I know not. He was with you at the time. Twas I that encountered the wanton hussy.''

''*What?*''

Kitt laughed at her shocked expression. ''Aye, Belle. She was as naked as a jaybird, too. Not pretty like the serving girl at Montjoy's—''

Belle grabbed him by the shoulders and shook him. ''Stop right there, Kitt! I do not want to hear one more word about your...new-found interest in women. Tis unseemly. You're still a baby.''

He glowered at her. ''Nay, sister! I am closer to my manhood than my cradle. Tis time that you, Mama and Papa realize that. With Francis in Paris and Papa strapped down in bed, tis only right that I came to your aid.''

''And what of Mark? Methought he was supposed to be my savior,'' she asked with a half-smile.

Kitt tossed her a towel for her wet hair. ''Jobe says tis blood that counts. I came for love of you. Papa is paying Mark a princely fee for your return.''

Belle could hardly speak for the sudden fury that exploded inside her. What a perfidious rat! Just when she thought Mark had finally attained some good qualities, she discovered that he was still the same self-seeking rogue he had always been—only worse.

This time, he had nearly stolen her heart.

''Tis a wonder he has lived this long,'' she murmured. When this nightmare was over and Bodiam was once again firmly in her hands, Belle vowed that Mark would rue the day he had accepted Papa's offer. "He'll soon find out that I am not a piece of chattel to be bought and paid for."

"Jobe says that women are always bought whether tis a dowry or—" Kitt had the prudence to shut his mouth when he spied the daggers in Belle's eyes.

"I do not give a squashed gooseberry what this buffoon Jobe says, Kitt. Just remember one thing—I will never become a man's property—most especially not Mark Hayward's!"

Mortimer sat hunched over his writing desk in the small garderobe off his bedchamber. He had no appetite for dinner, nor had he touched the early morning breakfast that one of the lackeys had delivered to his door. He ran his shaking fingers through his tangled hair as he stared at the sheet of blank paper before him.

What could he write to those infernal Cavendishes? How simple his plan had been twenty-four hours ago! Belle would be dead; her wasted body proof that she had died of grief for Cuthbert. A decent burial, condolences to her family, then the castle and its treasure for Mortimer. But now—?

Recalling the pile of ashes and duckling bones amidst her clothing, he shuddered. One thing was certain, he would never enter that room again. In fact he would order it sealed up. He wiped his sweaty palms on his dressing gown. What was he going to tell the world about the ungodly events of last night? He rubbed his eyes that stung from lack of sleep.

Belle died of a fever? Nay, twould set the countryside ablaze with fears that the strange sweating sickness had reappeared. Mortimer could not risk any close inquiries by the local authorities. An accident? Though he had staffed Bodiam with hirelings, he did not trust them beyond the limits of his purse strings. Besides, they had witnessed ghostly sounds and lights. He shivered.

A third alternative shot into his brain. Sitting back in his chair, Mortimer twirled his quill pen while he allowed his imagination to play out the full scenario. A sly grin fluttered on his lips.

Suicide! The very notion caused good people's blood to run cold. Even though King Henry had broken with the Pope, the condemnation of suicide was still universal. Anyone who took their own life flouted God's precious gift and was immediately damned to the eternal fires of hell. Suicides were not to be mourned, not to be given a Christian burial and the deceased's name was never to be spoken again. No corpse was needed, no burial—and no questions asked. Perfect!

Mortimer dipped his pen into the ink bottle, then began to write a sorrowful message to Sir Brandon and Lady Cavendish. As good, God-fearing folk they would never come down to Sussex to give their final farewell to their bastard daughter. To them, Belle must cease to exist—and Mortimer, her devoted brother-in-law, could lawfully claim Bodiam as his own.

I shall give my message a fortnight to reach Wolf Hall before I begin to tear this heap of stones apart. The brooch is mine at last!

Mark sauntered down the west gallery. Slowing when he neared the concealing tapestry, he glanced over his shoulder. Not a soul in sight. He knew he ran the risk of detection by visiting Belle in broad daylight but Mortimer's latest move made Mark's decision imperative. He slipped behind the thick tapestry and rapped softly on the door.

"Tis Mark," he spoke through the keyhole. "Hurry!"

The key turned in the lock. Not waiting for Belle to admit him, he ducked inside the door, bolting it behind him. Then he turned to her.

"We have a problem," he began, but the rest of his sentence lost its way. His breath literally stopped in his throat.

Seated on the foot of her bed like a nymph from a Greek vase, Belle brushed her long hair in front of a cheerful fire. The afternoon's sunlight turned her gleaming tresses into spun gold. After a good night's sleep and dressed in a clean blue gown, she looked new-made—and highly desirable. The square neck of her bodice did little to conceal the outlines of her firm full breasts. Mark's blood heated and his loins stirred at the sight. Great Jove! When had the chit turned into such a dazzler?

On the other hand, the fire storm in her eyes was anything but welcoming. "Exactly how much is my father paying you, worm?"

Mark whistled under his breath. How had she learned that piece of news? Kitt must have sneaked in to see her while Mark was in Griselda's clutches. He swept her a bow. "My deepest gratitude for your kind welcome, *chouchou*. Is this how you greet all of your knights-errant?"

She wrinkled her nose. "Answer my question, false cur! What riches did my father offer you to bring me home?"

Mark swallowed. He had not planned to tell Belle about the business end of this adventure. He knew she would take it amiss, yet now that particular sticking point had unsheathed itself. He switched his tactics. Offense had always been the best defense against Belle's tantrums.

"Tis barely enough for the trouble, I assure you," he replied with a twist of disdain.

Belle narrowed her eyes into dangerous slits. "Be precise! I want to know exactly how much my life is worth to you.''

Mark stepped closer, though he still kept out of the range of her claws. ''Your father thinks the world of you, but I am content to have a mere thousand acres of his estate lands.''

Rising, her body shook with her outrage. ''A goodly price—for a girl, I warrant, especially considering that she is a bastard,'' she snapped.

Ah! There's the core of her displeasure. Mark softened his expression. ''You are well worth twice that amount, *chou-chou.*''

Belle tossed her hair out of her face and lifted her chin. ''And what do you aim to do with this great wealth—if you manage to acquire it?''

Mark took another step closer. ''Build myself a fine manor house, marry a rich heiress and produce a long line of little Haywards.''

She arched one of her delicate brows. ''Of course! I had forgotten. You are nobly born though your behavior often gives the lie to that fact. No matter. Like all the rest of the noble peacocks, you run true to type. I suppose that this heiress of yours could be ugly, crook-backed and a dribbling idiot yet you would still marry her if she were rich enough and had the proper breeding.''

Mark's defensive anger turned to compassion. Belle's visit to King Henry's court must not have been a happy one for her once the truth of her parentage had become fodder for common gossip. How many slings and arrows of petty insults had she endured from those pompous popinjays?

Drawing closer still, he caught a faint scent of lavender in her hair. ''Then you are misinformed. Though I am but an impoverished younger son, I do have some standards.

I would marry a poor girl in only her shift if I loved her,"
he replied as his gaze bore into her eyes. "Why did Cuthbert Fletcher marry you, *chou-chou?*"

She looked away and rubbed the side of her nose, a sign
that told Mark he had cut too near the bone. Before she
had a chance to change the subject, he slipped his arm
around her slim waist and drew her closer to him. "All
those prattling fools at court must have had scales over
their eyes not to see you for the rare prize that you are."

Stiffening in his embrace, Belle would not look at him.
"Nay, they were all quite clear-sighted. They saw a commoner dressed up to ape a lady. Twas a very educational
time at Greenwich Palace. I had no end of young gallants
who wanted to show me exactly where my place in society
was—on my back in their beds!" A crimson blush stained
her cheeks.

A hundred curses trembled on his lips, but Mark refused
to unleash them. Had he been at court, he would have
challenged every last dog of them. Belle might try the
patience of a saint, but she was no lewd sinner.

"All except Cuthbert?" he prodded.

"Aye." She relaxed against him, spent by the strength
of her emotions. "He was kind, and did not care who
my...my mother was."

"So you married him." In gratitude, no doubt. Oh, poor
sweet Belle! "Did you love him?"

She spun out of his arms like a sudden whirlwind.
"How dare you ask me such a personal question!"

Mark's mood lightened. *She didn't!* He grinned at her.
"You know me, Belle. I can dare a great many things if
I put my mind to it. Tell me, did Cuthbert love you?"

"Of course he did!" she snapped.

Feeling more sure of himself, Mark again pulled her to
his chest and wrapped his arms around her. His body

throbbed at the stimulating contact. "And did he hold you in his arms like this?" He danced his fingers up her spine.

She shivered under his touch. "'Tis wrong to malign the dead," she murmured.

Mark swallowed a chuckle. He stroked Belle's cheek and traced her firm little jawline with the pad of his thumb. "And did blessed Cuthbert touch you like this?"

She gasped softly at his touch. "How can I recall anything when you distract me?"

Cuthbert was an ass of the first magnitude. Good!

Without pausing to give Belle any time to think, Mark lowered his mouth to hers. He brushed her lips with his as if he caressed a butterfly. She responded by rising on her toes to meet him. Encouraged, he traced the fullness of her lips with his tongue. Delicious and heady as new summer's wine. Belle slid her arms around his neck. Covering her mouth, he deepened his kiss. She parted her lips for him. His tongue explored the recesses of her mouth; the same mouth that had so often heaped abuse upon him in the past. His revenge was sweet. Passion's fire spread through Mark's body. His manhood rose with expectation.

The motley bed was too near and too tempting. Though he desired her with every fiber of his being, he knew he could not take her. Regretting his chivalry, Mark gently withdrew, nibbling her earlobe in passing.

"Did Cuthbert kiss you like that?" he whispered in a husky voice.

Then he stepped away before she noticed his physical state of arousal.

Belle opened her eyes, then moistened her kiss-swollen lips with her tongue. "Nay," she breathed. "That is, I do not think so." She snatched up her abandoned brush and began to pull it through her hair. "How could I possibly remember? Tis been a long time since anyone has kissed me.''

The jealousy that Mark had experienced at the mention of Belle's late husband now completely disappeared. He almost smiled but caught himself. Twas no time to gloat.

"You said we have a problem?" Belle asked abruptly.

Mark regretfully bade adieu to the last wisps of the pleasurable interlude. The mere thought of Mortimer's weaselly face damped his ardor more effectively than a bucket of ice water. "Aye," he replied. "Your knavish brother-in-law whispered to me that you killed yourself last evening.''

Belle blanched. "Suicide? Sweet Saint Anne!" She sank onto the edge of the bed.

Mark knelt beside her. "Aye. Tis a rumor that will run like wildfire through the shire in no time." He turned her face toward him. "Montjoy will hear of it and if the news doesn't kill that old man, he will write immediately to your parents.''

For once Belle offered no plan of action. She chewed her lip while she digested the horror of Mortimer's cunning lie.

Mark drew a small bundle from inside his sleeve. "Listen to me, *chou-chou.* I have brought paper, pen and ink. Write a few lines to your father to tell him you are well. I will take it posthaste to Montjoy to send north by a fast messenger. I know that you think me a rogue, but I would never wish for my Lord and Lady Cavendish to suffer one moment's pain on your account. In faith, your family has been more loving to me than my own—and that is the gospel truth.''

She stared deeply into his eyes as if searching for a sign of deceit, then she nodded. "Give me the pen."

While she scrawled her letter, Mark fed a few more logs

into her fire. Since her flue joined the larger one from the kitchen directly below them, her smoke would go undetected by Mortimer's henchmen.

Belle signed her name with her usual flourish. "There. Tis done." She folded the paper and handed it to him. "I trust you will not read it?" she asked with a challenge in her voice. "As if I could trust you at all, Mark Hayward. You kiss like a fox tasting the residents of a hen house."

He rolled his eyes. Belle would never change. Aloud, he replied, "You cut me to the quick, sweetheart. I have been a trusted member of the Cavendish household since before you were born. Indeed, your own father taught me the virtue of trust when he allowed me the pleasure of diapering you."

Her mouth dropped open.

Mark took advantage of her speechless shock. "Of course, I was only ten at the time and did not think that occupation much of a pleasure. By my troth, you were a foul little creature, *chou-chou*. But now..." He gave her a sly wink.

Belle swelled up like a wet cat. "I would break that thick pate of yours if the time were more convenient. Begone and count yourself fortunate. I swear, Master Coxcomb, you are the largest blot in my book of memory!"

Mark chuckled. "Sweet words from sweet lips." He unlocked the door. "Try not to miss me too much," he added and blew her a kiss.

"Go hug a swine!" she retorted just before the door shut behind him.

Chapter Ten

The purple-gray shadows of the season's early twilight crept across the moat when Mark returned from his visit to Montjoy. As he had suspected, the shocking news of Belle's self-inflicted death had already reached Hawkhurst by the time Mark arrived at the old steward's cottage. Once he had soothed Montjoy's fears, Mark had to endure a half-hour's sermon on the folly of Belle's plans. The young man did not admit to Montjoy that he agreed with him completely. With a final admonition to protect both the Cavendish children ringing in his ears, Mark rode back to Bodiam. Plans for tonight's haunting hummed in his brain.

As he unsaddled Artemis, he overheard the carpenter's apprentice recounting the castle's latest unrest to two appalled grooms. Mark moved nearer to listen.

"Barney's in the most parlous state, I assure ye," the apprentice gibbered. "Says he aged ten year this afternoon. Me own heart is still a-knocking in me chest. Pass me another jackmug, Dick. Look ye how me hands a-shake."

"Tell all," begged Dick while the other groom pulled a full measure of ale from a nearby cask.

Mark crept to the end of the stall.

The apprentice took a long drink. Then he continued his

hair-raising tale. "Ye know Master Fletcher was much undone by whatever was in that tower yonder?"

The other two nodded.

"So this forenoon he sends for Barney and tells him to
seal up the door of the garret room."

Mark swore under his breath. Inadvertently, he had put
Jobe in a dire situation.

The apprentice warmed to his story. "So me and Barney
spent all the livelong morning a-carrying stone up those
damnable stairs with nary a sound from the garret. The
door was locked tighter than a virgin. After dinner, we
mixed mortar and commenced to building a wall." He
lowered his voice.

Mark pressed his ear against the wooden panel of the
stall.

"Each time we went down for more buckets of mortar,
the wall *unbuilt* itself!"

Mark grinned. Well done, cunning friend!

The grooms gasped. "God's teeth!" muttered one.

"Aye, truly spoken, Frank! When we got back to the
top of them stairs, half the stones were—gone! Like that!"
He snapped his fingers. "No sign of 'em save bits of wet
mortar on the floor. And that door locked and as still as
death."

"So how did Barney get a broken head?" asked Dick.

"Ah! I was a-coming to that part." The apprentice
paused to take another drink. "We was getting on a-feared,
ye understand, and Barney is not a man to shrink at shadows as ye well know. So he tells me that we forget the
mortar, just pile up the stones and be done with the job.
Sooner the better, he says. So we did."

Mark released a little sigh. *Thank God for that small
favor!*

"We done a good job of it in no time," continued the

apprentice. "Afterward, we picked up our buckets and trowels, and we started down the stairs. We just reached the second landing when suddenly all them stones come a-tumbling down after us. Twas noise enough to wake all the dead in Saint Margaret's churchyard. I tell ye, lads, me hair about jumped off me head."

Mark covered his mouth to muffle his laughter.

The apprentice shifted closer to his grooms. "But that was not what did terrify us so."

"Nay?" breathed Frank. "Me? I would still be a-running all the way to Hawkhurst."

"What happened, Billy? Ye cannot leave us a-wondering," Dick pleaded.

Aye, what other prank did Jobe play on you?

Billy sucked in his breath. "When the last stone came to its rest and me and Barney was a-puzzling how this happened, the whole tower was a-filled with the most awful sound ever heard on God's green earth. Twas a howl from a demon, I swear to ye. About froze me blood on the spot."

"Jesu!" Dick whispered.

"I nearly flew down the rest of them stairs. But Barney tripped over one of the very stones that we had piled up so high. Fell head over heels after me. Knocked out cold by the time we both reached bottom. And that...that hell-sent scream was still a-following us."

Having heard enough, Mark quietly withdrew to the far end of the stables.

"May I be struck by lightning if I ever venture up them stairs again!" Billy swore to the others.

"Amen to that!" Dick and Frank replied.

Mark stole out the stable's side door. He paused near the archway to the "haunted tower" and pretended to inspect the soles of his boots. When he was sure that no one paid him any attention, he slipped into the tower and bounded up the spiral stairs two at a time.

As Billy had described, a number of rough-hewn stones littered the way. More stones, an overturned mortar bucket and one of the workmen's caps on the topmost landing gave further witness to the story. With a chuckle, Mark rapped three times on the door. "'Tis Mark," he said softly.

Jobe welcomed him with a broad smile. Neither man spoke until Mark was inside the chamber and the door once again bolted and barred against dim-witted intruders.

Mark clapped his friend on the shoulder. "How now, Jobe! What tales I have heard of you!"

The African laughed deeply. "I trust my fame will stretch across the whole castle."

"You are too modest, my friend." Mark grinned at him. "By daylight I warrant the whole shire will hear of the strange howling spirit of Bodiam. By the rood, Jobe, what sound did you make that so frightened the poor carpenter and his apprentice?"

Jobe shrugged. "'Tis nothing much—only the mating cry of the monkeys who inhabit my homeland. The stone walls of the tower made a fearsome echo."

Mark joined him in his laughter. "'Tis a noise that I must hear one of these fine days, but not now. We have more serious work to do."

The African nodded. "What new devices shall I work for this evening's pleasure?"

Mark rubbed his chin. "The hoofbeats, of course," he began.

Jobe grinned. "Young Kitt will like that. He played them well last night, methinks."

"Aye," Mark agreed, "but put him on the east battlements this time. Then tomorrow night on the north side and the night after on the south and so on. And, I pray you, do not allow him to become carried away by his music. Twould be doomsday if he were caught.''

The giant nodded again. ''And for myself?''

Mark chuckled. ''Mistress Sondra Owens, whom folk hereabouts thought was a good witch, used to tell us of the Bodiam Knight. She said that in olden times he walked the battlements, beating a drum to frighten away his widow's suitors.''

Jobe picked up his water bucket and inspected it with care. ''This will do if I can find a good piece of leather for the drumhead.''

Mark rubbed the bridge of his nose. ''If my memory serves me well, there used to be several drums of different sizes left in the minstrel's gallery above the hall.''

''I will stroll in that quarter after supper. Anything else?''

''Another monkey howl or two if the mood suits and the company is right.'' Mark grew more serious. ''There is one great boon I ask of you, my friend.''

Jobe lifted a dark brow. ''Ask. You know I am yours to command.''

Mark snorted. Jobe's insistence that he owed him a blood oath made Mark feel more than uncomfortable. Though he had tried to dismiss Jobe's bond, the proud man would not hear of it. A life for a life, Jobe had insisted. Mark knew the African would stay by his side until that debt was paid.

''I suspect that Mistress Belle will soon grow weary of her little hiding place. She hates to be restrained. I fear that she will take it into that willful head of hers to roam around the castle, stirring up mischief of her own.''

Jobe's grin widened. ''Then she shall have a second shadow.'' He laughed in the back of his throat. ''A very large, black shadow.''

Mark gave him a wry look. "Do not be lulled by her winsome looks. Belle is more slippery than an eel in jelly and twice as cunning as any creature you have ever met."

"Sounds like good sport."

Mark gripped the other man's forearm. "Be gentle with her, though she spits and claws you like a cat. She has been ill-used."

Jobe drew himself up to the top of his six-foot, seven inches. He struck his massive chest. "I vow to treat her as my own." He chuckled. "Do you think I do not know how to win a woman's heart?"

"You don't have to win her heart," Mark snapped. "Just keep her out of trouble. You will find that to be ample work, I assure you."

Jobe merely laughed again. "I like a challenge."

Mark saluted his friend, wished him well and left Jobe to manufacture his makeshift drum. Why should Mark care who won Belle's heart? All he desired was to preserve her skin in one piece. If Jobe wanted to woo a wildcat, he was welcome to try it. He would soon find that Belle was considerably more than a handful. Thinking these and other gloomy thoughts, Mark stomped up the postern tower's stairs to his guest chamber where he changed into his gaudy wooing suit. Another eternal evening in Griselda's sniveling company.

No reward is worth this!

As the cloud-covered sun sank below the treeline across the river from the castle, Belle fumed in her cell. This room was only a shade better than the last closet she had been caged in. Kitt had come twice today and the second time he had paused only long enough to hand her a tray with her dinner under a napkin. Before she could ask him the latest gossip or even thank him, he disappeared on the other side of the tapestry.

"I am heartily tired of playing this waiting game," she told Dexter, who snoozed on the end of the bed. The cat twitched one of his pointed black ears. "Tis time I did a little haunting myself. Mark and Kitt can't have all the fun."

Since she was supposed to be dead, Belle now had the perfect opportunity to play her own ghost. She glanced down at her borrowed gown. Though it was blue, it should be dark enough to meld into the evening shadows. But what about her hair? Her golden crown would shine like a candle should it catch a light.

"Perchance twill look like a halo," she suggested to Dexter as she quickly braided it. "Although I suspect suicides don't merit halos," she added, wrapping the braid around her head. "But then again, no one will notice me as I intend to be invisible." She skewered her bodkin into the tight coil. As weapons go, the long thick pin wasn't much, but she knew it would inflict painful damage if she stuck it in the right spot of a man's anatomy.

With excitement swelling in her breast, Belle unbolted her door. Then she stood completely motionless for a moment with her hand on the latch. "Wish me luck," she whispered to Dexter. Taking a deep breath, she cracked open the door.

Nothing smelled so sweet as the fresh air of freedom. Belle listened for any sound that would betray a nearby presence, but heard nothing except her own heart hammering in her ears. Just before she closed her door, Dexter squeezed his ponderous body through the opening. Without waiting for her, he meandered out of her sight on his own quest.

Keeping herself as flat as possible against the wall, she

inched along the back of the tapestry. She peeked out, looking first one way then the other along the empty gallery. Below her she heard the muffled sounds of the cook and the scullery boys in the servants' kitchen. The flambeaux in the courtyard flickered through the mullioned lancet window. Grinning to herself, Belle slipped away from her nest. Nothing to it! Twas just like her childhood days when she had crept about the castle on one of her many secret jaunts.

As Belle glided down the gallery toward the southwest tower, something stole up behind her and enveloped her in a dark cape. For a fleeting instant of fear she thought she had been attacked by a real ghost. Then a large warm hand covered her mouth and muffled her gasp of surprise. As she fought to free herself from the cape's black folds, she felt herself pulled backward. She tried to reach her bodkin, but her captor pinioned her arms to her sides. Baring her teeth, she bit the nearest finger over her mouth.

Her abductor swore in a strange tongue but did not relinquish his steely hold on her. Realizing that her attempts at escape were futile, Belle grew very still and waited for an opportunity to bolt. She heard a door open. Then the man stepped inside taking her with him. A strong aroma of lavender filtered through the folds of the cape. Belle realized that they were now wedged inside the linen cupboard that had been built into the castle's outer wall.

"Be still, Mistress Belle," a very deep voice murmured in her ear. "I am a friend of Sir Mark Hayward and your brother Kitt. Make no noise."

Though the mysterious stranger lifted away his cape, Belle could see nothing in the inky confines of the tiny recess. By the feel of his arm around her waist, she realized she was in the company of an exceptionally large man.

"How dare you detain me in such a rough manner?" she whispered.

He rumbled a low laugh. "I am very bold," he replied in a lilting accent that she could not identify.

"Aye, and a knavish cur as well!" Belle retorted, still keeping her voice low. "I should have expected something like this. Mark always did consort with rogues and thieves."

Her taunt only made him laugh again. "I am the very best of both," he agreed.

Belle tried to pull herself out of his hold but found it impossible. "Pray tell me, whom do I have the dubious pleasure of addressing?"

"I have a very long name, mistress. Most of it you could not pronounce. Some English address me as an Ethiope; others swear that I am the son of the devil. You may call me Jobe."

"You!" she squeaked. "The very one who has corrupted my little brother, teaching him to swear and steal."

"And lying too," Jobe added with another chuckle, "but Kitt still needs more practice at that art."

"I would scratch out your eyes if I could! Kitt is nothing but a baby." She tossed her words over her shoulder at him, wishing that each one were a stone.

"Nay, little mistress," Jobe whispered in his honey-rich voice. "Kitt is almost a man. He needs to learn the ways of the world."

Belle curled her lip. "From you?"

"None better," he replied. "Shhh!" He put his hand back over her mouth. "Do not bite me again, lioness, or I will bite you back and my teeth are very large."

Belle started to sputter a protest, but then she heard the scrape of spurs on the oak floor of the gallery. She stilled, barely daring to breath. Someone strolled along the corridor at a leisurely pace. Her heart almost stopped beating when the man paused outside the cupboard door. Jobe tightened his arm around her waist. He took his hand away from her mouth. Belle could sense rather than see that he slipped a dagger from a sheath. After another breathless moment or two, the unseen person continued down the gallery toward the middle tower.

"Greetings, Dexter," the stranger said. "Have you been behaving yourself, hmm?"

Belle did not recognize the man's pleasant voice. Perhaps Mortimer had called for a member of the local clergy to cleanse the castle from the taint of her presumed suicide.

"You *are* a good boy," the man continued. "Keep a sharp watch now."

Then he moved out of her hearing. Jobe maintained his vigilance for a few minutes longer before he relaxed his grip on Belle.

"Tell me, little one," he asked. "Where would you be now if that man had met you on the stair?"

Belle swallowed several times in an effort to regain her control. "I would have ducked out of sight long before he could spy me. I know every bolt-hole in Bodiam."

"Then let us visit a few of them," Jobe suggested. "Perchance one or two may be put to good use by we spirits of the night."

After ascertaining that the gallery was now empty, Jobe and Belle stole out of the cupboard. In the dim light of the courtyard torches, Belle finally got a good look at her companion. She nearly screamed, but Jobe silenced her cry with his hand.

"You're black!" she breathed when he released her.

He bowed to her. "As my esteemed ancestors were before me. I am from a different world than you."

She swallowed. "The one below this earth?" She could

not tear her gaze from his gleaming ebony skin, the golden hoop in one ear and the bandoliers of sharp daggers that crisscrossed his broad chest. "Are you from hell itself?"

Jobe grinned, then shook his head. "Nay, little one, I speak only of Africa and its golden joys. There is my heart's home."

"You speak our language well," she remarked.

He inclined his head. "My thanks to the Creator for giving me a good ear. I learned Portuguese from my captors, Gaelic from the Irish and three years in Mark's company has taught me English. Shall we proceed, mistress, afore unfriendly eyes discover us?"

Her heart still thumping in her throat, Belle led the way toward the great hall where supper was in progress. When they drew near to the rear of the minstrel's gallery, Belle signaled a halt. She turned one of the apples carved in the decorative panel, and a secret door sprang open. Jobe returned her grin as he squeezed himself into the narrow compartment. Once Belle shut the door, it became almost as dark as the linen cupboard had been.

Standing on tiptoe, Belle whispered to Jobe. "The original owner of Bodiam was a master brigand. He won his title and fortune by riding roughshod over half of France as well as a good many of his neighbors here in Sussex. In short, he trusted no one, not even his own flesh and blood," she related. "He built a number of these spy nests within the walls so he could see and hear what his family and retainers said about him. Watch now for the light."

So saying, Belle moved her hand along the surface of the wall that faced the hall below them. When her fingers touched a raised piece of wood, she slid it to one side. A long sliver of light from the hall's candles pierced the darkness.

"Bem! Tis good," breathed Jobe. "But why do they not see this hole in the wall?"

"Tis masked amid the linen-fold carving on the other side," Belle replied. She peered through the oillet at the high table, then swore under her breath. "Froth and scum! Look how Griselda fawns over Mark. She is practically chewing on his ear. And she is rustling about my home in a most costly silken gown. I wager tis not yet paid for."

Supper was more dismal than usual. Even the cook's offerings lacked his usual flair. The baked tripe pie did not sit particularly well in Mark's stomach. Meanwhile the great chamber buzzed, not with music or song, but with whispered stories of the latest excitement within Bodiam's crenellated walls.

Griselda leaned heavily on Mark's shoulder. "Did you hear it too?" Her breath smelled of too much wine.

Mark lounged against his high-backed chair, crossed his ankles under the oaken table and decided to play the fool. "Hear what?" he asked loudly.

Emitting a high-pitched squeak, Griselda looked over her shoulder into the shadowed corners of the large chamber. "Last night—the hoofbeats," she whispered.

Mark spied Kitt's suppressed grin as the boy served them cold strips of smoked pike fish floating in some grayish sauce. Mark scowled both at the food and at Kitt's obvious eavesdropping. *He will give our game away if he doesn't learn to hide his thoughts.*

Aloud, he replied, "In faith, sweetheart, I had just managed to fall asleep when some disturbance awoke me. Methought twas a late night visitor for your brother."

"Would that it had been," Mortimer remarked with a glare at his sister. "As I told you before, my lord. Twas nothing."

"Aye, you did, but when I returned to my chamber, I

found that someone had strewn all my clothing on the floor." Let everyone digest that nugget along with the unspeakable fish, he thought.

Griselda dug her nails into Mark's arm. "God save us, Mortimer!" she squealed before he could shut her up. "Twas the same with me this forenoon." Her pale eyes grew enormous. "When I opened my clothes chest, I found that everything had been turned inside out!"

Good boy, Kitt! You'll become a proper rogue yet!

Mortimer tossed Mark a meaningful look. "My sister has no lady's maid at the moment," he ventured to explain. "Tis no wonder her fripperies have become disarrayed. I trust nothing was stolen from *you?*"

Mark shook his head. "Nay, methought twas a prank...." He leaned his elbows on the table then continued in a very loud whisper, "Then I heard the most ungodly caterwauling coming from...from the privy hole in my alcove."

Will, the potboy, dropped his serving platter with a loud crash. The hall grew deathly still. Only the hiss and pop of the logs on the fire broke the silence. Mark waited to see who would speak first. *This game grows more interesting.*

Mortimer wiped his face with his napkin. "The wind," he snapped. "It sometimes blows through the chinks and holes in the most unnerving manner."

"Tis the self-same howling as the carpenter and his prentice heard this afternoon," the steward ventured from one of the lower tables. A number of the other retainers nodded their agreement. "Scared the wits out of both of them."

"Bewitched we are," muttered the grizzled marshal. He signaled for more ale in his cup.

"Oooh!" Griselda clung tighter to Mark's arm. "Tis true, I fear. Tis Belle Cavendish bewailing her d...doom!"

Mark lifted his brow. "There, there, my sugar comfit," he crooned. "Do not be afeard. Who is this Belle?" he asked Mortimer.

The man glared at Griselda before he answered. "Tis she whom I told you of. The one who...ah...died suddenly last evening. A bad business—not to be spoken of, if you grasp my meaning."

"My condolences," Mark murmured to no one in particular. *There is no hole in hell hot enough for you, Fletcher.*

Squealing again, Griselda made the sign against the evil eye. "She haunts us, I just know it."

Now to play my ace card. "That is hard news indeed— especially since the feast of Samhain draws apace. Tis the time of year when owls cry out deathly warnings, ghostly dogs howl, witches fly to the moon on broomsticks and goblins wander over hill and dale."

Mortimer fidgeted in his chair. "Fantasies for children and other weak-minded creatures!" He gave his sister a lethal stare.

Mark put his arm around the shivering Griselda. "Not so, Mortimer. In times past, I had heard but did not myself believe the tales of spirits who walked abroad on the night before All Hallows Day. But in my travels since then, I have witnessed many great wonders so that now. . ."

Pausing, he looked around the hall. Every eye was upon him. He sensed that every ear strained to catch his next words. "Now I do believe that the dead visit us on that fearful night."

"Angels preserve me!" Griselda threw her arms around his neck and practically crawled into his lap. She clasped him like a vine around a tree trunk.

Mortimer drained his wine cup and poured himself more before Kitt could serve him. "Old wives' tales!" His hand shook as he lifted his drink.

Mark shrugged. "Be that as it may, but one cannot be too careful at this time of year. Might I make a suggestion?"

"Aye, speak, my lord," said the steward. Several members of the household banged the table with their cups and knife handles.

Mark addressed the castle's retainers. "Have no fear, my good people. There is a remedy to keep this house and all who dwell within it safe from goblins, ghoulies and other creatures that live in the shadows of graveyards."

"Tell us!" the men shouted.

Mark glanced at his ashen-faced host. Mortimer nodded and drank more wine. *This plays out even better than I had hoped.* "Master and Mistress Fletcher should hold a goodly feast here on All Hallows Eve. Invite all your friends and neighbors. Aye, even the good, god-fearing folk of Hawkhurst should come. Fill this hall with many friendly faces."

"Sounds expensive," Mortimer mumbled.

"Nay, tis a blessing," Griselda retorted with rare spunk. "Twill save us from…that evil one." She bit her lower lip. "What must we do at this gathering?"

"Why, we will make merry with a great deal of noise," Mark replied, his imagination embellishing the folklore Mistress Owens used to tell on dark nights.

"We must fill the hall with many burning tapers and keep the hearth fire high to ward off unwholesome spirits. The cook should prepare foods in thanksgiving for your good harvest—dishes that feature apples and nuts particularly. You should leave a dish of cream on every hearth in the castle—to appease the goblins lest they do us mischief.'' Belle's fat cat should appreciate that touch.

Mortimer swore into his cup but made no other objection.

Mark continued to elaborate. ''We will play games like Hoodman Blind, dance country jigs and enjoy a clever entertainment—anything that keeps us cheerful until after the midnight hour. Everyone will wear masks so that the spirits will not know who we are. Twill be goodly sport. Oh, and all the doors must be unlocked,'' he added.

Mortimer narrowed his eyes. ''Why?''

Mark gave him a superior look. ''So that the spirits will be able to flee this place without hindrance.''

Griselda nodded so hard that her headdress wobbled askew. ''Aye! Tis a good idea. Everyone knows that Bodiam is haunted by the ghost of a great Black Knight.''

Mark pretended surprise. ''How now?''

Griselda curled into a ball in his arms. ''They say that on All Hallows Eve he rides, dressed in full armor, through...through this very hall!''

''Tis true enough,'' murmured the steward. ''I myself have heard this tale.''

Mortimer glared first at his sister, then at his steward. ''Tis confections of the imagination to frighten small children into early bedtimes. I'll hear no more of this talk— and there will be no Samhain feast, sister. I'll not have my house filled up with a lot of hungry, thieving knaves.''

At that moment, one of the candles in the candelabra on the high table snuffed itself out. Even Mark was taken aback since there was no draft blowing through the chamber. Mortimer stared bug-eyed at the smoking candlewick. Just then Griselda screeched and rubbed her arm.

''Something stung my hand!'' she yowled.

"Tis too late in the night for bees," Mark muttered, glancing around.

A second candle winked out.

Rising from his chair, Mortimer thumped his fist on the tabletop. "Who did that?" he bellowed.

From the pierced wooden screen at the end of the hall, low laughter began. It rose in volume, then suddenly turned into the most fearsome hooting and howling that Mark had ever heard. The sound reverberated off the vaulted ceiling and reechoed down the large chamber. The potboys scattered to the safety of the kitchens. The castle retainers fell over the benches in their haste to escape the terrifying noise. Mortimer staggered back into his chair. Griselda swooned, her head falling heavily onto Mark's chest.

The tiny hairs on the back of Mark's neck prickled. Even though he suspected Jobe at work, he had to admit that the monkey call was more than enough to chill the blood. Just then a small pellet hit him squarely between the eyes. Though the missile stung, Mark knew exactly what it was. He scanned the dark recess of the empty minstrel's gallery. Jobe was an expert at blowing dried peas through a hollow reed. At that moment, the last candle's flame disappeared. Mark heard the tiny sound of a pellet bouncing along the table.

Well aimed, my friend!

Behind the paneling, Belle muffled her giggles with both of her hands. Below her, the hall emptied like the outgoing tide at Winchelsea. With a wide grin, Jobe slid his blowpipe back into his belt.

"Most excellent sport!" he whispered.

Chapter Eleven

As the last stroke of midnight died away, the phantom hoofbeats once again echoed in the courtyard. The hardened men-at-arms on guard reacted with something close to panic. Even though she had known what to expect, chills ran down Belle's spine. From her vantage point in the deserted garret of the western mid-tower, she hovered in the shadows as she observed the accelerating chaos sixty feet below her. Sitting on the wide window ledge, Dexter surveyed the scene with his unblinking golden eyes.

"Kitt should be abed," she remarked to the cat, "instead of staying up half the night and banging two bowls against the wall. He will be impossible to live with once he returns to Wolf Hall. You mark my words."

Dexter washed a milk-white paw.

Belle tried to locate her little brother's hiding place in the tower opposite her, but she could not discern his movements. Meanwhile, the action in the courtyard mounted.

"By my life!" cried one of the grooms to the yawning blacksmith, "I swear I saw it fly right by me. A ghostly horse caparisoned for a joust, he was."

"Nay," shouted a stable hand. "'Tis a great water horse come out of the river yonder. Ye can smell him!"

"'Tis two, three or more!" exclaimed a quaking lackey. Will nodded his curly head in stupefied agreement.

"Search for the beast!" ordered the marshal, but no man dared to obey his command.

Just then, Mortimer, attended by the steward, Fowler and a gaggle of gaping underservants, came through the wide arched doorway. Planting himself on the top of the broad steps, he attempted to quell the rabble.

Belle giggled. "Hoy day, Dexter! Look at his spindly legs!" Clad only in his nightshirt, Mortimer reminded her of a ruffled stork. "He must stuff padding down his tights to give himself a fine shank. I knew of many a dashing fop at the king's court who did that."

Dexter paid her no mind. Instead he cleaned his other forepaw until it gleamed as white as its mate.

"How now?" Mark's voice rose above the general din. "What is all the fuss this time, Mortimer? Lose another horse?"

The hoofbeats suddenly ceased.

Belle drew closer to the window. "Mark doesn't know I am up here," she explained to the disinterested cat. "He thinks I am tucked away in my trundle bed like a good little girl. Pah! He should know better than that by now. He should—Great Jove!"

Mark moved into the circle of torchlight. Practically naked, he was dressed only in his burgundy-and-gold striped tights, a sight that literally snatched Belle's breath away.

Where had the gangly, wiry youth of her childhood days gone in the last eight years? The powerful, well-built man that Mark had become claimed her riveted attention. Something fluttered in the pit of her stomach as she watched him take command in the courtyard like the lead performer of a court masque. His mere presence compelled the attention of the jittery rabble.

The firelight caught the flash of his dark eyes and caressed the rippling muscles of his broad, bare chest. Belle could not suppress a sigh when she recalled how he had so recently held her close to his heart. But Mark had been decently clad then, not looking like he had just stepped down from a Grecian pedestal. The tight hose outlined his muscular thighs and sturdy calves to perfection—no padding needed there. And the bulge between his legs? Positively scandalous! Belle could not tear her gaze away from him. Her knees trembled. She swallowed hard.

"I hope that he has not come fresh from Griselda's bed!" she sputtered to Dexter. "Not undressed like that! *Oh, la, la! Quel magnifique!*" she added, lapsing into her mother's French tongue. Hot jealousy welled up inside her. She tried to ignore its sting. *Mark is not the least bit interested in Griselda.* Belle did not want to admit—even to the cat—how much his handsome body enticed her. Her cheeks flushed. Be sensible, she scolded herself. Mark was only her father's hireling.

A sudden booming from the south battlements startled her. Jobe must have found the kettledrum in the minstrel's gallery. Its deep tone throbbed in the night. Everyone froze in place. Belle's heart beat in time with its rhythm. Pandemonium broke out in the courtyard below her.

The men and boys scattered in every direction like a disturbed hill of ants. Several shouted to lower the drawbridge; they would not stay a minute longer inside Bodiam's haunted walls. Others dropped to their knees gabbling disjointed prayers. Many fled back to the safety of their beds. Belle closely watched Mortimer's reaction.

"Fly now, you dissembling cur! Leave my home!" she whispered.

Dexter crouched as if he would spring out of the tower window.

Mortimer stiffened as his craven minions scuttled away from the mysterious drumbeat. He paled, flinched but held his ground. His knobby knees shook beneath the hem of his nightshirt. Surveying the shambles of his domain, his eyes narrowed and his mouth thinned with anger.

"Pernicious bloodsucker!" Belle hissed under her breath. "Not afraid yet? Your greed still holds you in its thrall? This little dance is only the prologue. Fear me, brother-in-law. I am the broom that will sweep this castle clean of such filth as you Fletchers!"

The distant church bells pealed the hour of two after midnight before the castle settled down to an uneasy rest. Long before then Belle and Dexter had returned to their snuggery. Too excited to sleep, she stirred up her fire and waited for the friendly "spirits of the night" to come bragging of their exploits. Dexter curled into a large black-and-white ball. He barely moved when someone finally knocked on her door.

"Tis Mark," he said in a hoarse whisper. "Are you still awake?"

A warm glow flowed through her at the sound of his voice. *I must be losing my mind. He is only a land-hungry mercenary.* Yet her fingers trembled as she unbolted the door. He slithered inside like the shadow he pretended to be. She noticed with a twinge of disappointment that his handsome body was now modestly covered in dark clothing. To shield her true emotions, she assumed her usual mocking tone.

"How goes the haunting? Or were you too busy with the fair Griselda to notice?"

He made a face, then flashed her a smile. "Twas a most satisfying sight, *chou-chou*. You should have seen it!"

Wouldn't you be surprised! "Oh?" she asked with an

arched eyebrow. "Do you speak of Griselda in the throes of a love frenzy or the ghost of the Bodiam Knight?"

"You minx!" Mark caught her in his arms and whirled her around the tiny space. "Let us not speak of Mistress Fletcher. Her face alone curdles fresh cream in a churn. I last saw her after supper when I dumped her on her bed—not *in* it. She was quite unconscious at the time. Here!"

He plopped Belle down in front of the hearth then took off the wineskin that hung from his shoulder on a crimson cord. "A sweet vintage claret from your very own cellars. Let us drink to the ghostly horse and the drummer upon the battlements. God's teeth, Belle! Twas a masterpiece of confusion! You should have seen those pullets run!"

He took a deep drink before he passed the skin to her. The cool wine soothed her tight throat. The knotted muscles in her shoulders relaxed under its influence. "And Mortimer? Did he run?"

A frown creased Mark's features. "Nay! At first methought he would, but he held himself in check, though he shook like a leaf in the November wind. But fear not, Belle. I have laid the groundwork for even further mischief."

Belle folded her arms across her breasts as if to keep her traitorous heart from flying out to him. "My, my! How your tongue wags!"

Mark tossed her a boyish grin, one that she found far too appealing for safety's sake. "Cool your temper, *chou-chou*. I have but toiled in your service." He drew closer to her and circled her waist with his arm. "Mortimer is shaken and methinks he will lose a number of his men after tonight's work." He smoothed a wisp of her hair across her forehead. "Thanks to Jobe and Kitt, Mortimer will fall into the trap that I baited at suppertime."

Just as I am falling into your trap, you thief of hearts!

She wiggled out of his embrace and swept up the sleeping cat in her arms. Dexter's effect on Mark would keep that swaggering rooster at bay. "What ploy now rattles around that brain of yours? Or are you only thinking of my father's rich land and your future rich wife?"

Mark winced as if she had shot him with an arrow. He whistled through his teeth before taking another drink from the wineskin. "What did you eat for supper, Belladonna? Fire and brimstone? Exactly what have I done recently to deserve this disdain? I have half a mind to leave you to do your own haunting."

In a crystal-clear instant, Belle remembered the last time she had seen Mark eight years ago. His expression had been the same mixture of disbelief, anger and pain when she had rebuffed his amorous advances and pushed him out of the tree. The resulting fall had broken his sword arm. Belle had regretted her action immediately, but her pride kept her from admitting it to Mark. Nor did her fear of her father's anger allow her to admit her responsibility for the mishap.

Belle bit her tongue. A wise woman never made the same mistake twice. This time she would apologize for her sharp rebuke. Still holding the cat, she sat down on the foot of the bed and patted the place beside her.

She flashed him a half smile when he joined her. "The hour is late, Mark, and I am at sixes and sevens. Forgive me . . .that is, my words. In faith, I am grateful for all that you and Jobe are doing on my behalf—even if you are corrupting Kitt in the process," she added.

Mark moved to put his arm around her shoulder, but he sneezed instead. Turning away from her, he blew his nose. "A plague on your cat," he muttered.

Belle stroked Dexter's long back. He purred in his sleep.

"Tell me of this trap you have set," she suggested in her most winsome tone.

Mark moved farther away from Dexter before answering. "Mortimer will hold a feast on All Hallows Eve to appease the restless spirits of the castle. I have already put a number of ideas into Griselda's ear. She is so terrified of her own shadow, methinks she will implement them all."

I wonder what sort of ideas you would put into my ear if I ever gave you half the chance? Belle banished that intriguing question before it had time to take root in her imagination. "Tis good for a start," she conceded.

Mark sneezed again. His eyes watered. "Sdeath, Belle! I must depart before I go blind or cease to breathe." He sneezed a third time. "Adieu!" He backed toward the door.

I can't let him leave while he still thinks ill of me. "Wait a moment, Mark!" Belle dropped Dexter back onto the bed.

He had already opened the door. He drew deep breaths of the cold night air that hung in the long empty gallery. Belle took his warm hand in hers. "You did right well tonight, Marcus," she whispered. "I am grateful."

He wiped his nose then slowly raised one of his dark brows. "Grateful?" he repeated. "You have never been grateful for anything in your life, *chou-chou.* As I recall, you played the Amazon princess and treated the rest of us as your slaves."

His barb hit home. Belle tried to think of a proper retort without stinging his vanity any further. "Twas a childish game." She looked deeply into his liquid brown eyes. "And I am not a child any longer," she murmured.

An indefinable sensuous spark passed between them. His steady gaze bored into her, causing a tingling sensation

at the base of her throat. Without speaking, he drew her
into his arms. Her skin prickled at his tender touch. Rising
on her toes, she wrapped her arms around his neck and
buried her fingers in his thick dark hair. His breath softly
fanned her face as he bent down to her.

"Tis true, sweetheart, you are all woman now—and I
am a man."

His mouth closed over hers. She melted under his gentle
assault, and gave him her kiss in return—lingering over
his lips, savoring every sweet moment of the encounter.
Lights flashed behind her closed eyelids. Something
buzzed in her ears. Though her eager response to the magic
of his lips shocked her, she pulled him closer to her. He
deepened his kiss as if he would plumb the depths to her
very soul. Her thoughts spun like a whirligig. She clung
to him lest she melt away.

After endless moments, he slowly withdrew, leaving her
mouth burning with his fire. "Ah, Belle," he murmured,
his breath warm against her ear. "You have witchcraft in
your lips."

Then, with a quick peck on her nose, he set her back
on her feet. Still reeling from the impact of their passion,
Belle opened her eyes.

Mark stood at the edge of the tapestry. "Knew you
couldn't resist me for long." He winked at her, then disappeared around the embroidered cover.

Belle touched her still-burning lips. "Don't begin to
strut just yet, my Lord Hayward," she whispered.

Her hands filled with missives from the south, Kat burst
into Brandon's sickroom. She gave her dozing husband a
gentle shake.

"What?" he mumbled, rubbing the sleep from his eyes.
"Tis supper time?" he added with a hopeful expression.

Despite her anxiety, Kat smiled at him. What a lovable bear he was! "Not yet, my darling, but there is news to chew on, and such news that you will never believe." She waved the letters under his nose. "At this rate, I shall have to erect a postbox at the gate to catch them all."

Brandon pulled himself into a sitting position. "From Montjoy again?"

Kat nodded. "Aye, him, as well as from Mark, Kitt, Belle, thank heavens, even old Andrew. And there's a particularly vile one from Mortimer Fletcher."

Brandon narrowed his eyes. "Bad news?"

Kat fanned herself with the letters. "That depends upon which one you read. They are written in every humor—and then some."

"Are the children safe? Tell me that first."

Kat shuffled through the pile until she located Belle's brief note. "Methinks so, but you be the judge. Belle writes that she is well no matter what other news we may hear of her and—attend to this part, Brandon—she says that 'the rumors of my recent death are all false.'"

Brandon rubbed his temples. "Belle always enjoyed courting an air of mystery. Does she elaborate?"

"Nay, though she does end with this interesting note, 'Mark is not as bad as I once thought him to be, even if you are paying the jackanapes.'"

Brandon grinned. "That's my girl and no mistake. I would have hated to be in Mark's shoes when she learned of my offer. It must have set her pride back a notch or two."

Kat shook her head. "Mark was a fool to have told her."

"Methinks he didn't. What does Kitt write?"

Kat smoothed out his letter on her knee before handing it to Brandon. "I shall not deny you the pleasure of deciphering it yourself. His penmanship is only a shade less shocking than your own.'' She smiled. She would preserve Kitt's first letter to his parents in her jewel casket, shocking penmanship and all.

Brandon squinted at the scrap of paper. ''Hoy day, Kat! Tis enough to make a scholar weep. 'To Mama and Papa, I send gratings. Feer not fur me. I am rite wele in spirit and in bodie.''' Pausing, Brandon gave his wife a sheepish look. ''Methinks we have been a bit slack with Kitt's schooling. He goes on to say, 'Belle is safe and we are having xcellent sport.' What the devil does *that* mean?''

Kat shook her head. ''I know not, save that each one of these letters gives me cause for some concern. Pray continue. You are translating Kitt's prose much better than I could.''

''Hmm. 'I will rite more a nun. Yur most loving son, Christopher Cavendish. By the way, I am lerning how to be a...''' Brandon sounded out the word slowly. ''God shield us from such scribbling. Methinks he says he is becoming a warrior though his spelling is almost beyond belief.''

Kat arched her brow. ''Tis not how Kitt spells the word that worries me half as much as what he might be doing to become one. Sweet Saint Anne, Brandon! I fear our baby will injure himself in some madcap escapade. Trust me, I will put a very large flea in Mark's ear when next I clap my eyes on him.''

Brandon had the cheek to laugh at her maternal misgivings. ''Hold your ire, sweetheart. Our son needs to stretch his wings. Methinks we have coddled him too long. In fact, I intend to ask Mark if he would take Kitt as his squire.''

Kat glared at her husband. ''You are moonstruck!''

He chuckled. ''Time will tell. What does Mark write? His spelling should be more readable, though I admit I did not give it much attention when I had him under my tutelage.''

Kat decided not to agitate Brandon any further on the matter of Kitt's future—at least not until Brandon could stand upright. Then she would speak her mind in full. She unfolded Mark's letter.

"He sends the usual salutations, then says Belle is safe 'for the moment.' My mind misgives what that arch phrase might mean. He goes on to say that there have been 'complications of divers sorts' and that we are not to believe a word we might hear either of Belle's death—or of his own betrothal!''

Brandon furrowed his brows. "What the hell is going on at Bodiam?''

"My thoughts exactly. We should never have sent Mark and that…that blackamoor down there. They have made a complete dog's breakfast of the whole matter.''

Brandon took her nearest hand in his and kissed it. "Tush, my love. The fault lies not with Mark, but with his charges. After all, he is saddled with two Cavendishes and you know what a stubborn lot we are.''

Kat softened a little under the gentle pressure of his lips on her skin. It had been over six weeks since they had last shared a bed and she missed him sorely. She was half-tempted to—

She gave herself a shake. "Mark ends with his hopes for your rapid recovery. That's it. No explanations, no details. Nothing! I could just scream.''

Brandon turned her hand over and caressed her palm with his warm tongue. He shot her a mischievous glance. "Does Montjoy fill in the gaps?" he asked.

Kat shivered, then she frowned when she thought of the old man's message. At least, Montjoy wrote with a good hand and understandable spelling. "Doom and gloom, as is his usual habit, but he does say that Mortimer has filed for Bodiam's ownership due to the death of the castle's late owner.'' She pursed her lips. ''He'll claim Bodiam over my dead body!''

''God help Master Fletcher,'' muttered Brandon. He nibbled on her fingers.

Kat found it increasingly difficult to concentrate. ''Brandon! I pray you pay attention.''

He sighed but did not let go of her hand. ''What else does your worthy steward say?''

''That Mark and the son of the devil—that must be Jobe—have embarked upon a hare-brained scheme and that Belle is their leader in the enterprise. Montjoy predicts disaster will result.''

''He would,'' Brandon remarked. ''Anything else?''

Kat snorted. ''Of course not. He leaves us dangling like trout on a line. Oh! He can be the most infuriating man— besides you.''

Brandon stared at the two remaining letters. ''Which one next?''

Kat decided to save Mortimer's for last. She opened Sir Andrew Ford's note. ''Uncle Andrew is almost as bad as the rest of them. He tells us to 'be of good cheer' and that Mark is a most excellent young man.''

''I always thought so myself,'' Brandon agreed.

Kat rolled her eyes, then continued. ''He further writes that he has been creating 'many unusual fireworks for Mark's grand illumination.' Now I ask you, Brandon. What can he possibly mean by that?''

He shrugged. ''Mark's wedding perchance? Who knows? I agree with you, my love. Something strange is surely afoot at Bodiam, though I have not got the least idea what it might be.''

Kat took a deep breath. ''Then this letter from Mortimer

will confirm your worst suspicions. Tis a foul piece of work, I assure you."

"Mortimer himself is a foul piece of work. Read on."

Kat cleared her throat. "'To my Lord and Lady Cavendish, Wolf Hall. I fear I must send you tidings of the most doleful nature and so I will be brief. On the evening of the twenty-second of October, your daughter, deep in grief for my poor brother, did take her own life—'"

"What!" Brandon sat bolt upright in his bed. "The devil take him! What does that moldwarp think he is doing?"

Kat jumped up and eased Brandon back against the pillows. "Soft, my darling. Remember, tis not true. Belle is very much alive and up to mischief. I'll warrant that she is the mastermind behind this ruse."

Brandon stroked her cheek. "Ah, Kat! I am glad of your clear head. What wickedness bustles about this old earth! There, I am calm now. Read me the rest of this knave's puling lie."

Kat curled up beside him. "He continues that 'I have disposed of her earthly remains as is fit under these most grievous circumstances—'"

"I'll gladly dispose of Fletcher's earthly remains," Brandon growled.

Kat kissed his brow to soothe her husband, then she read, "'...and will administer Bodiam Castle as it is now my right. I would offer you my condolences, but the church's teaching forbids me do so. I remain your most obedient servant, Mortimer Fletcher.' Oh! The man has the heart of a snake. What kind of monster would send such a letter?"

Brandon put his arm around her and drew her closer to him. Kat pillowed her head on his shoulder. "What if we had not received Belle's letter first?" she whispered.

"Tis why I am right glad that Mark is there with her," he replied. He kissed her forehead.

"But what should we do, Brandon? I cannot bear to sit idly by while our children dance a galliard with danger."

In answer he gave her a deep kiss that heated her blood. "Then let us not be idle," he murmured. "First, you will physic me with the pleasure of your sweet body—"

"Brandon!" she gasped as he caressed her breast. "You are supposed to lie still."

"And then we will take a little ride to the south—"

"You cannot possibly sit on a horse!" Her mind clouded with the insistence of his love-making.

He chuckled in the back of his throat. "Oh, there are a great many things methinks I can do when given the proper incentive. Very well, we will go to Bodiam in a wagon." He rained kisses on her eyelids and nose. "And there we will take our children in hand and afterward we will hang up Mortimer Fletcher by his heels from the portcullis. Mmmm! Give me your mouth, my love."

"Brandon! You are completely impossible!"

"True, sweet Kat. I am a Cavendish."

Chapter Twelve

Immediately after finishing his breakfast, Mortimer requested Mark to join him in the estate office. Dreading the subject of the coming interview, Mark followed the man into the small chamber off the hall. Mortimer closed the thick oaken door, then seated himself behind his counting table. He graciously offered Mark the better chair.

He looks like he's had even less sleep than me.

Mortimer's eyes were red-rimmed and deep shadows hung under them. Mark assumed a pose of casual nonchalance.

"Ah, Fletcher! How I envy you!" he began before Mortimer could open his mouth. "The Sussex air is most marvelous for my health and constitution. By my faith, my appetite has much improved and my sleep sweeter since I have come here."

Mortimer stared at him with utter disbelief etched on his pasty countenance. "Surely you jest with me, Sir Mark. You too have been awakened by the sounds in the night."

Mark gave him a wry look in return. "Aye, your minions make a great deal of noise over a wayward horse that bolts from his stall on occasion."

"But the hoofbeats?"

Mark shrugged. "I have heard nothing but a great deal of shouting. Indeed, my squire has enjoyed the show immensely," he added.

Mortimer wiped his face with a sodden handkerchief. "And the drumming? What of that?"

Mark laughed. "Peace, friend! Do not remind me. Tis true. I tend to drink too much of your good wine at night. The drumming in my ears is my just penance."

The other man turned a sickly mottled color. "Nay! I speak of the drum upon the battlements."

Swallowing his grin, Mark shook his head. "I heard nothing."

"Last night at supper, the candles went out suddenly."

"Twas a puff of ill wind."

Mortimer grew more agitated by the minute. "That howling! You could not have missed such a hell-sent noise."

Mark pretended to ponder the question. "Nay, I recall no howling. Is there a dog in pain? In faith, I have seen no dogs since my arrival. Now there is one large, overfed cat. Did it howl, by any chance?"

Mortimer gave him no answer. Rising, he paced to the narrow window that overlooked the moat. He clenched his hands behind his back. After a few moments, he spoke again.

"I pray you excuse me, my lord. I have not…been well of late."

Mark smiled inwardly. "I am most sorry to hear of it. Perchance you need a change of scenery," he suggested.

Mortimer turned back to him. "You have hit the nail upon its head, my lord. In truth, I am heartily sick of this heap of stones. The sooner I can return to London, the happier I will be. I was not country-bred."

Mark placed his elbows on the table. "Then why do

you infect yourself? Leave tomorrow." *And make Belle a most gladsome lady.*

He shook his head. "Alas, my affairs here are not yet...concluded."

Mark scented a secret in the air. "Then leave Bodiam and its management to me as Mistress Griselda's dowry. As your brother-in-law, I will tend to these tedious problems. Unlike you, I was born to this way of life."

Again, Mortimer shook his head. "Gladly I will leave the estate to you, my lord. Indeed, that is the very nut and core of what I wanted to discuss with you this morning, but for the moment, this castle is my...concern, though it gives me sleepless nights and restless days."

Then prepare yourself, knave, for you have not yet experienced all that I have planned. Aloud, Mark said, "Ah! The dowry! Now you are speaking my language. I take it that the...entanglement that we mentioned a few days ago is resolved?"

Mortimer mopped his sweating face again. "Just so, my lord," he replied in a hoarse whisper. "And I beg that you never bring up that particular subject again."

"Done," Mark said through thin lips.

Mortimer returned to his seat. He drew out a paper from the stack on the table and passed it to Mark. "'Tis the marriage contract that I prepared yesterday." He pointed to the third paragraph of the densely written sheet. "Here I have spelled out all the lands and entitlements that I will give you as my sister's dowry. You will find that I have been most generous."

Mark scanned the page. Mortimer's use of legal terminology surprised him. As a member of a prosperous wool-merchant family, Mortimer had obviously become well-versed in complex business transactions. One thing was certain in Mark's mind. He would not sign any document—particularly one with the words *marriage bond* and *matrimony* in the text. He pretended to read it with difficulty.

"Hoy day, Mortimer! Tis a weighty piece of writing here, and I must confess that I always was lax in my book-learning. Allow me to peruse this in private. I am sure tis proper to the letter and form, but I must study it before I sign. As a man of business, I am sure you understand."

A shade of annoyance crossed the other man's face, but he nodded. "Of course," he agreed with reluctance. "Take your time, my lord, though I must warn you that my sister grows impatient to announce the banns. The season of Advent draws nearer and she wants to be well married before then."

Mark folded the paper and stuck it inside his jerkin. "Aye, Mistress Griselda has told me often enough." *She has whined about it unceasingly in my ears.* He swallowed. "Then to soothe her anxiety, let us announce our betrothal at your feast on All Hallows Eve."

Sdeath! I cannot believe I just said those words!

"Agreed!" Mortimer held out his hand to shake on the pact.

Mark accepted his sweaty paw with loathing. Then he rose and beat a hasty exit saying that he wanted to ride over the property to inspect it. By the time Mark had returned to his own chamber, his temples throbbed with the beginnings of a nasty headache. He stuffed the marriage contract deep into his clothes chest, then he collared Kitt in the gallery.

"Where to?" the boy asked, eager for an outing.

"To Hawkhurst," Mark muttered, "though I wish it were to the ends of the earth."

The visit to Montjoy's cottage was a great success as far as Kitt was concerned. The winsome Ivy deigned to give the fledgling swain a peck on his cheek when he carried water from the well for her. For Mark it was another matter. The package that he expected from Sir Andrew had not yet arrived, nor was there any word from the elderly knight. Mark needed some time to acquaint himself with the mysteries of Sir Andrew's fireworks before he unleashed them on the unsuspecting population of Bodiam. And time was running out—especially since he was now doomed to betroth a harpy on All Hallows Eve. Then there was the feast itself.

"I need turnips," he told the old steward. "Fifty pounds more or less and soon."

Montjoy lifted one shaggy brow. "Are they starving at the castle?" he inquired mildly.

Mark grinned. "Nay, tis for Kitt." He glanced across the room at the boy who was deep in conversation with Ivy.

Montjoy nodded. "Ah! A growing lad's appetite, I vow."

Mark's grin widened. "Methinks he will grow heartily sick of them soon enough."

After enduring Montjoy's usual stern lecture concerning the care and protection of the Cavendish offspring, Mark dragged the besotted Kitt away from the fair Ivy's charms. Mark promised himself to give his squire a man-to-man talk in the very near future before the boy did something rash. After all, Kitt was a Cavendish and Mark was well acquainted with that family's quirks and passions.

They arrived back at Bodiam in time for the noon dinner. Kitt, still wrapped in a cloud of first love, stumbled through his table service with more than the usual number of mishaps. Griselda, buoyed by the news that her betrothal was closer to its dreaded consummation, talked nonstop during the eternal meal. Afterward, she insisted that Mark help her plan the feast. Despite his need for a long nap, he agreed. The opportunity to orchestrate the event to his benefit was too good to pass up.

Griselda's unusual industry surprised him until he realized that for the first time since she had arrived at Bodiam she had something constructive to occupy her mind. Up until now she had spent her time bemoaning real and imagined slights. As soon as the remains of the sweet course had been swept from the board, Griselda grabbed Mark's hand and pulled him into the seldom-used withdrawing chamber. She had already made out a number of lists that were scattered around the surface of a long refectory table that was the room's main furnishing.

Griselda pointed to the nearest piece of paper. "Here are some of my ideas for a proper menu. What do you think?"

Stifling a yawn, Mark scanned it. "Steamed cabbage pudding, roasted venison, tarts with apples and raisins, soul cakes with walnuts." He gave her a smile. "Tis a goodly fare indeed. And the drink? Your guests should be well provided with good cheer." *And well pickled by the witching hour when the ghost comes a-calling.*

Griselda giggled through her nose. "Ale, claret for the gentry and mulled cider all round."

Mark nodded. He would make sure that the cider was mulled with some potent sackwine. The more befuddled the guests were, the more believable his haunting would be.

Griselda snatched up a second list. "And here are some of the entertainments I have devised." She frowned. "I would dearly love a trained bear. Do you think we could find one in time?"

Mark shuddered inwardly. Such an unpredictable animal

as a bear might queer his whole plan. Besides it would terrify Dexter into hiding and the cat's presence would be required on this occasion.

"Nay, sugared nymph," he murmured, kissing her fingers. They were still greasy from dinner. "I must confess that I am mortally afeared of bears. Will a juggler do instead?"

"But I had my heart set on a bear," she pouted.

He sighed and pulled her closer. "Methought you had your heart set only on me."

She brayed a discordant laugh.

Mark removed himself from her grasp and pounced upon a drawing. "What is this?" He held up the paper.

Griselda blushed red. "Tis a mere jotting of mine," she simpered. "Tis a design for a mask. What do you think? I know of a most excellent mask-maker in London who could do it if we send this to him in time."

Mark studied the bizarre sketch. It looked like a badger with feathers but it had distinct possibilities. It completely covered both the face and hair. He gave her a smile of genuine approval.

"You possess a remarkable talent, my tricksy sprite. By my troth, I do not believe I have ever seen the like before—not even at one of the king's masques."

She clapped her hands. "Truly?"

"I swear it upon my soul. Pray, can you design others in like fashion? Twould make a great show if all the guests were so disguised. Think of the merriment we will have trying to guess who is who."

She nodded but did not rise to his compliment as Mark had expected. "Aye," she replied with a deep sigh, "but there is one sticking point."

"Money?" he asked faintly. His own purse was practically empty.

She waved away that objection. "Nay, tis the guests." She pointed to yet another list with only a few lines written upon it. "I fear we are sadly lacking in that quarter. We have not resided in this area for too long and my brother..." She gnawed her lower lip.

Mark again put his arm around her bony shoulders. "You may tell me, Griselda. Am I not your man?" *Lightning will strike me dead for that lie.*

She rested her head on his shoulder. Her hair under her coif smelled of tallow grease. "When we first came to help nurse poor Cuthbert, Mortimer would not admit any visitors while my brother was so ill." Her eyes filled with tears.

By the rood, she must have actually loved the milksop. Mark gave her a little squeeze to comfort her—and to encourage her tale.

She dabbed her eyes with the end of her sleeve. "Then, after Cuthbert died, we could not entertain because we were in mourning. Then Belle—" She glanced over her shoulder, and made a quick sign against the evil eye. "I mean, my sister-in-law grew quarrelsome and out of sorts with her grief, so Mortimer was compelled to put her to bed in a dark room until she recovered her wits."

"Just so," he murmured. Mortimer's double-dyed villainy became much clearer. Mark would suffer no pangs of remorse when he frightened the man senseless. Mayhap, Belle's "spirit" should return to haunt him. Twas an intriguing thought.

"Mortimer dismissed all her servants lest they annoy her. Instead he hired his own men." She dropped her voice to a whisper. "In faith I do not like them one little bit. They are nothing but knaves and varlets and they frighten me."

"They will soon be gone," he promised her.

"Since then Mortimer has shut the gates to all but the vendors. It has been very dull here—until *you* came, just like a knight out of a troubadour's ballad."

Mark felt a little sorry for her—though not enough to make him forego his plans. Griselda's future was not his concern. She'd be far happier back in London anyway, he told himself.

"Fear not, my delicate primrose. I have an idea that will fill your hall to overflowing—and gain good opinions of you from all the countryside."

"I pant to know," she murmured, batting her eyelashes at him.

He groaned to himself. *Tis my punishment for a lifetime of swearing false love to innocent maids.*

Ignoring her attempt at seduction, he rattled on. "Allow me to take this task in hand. I will ride to Hawkhurst and acquaint myself with your neighbors. After all, they will soon become my neighbors as well. I will invite the country folk to help us celebrate the harvest and to join in our dancing."

"Oh me!" she wailed.

His heart sank. "Tis not a goodly plan?" He needed to smuggle the former castle servants back into Bodiam if his haunting was going to work.

Griselda flopped down on a nearby bench. "Tis not the guests. You said dancing and I…I cannot dance a step." She burst into gushing tears and buried her face in her hands.

Mark released a sigh of relief. He went down on one knee beside her. "Is that all, sweet cuckoo-bud? Then dry your eyes. I am a dancing master of the first degree. We have a week to practice. By All Hallows Eve your feet will be the lightest in the hall."

She stared at him through a thick sheen of tears. Her lower lip quivered. "Tis true?"

"Aye, truly," he replied. At least this was one time that he did not have to lie. Everyone who lived at Wolf Hall knew how to dance well. The Countess of Thornbury had insisted upon it.

"May we start today? This minute?" She pulled him to his feet.

Mark kissed away his last hope of a late-afternoon nap. "On one condition, pigeon-egg of mine. First we design more masks so that I may send to this wonder-maker of yours in time, then we will dance."

Griselda showered him with foolscap. "Twill be done in a twink. I have many ideas that will please you, sweet Mark." She screeched another giggle. "Perchance we can do a different kind of dance anon—in the privacy of your bed?"

God shield me!

Fortunately for Mark, though not for his feet, Griselda proved to be a slow but determined learner. Hour after hour he pushed her through the steps of a simple galliard, a bransle and the stately pavane. Kitt was sent scurrying to the minstrel's gallery to retrieve a recorder. The boy naturally dallied in his journey, leaving Mark to hum a melody over and over again until Kitt's return.

Kitt's repertoire of tunes surprised Mark. He had thought that the boy had done nothing during the first eleven years of his life but sit within Kat's reach and eat sweetmeats. Twilight and the approach of supper time called a halt to the proceedings. With barely a backward glance, Griselda dragged herself upstairs to prepare for the evening meal. All thoughts of an amorous interlude had thankfully flown from her head. His feet numb from dancing on a stone floor, Mark could barely climb his own stairway. He threw himself across his bed with a groan.

"Wake me in a half hour, Kitt. God's teeth! I am exhausted."

Kitt rinsed his face in the basin. "Jobe stopped me outside the minstrel's gallery. He wants to speak with you."

"Now?" Merciful heaven! What had Mark done to deserve this day? If he didn't get some sleep soon he would be in no shape for tonight's ghostly surprises. "What does he want?"

Kitt dried his face. "I know not, and now I must go to the kitchens to fill my ears with more of the cook's abuse. Ask him yourself." The boy banged out of the room.

The African's low laughter caught Mark unawares. He opened his eyes in time to see Jobe emerge from the privy alcove. "Your pardon if I don't get up to greet you, my friend. You see before you a man worn to the very nub."

Jobe flopped down beside him. "Ah! I had forgotten what a mattress felt like."

Mark cast him a sidelong glance. "Are you complaining of your royal accommodations in your garret hole? Perchance you would like to woo Mistress Griselda in my stead?"

Jobe chuckled causing the bed to shake. "Nay, *meu amigo*. I leave that pleasure to you."

Mark yawned. "So what is amiss?"

Jobe laced his hands behind his head. "A most interesting thing, methinks. Two men are digging up the cellar next to the chapel crypt."

Mark rubbed his aching eyes. "Whyfor?"

"Ah! That is the question," Jobe replied. "I bided my time in the shadows and listened. They are most unhappy to toil down there day after day. Indeed, they filled the air with curses against Master Fletcher, though he pays them well enough for their trouble."

Mark turned on his side to face his friend. "What do they seek?"

Jobe shrugged. "They do not know, save that it is in a small chest. After a while I grew as tired as they, so I gave them my lovelorn monkey call. Alas, they were not in a loving mood." He laughed. "They ran like children who have spied a mamba snake."

Mark rolled onto his back and stared up at the bed's green velvet canopy. He knew that cellar but could not understand why anyone would have such a keen interest in the place. In the distant past, it had once housed plunder that Bodiam's original owner had stolen while adventuring in France. During Lady Kat's tenure, the low dusty vault stood empty unless the year's grain harvest had been especially good.

"Most interesting," he agreed. He would ask Belle about it when he saw her later this evening. "And how fares Mistress Belle?"

Jobe flashed him a grin. "Ah! She is a lion cloaked in a woman's fair skin."

Mark rolled his eyes. "What did she do this time?"

"Took a bath."

Mark bolted upright. "Fire and brimstone! Just like the minx. Where? When?"

"When she grew tired of watching Mistress Griselda climb all over you during the dance instruction. Indeed, your sweet Belle has a goodly range of oaths—and some in French as well. I was most impressed."

Mark fidgeted with the silken bed coverlet. "And just exactly where did she take this bath?"

"In Mistress Griselda's chamber."

Mark could do nothing but gape at him. Belle had always loved to court disaster but this was going too far. "Did *you* fetch the water for her?" he snarled.

Jobe looked too pleased with himself. "Nay, she called through the door to one of the serving boys to prepare the bath. By my troth, she is a good mimic of Mistress Griselda's shrill tune. Then she hid in the privy until the tub was filled. After that, she helped herself to soap, comb and brush—even a new shift and gown from Mistress Griselda's chest."

Mark wanted to wring Jobe's neck. "And just where were you when the little gamester was in her bath?"

Jobe sighed. "Alas, in the privy alcove and sworn upon my honor to stay there until she called. And, upon my honor, I did so—though I must admit, twas tempting to take a quick peek."

Mark closed his eyes and tried to imagine the scene. "I am right glad you were there." *And not I. Since I have no honor, I would have taken a good long look.*

"Love is the most excellent sport of all," Jobe remarked.

"Don't entertain any fantasies on my behalf. I am not in love with anyone—and certainly not with Mistress Belladonna! I am just here for Sir Brandon's reward."

The African merely laughed in his face.

Chapter Thirteen

The rain began to fall on Bodiam at twilight. By late evening it had increased to a miserable downpour, effectively canceling the ghost's midnight performance, much to Kitt and Jobe's disappointment. Kitt trudged off to his pallet and was soon in deep sleep, no doubt dreaming of the delectable Ivy. Jobe consoled himself by harassing the soaked men-at-arms with his blowpipe. On the other hand, the inclement weather was a relief to footsore Mark. It promised him his first decent night's sleep since he had arrived at Bodiam. Leading a double life was exhausting. He would visit Belle for a brief moment to make sure the little vixen was safe in her hideaway before he sought his own bed.

Mark's good intentions flew up the chimney the minute he saw Belle framed in her doorway. Thanks to good meals and restorative sleep, her natural beauty had blossomed. Her unbound golden hair shimmered in the firelight's glow; its wispy tendrils caressed her cheeks. When she greeted him, her skin flushed becomingly like sunset reflected on virgin snow. The beginnings of a smile tipped the corners of her lush mouth. The wild sapphire of her eyes mellowed when she looked up at him. His gaze wandered past her slender neck to the pale satin skin of her half-hidden breasts. A fierce rush of passion took hold of him.

Belle raised one eyebrow with amusement. "Are you coming inside or merely gaping at me like a marvel at a fair? Should I charge you a ha'penny for the privilege?"

Mark swallowed the hard knot in his throat. What he wanted to do was to sweep her in his arms, kiss her into a half-swoon then lay her on her bed and spend the night making sweet love to this delectable creature. Since he knew that option was an impossibility, he blurted out, "Did you know that there are two men digging up the old storage cellar by the crypt?"

Belle cocked her head. "And so the worm turns again," she murmured to herself.

Locking the door behind him, Mark mopped his brow. He felt hot and cold at the same time. An ache settled in his loins. He tugged at the hem of his loose thigh-length overcoat and prayed that it covered his growing arousal. He glanced around the room in search of the cat, but for once Dexter was not present. Mark leaned against the chimney hood and attempted to look at ease.

"Does this worm go by the name of Mortimer Fletcher?" he asked. "Jobe overheard his minions speak of a small chest. Have you any idea what it might contain?"

Her eyes darkened. Her mouth curled back as if she tasted a bitter root. "Aye, tis the Cavendish jewel he seeks. I should have guessed his true intent."

Mark drew in his breath. "Do you speak of your grandmother's fabulous brooch?" He had seen the Countess of Thornbury wear it on special occasions during the years he had lived under Wolf Hall's roof.

Belle nodded. "The same."

He whistled through his teeth. The pigeon's-egg-sized ruby was worth a kingdom alone, yet an equally impressive teardrop pearl dangled from the gem's gold setting. He licked his dry lips. "Tis here at Bodiam?" he asked in a hoarse voice.

Again Belle nodded, then she lifted her face to meet his startled look. "Tis mine," she said softly. The challenge in her tone was clear. "Grandmamma gave it to me as a wedding present."

Mark opened his mouth to babble something appropriate, but absolutely nothing came out. He wished he had a cup of wine. Even mere water would do.

She stiffened. "I perceive that you are surprised by my grandmother's generosity," she remarked with a cold edge in her voice. "No doubt you wonder why on earth she would give a bastard such a precious heirloom when she has two nobly born daughters-in-law."

"That thought never crossed my mind," he lied. He flashed her a friendly smile, but Belle saw through him as if he were made of glass.

"Do not play the fool with me, Sir Mark Hayward," she stormed. Her fists balled at her sides. "Your face is the mirror of your mind—always has been. I could read you like a book since I was eight and was no longer under the thrall of your so-called superior wit."

He flinched inwardly at her biting words. As in the past, he retaliated in kind to protect himself. He crossed his arms over his chest. "Very well, Mistress Cavendish. Since you are so brilliant, pray enlighten my dull brain. Why did my lady Countess bedeck you with her treasure?"

A scarlet blush stained her cheeks. She blinked her eyes several times in rapid succession. Mark immediately regretted the visible hurt he had inflicted. Before he could beg her forgiveness, she snapped, "Because the good Countess is a bastard herself."

Mark felt as if he had been gut-punched. He flopped into the chair by the hearth. "Never!" he breathed. Lady Alicia was the most noble woman he had ever known.

Belle sneered at his disbelief. "How now, jolt-head? What did you mutter? That I lie? Ha!" She snapped her fingers under his nose. "Do you think for one fleeting moment that I would besmirch my good grandmother's reputation to you for the sole pleasure of seeing you goggle and gasp like a beached salmon?"

Mark grabbed her hand. Despite her lively resistance, he pressed it to his lips and kissed her whitened knuckles. "Nay, *chou-chou,* pray pardon my poor manners. I am a jackass of the first magnitude." When she slowed her struggle against him, he caressed her hand again.

Belle rubbed the side of her nose. "I am not won by your rabbity lips," she retorted, though her shoulders relaxed.

Mark turned her hand over and planted another kiss on the soft skin at her pulse point. "And I do not seek to buy you," he replied, searching for some glimmer of forgiveness in the blue fire of her eyes. "You are not a woman to be set out in the marketplace, but a jewel bestowed upon only the most fortunate."

She snorted. "Don't you ever grow tired of hearing yourself prattle? How many women have you whispered that endearment to?"

He drew her closer to his side. "None, and that is God's own truth." He gave her another smile. "Tis not my habit to insult a member of the fair sex. Will you forgive my words? If they were written down on a piece of paper, I would tear them into shreds."

Amusement flickered across her face. "Good quality paper is very expensive," she remarked.

He grinned. Knowing Belle, this was as close to absolution as she would give him. He gently pulled her into his lap, though he resisted the urge to press his advantage. Belle perched on his knees with her hands folded primly together. She stared into the fire with a faraway look in her eyes.

After a short while, she broke the silence. "I was as shocked as you when Grandmamma told me her secret," she began in a hollow voice that seemed to reach across a far distance. "'Twas the night before my wedding. The whole family was gathered here at Bodiam for the ceremony. When Grandmamma took me into the solar, methought she intended to reveal the mysteries of the bedchamber—which I had already learned from years of observation." She shot him a sidelong glance full of mischief. "I must confess, Marcus, your amorous antics were particularly educational."

Mark groaned, but had the good sense not to press her for dates, places or partners. He really didn't want to hear the history of his misspent youth fall from Belle's sweet lips.

She continued. "Instead, Grandmamma handed me a blue velvet bag. When I opened it, I could not believe my eyes. My wonderment increased a hundredfold when she told me that her beautiful brooch was mine to keep. I...I wept." Belle chewed her lower lip.

Mark shifted her a little closer to his chest. *So would I,* he thought, *though not for the same reason.*

"When I told her that I could not possibly take it...because of my birth, she smiled and shook her head. Then she told me that she too was a bastard. At first, methought she teased me to take my mind off the day to come. Instead she told me the most marvelous tale how her father had been a great nobleman of the land while her mother was the wife of a goldsmith. Her mother disappeared after giving birth, but her father put Grandmamma into the safekeeping of his brother. He in turn gave her to another goldsmith and his wife to rear. The brooch was her father's dowry for Grandmamma.''

Mark tried to imagine what the gruff old Earl of Thornbury must have thought the first time Lady Alicia told this tale and showed him the mind-boggling gems.

Belle softened. ''Grandmamma told me that when my father brought me home, she knew exactly to whom she would pass on her brooch. She said we were much alike and needed to stick together.'' Belle turned to look fully into Mark's eyes. ''Can you even begin to guess how much her words meant to me?''

He nodded. ''More than the price of the ruby and pearl, I expect,'' he replied. ''And did you wear the brooch when you married Cuthbert?''

She tossed her head. ''Aye, and his eyes nearly popped right out of their sockets. In fact, he did nothing for the rest of our wedding day but ogle the jewel.'' Her eyes narrowed. ''And so did his brother now that I think of it.''

Mark slipped his arm around her tiny waist. How delectable she was! ''Mortimer?'' he asked, though he knew the answer.

''And Griselda too. The whole Fletcher clan practically slobbered down my bodice.'' She wrinkled her nose.

''Obviously an ill-mannered family,'' he remarked. If I had been your bridegroom, I would have dispensed with your gown and kissed your sweet paps. And ogled the brooch on another day.

She nodded. ''Exactly what I thought. When the time came for me to withdraw to the bedchamber, I made a little detour.'' A secret smile ruffled her lips. ''The Cav-endish jewel went into hiding and there it has remained. It nearly drove poor Cuthbert to distraction trying to guess what I had done with it. Twas a jest to tease him about it.'' She gave a small sigh. ''I suppose I would have told him eventually—but he died.''

Prudence restrained Mark from inquiring the jewel's current whereabouts. Instead, he mused, ''This must be the real reason why Mortimer dismissed your servants and why he is so anxious to possess the castle. Only today, he confessed to me how much he hated living in the coun-try.''

Belle applauded him. ''Bull's eye, Mark! The man does not care a dented groat for this wonderful old home—only for the brooch. In faith, I wish there truly was a real Black Knight who would protect Bodiam from Mortimer's foul designs! Instead there is only me.''

Mark traced her lips with his fingertip. ''You forget that you have us to help you now.'' He chuckled in the back of his throat. What enticing lips she had! How close they hovered to his! A little kiss would not be out of place.

''Ah, *chou-chou*, what a piece of work you are! Not only did you inherit your mother's beauty but also your father's quick wits as well.'' He lifted her chin to kiss her.

Belle shook him hard by the shoulders. ''My mother? How on earth do you know what she looked like?''

Mark heaved a sigh of regret for his missed opportunity. ''Because I met her,'' he replied peevishly. ''And she was a lot nicer than you are!''

Belle blinked at him, her face a picture of confusion. ''You must have been a baby at the time,'' she insisted.

Mark rested his head against the back of the chair. ''Twas June of 1520. I was seven and had been fostered at Wolf Hall for less than a month. Sir Brandon and your uncle were created knights on the feast of Saint George and the old earl gave me to your father as his page boy. Since he had no squire, Sir Brandon told me that we would grow to learn our duties together.''

Belle said nothing. Instead, she slipped off his knee and knelt down on the hearth where she studied the low flames. Mark yawned. The sleep he had eluded all day finally caught up with him. He eyed Belle's bed, not with lustful intentions but with an overwhelming desire to stretch himself out on its inviting mattress. When Belle gave no indication that she noticed him, Mark eased himself down on top of her blankets. He would rest his eyes for just a minute while he gathered his strength to crawl back to his own chamber. The feather pillow welcomed his head.

''Mark?'' Belle's soft voice intruded in his half dreams.

''Hmm?'' he replied.

The mattress shook as she lay down beside him. ''Tell me about my mother. Please,'' she added as an afterthought.

Mark rubbed his eyes and tried to compose his answer.

''What did your father tell you?'' he hedged. He yawned again.

Belle rubbed the side of her nose. ''Not much. When I was little, methought his silence indicated his great sorrow for her death. Of course, I had presumed that they were legally wed.''

He detected the bitterness in her voice. ''When did you learn otherwise?''

''Two summers ago, when King Henry commanded the family to come to court for his wedding to Catherine Howard. I remember how unusually hot the weather was.''

Mark did a quick mental calculation. ''You must have been nineteen.'' Why had Brandon waited so long to tell her the truth?

She nodded. "Before we left Wolf Hall, Grandmamma took me aside. She said that there would be many people at court who knew the story of my parentage."

Mark agreed. Brandon Cavendish had been a shining light during the heyday of Great Harry's glittering court in the 1520s. As both his page and later squire, Mark had reveled in his lord's popularity. It was a memorable day at Hampton Court when the curly-haired souvenir of Brandon's youthful fling with a French vintner's daughter arrived unannounced in the middle of a royal summer's-day frolic.

Two French nuns from a convent located outside of Rheims appeared in the Great Hall armed with a two-year-old cherub and asked for a nobleman by the name of Brandon Cavendish. The whole court erupted in roars of laughter when the holy women of Mother Church presented the speechless rake with his daughter, LaBelle Marie Cavendish. Mark, then a feckless ten-year-old, had joined in the universal merriment.

Belle thumped him on his chest. "Tell me all, Mark. I don't even know her name."

He instantly snapped wide awake. *Blast you, Brandon! This tale should have been your office, not mine.* "Yvette," he replied, picking his words with care. "She was French."

Belle played with his wrist laces. "So Grandmamma told me. She said I was conceived during the great fortnight when the French king met our king on the Field of Cloth of Gold."

"Aye." Mark closed his eyes and conjured up the images of that magnificent event from his memory. "Twas a time of feasting, tournaments, great displays of pageantry, fine clothes and non-stop merriment. Heady stuff for a small boy, I assure you."

Belle snuggled next to him. "Grandmamma said that Papa and Uncle Guy were the best jousters there, besides King Henry of course. She told me that they won dozens of prizes."

And dozens of women as well. Roosters in the henhouse—both of them. The Cavendish brothers, flushed with their youth, vigor and unusual good looks, made conquests at every turning. It was no wonder that the sixteen-year-old Yvette was swept off her feet and into Brandon's tent.

"Can you remember what she looked like?" Belle whispered.

Mark put his arm around her and pillowed her head on his shoulder. "Methought she was the most beautiful woman I had ever met in my life."

"Cross your heart and hope to spit?" Belle murmured.

Mark smiled. "Truly. I remember that her golden hair hung down to her waist when it was unbraided. She smelled good—like lavender and honey. And her laughter reminded me of silver bells tinkling in the breeze. She was warm, kissed me a lot and called me *un petit chou-chou.*"

Propping herself on her elbow, Belle stared at him. "But that's what you've always called me. My mother said that?"

Until that moment, Mark had never considered why he had chosen that nickname for Brandon's little French waif. "Aye, twas lodged in my memory, I expect. I also recall that your mother stuffed me with sweetmeats. I liked that part best of all."

Belle drummed her fingers on his buttons. "You haven't changed much since then." She paused, then asked with a light tone, "Did Papa love her?"

Mark swallowed. How could a seven-year-old tell the difference between love and lust? "He gave her pretty gifts and squired her about the English camp just as if she was the grandest lady there.''

"But she wasn't a real lady, was she?" Belle prodded. ''She was just a commoner?''

Mark wished he could tell her that her mother had been of royal birth instead of a barefoot country wench. ''She came from a fine merchant's family in Calais,'' he muttered quickly. ''But I thought she had descended from heaven,'' he added. How he had idolized her then!

Belle polished the nearest button with her thumb. ''If Papa loved her so much, why didn't he bring her back to England when the royal meeting was concluded?''

I was afraid you would ask that question. Mark ran his tongue over his dry lips. Noblemen never married common lightskirts.

''Your father didn't know that she was pregnant with you or I am sure he would have,'' he stumbled through his reply. ''Besides, methinks her family objected,'' he added throwing his caution to the wind. *I have spun enough tales this fortnight to roast me for a thousand years. What is one more now?*

''Ah,'' she said, more to herself than to Mark. She polished another button. ''Then how did Papa find me?''

You found him. Mark considered a number of answers but decided to stick close to the truth. No telling what Belle might have learned during her short stay at court.

''Your mother gave birth to you in a convent near Rheims. The good nuns knew that your father was a member of King Henry's court and Yvette had told them his name.''

''Before she died,'' Belle inserted.

Before she walked out the door without a backward glance and left you to fend for yourself. Mark ignored her question. "The holy sisters had few resources. It took them nearly two years to locate your father."

She twirled a lock of her hair around her finger. "I was told by a goodly number of courtiers that my first appearance before King Henry was the grandest jest of the season."

Mark closed his eyes. *Forgive me, sweet Belle, but I laughed louder than all the rest on that fateful day.* "Twas no laughing matter for your father. By my troth, I have never seen a man grow so besotted as Sir Brandon did the first time he laid an eye on you."

She propped herself up on her elbow and stared into his face. "Is this really true, Mark?"

He chuckled. "Cross my heart, *chou-chou.* He took you in his arms and hugged you until you protested with a howl. When the laughter died down, he held you aloft so that the whole court could see you. 'Behold the fairest maiden in all England,' he cried out."

Belle shivered in Mark's embrace. "I did not know that part."

"And from that day to this, you have been the darling of his heart. And that is God's own truth, Belle."

She sighed. "Poor dearest Papa! I have led him a merry jig."

Mark relaxed further into the mattress. "That you have, *chou-chou.*" Now that the ticklish storytelling was over, he allowed himself to drift toward sweet slumber. Curled next to him, Belle felt so comfortable, so right.

"I knew I had been born in a convent," she suddenly remarked, jarring him. "I was always afraid that the family would grow tired of me and send me back there. Could you imagine me as a nun?"

"Never," Mark murmured.

"That is why Bodiam is so important to me. Tis my

safeguard against exile into oblivion. Tis my only refuge. Can you understand that, Mark?''

He tried to pay attention but his need for sleep proved too powerful. ''Understand...'' he mumbled.

Just before he completely lost consciousness, Belle whispered in his ear, ''Thank you for telling me, Mark, even if parts of your story were very pretty lies.''

Chapter Fourteen

Belle settled into the crook of Mark's slack embrace. His heavy breathing told her that he had slipped into a deep sleep. The fire in the hearth burned itself out, yet she still lay awake pondering the mysteries of her childhood. Only when the night's chill penetrated her clothing did she rouse herself. She unfolded one of her spare blankets and laid it over Mark. She had not realized how tall he had grown until she noticed that his boots hung over the bottom of the bed. Gently she pried them off and set them side by side on the floor.

A few embers still glowed, casting a feeble orange light. Belle stood over Mark's sleeping form and gazed down at the man she had teased and exasperated for so many years. In slumber, his face appeared more youthful. His boots reminded her of the time she had poured honey into his new shoes. In return, he had tossed Belle into the moat. After Papa had fished her out of the green waters, he had ordered Mark to trudge around the courtyard while carrying a heavy log on his shoulders. Mark's punishment had lasted three hours, though the fault had been hers entirely. Though his shoulders ached for a week, the squire did not breathe a word of her prank—not that day nor ever after, but she would never forget the angry look in his eyes. No wonder Papa had had to bribe him to come for her!

Belle swept an errant brown lock from his forehead. How many times had she watched her young nursemaid run her hands through Mark's thick hair? How they both had laughed! How Belle had longed for Mark's warm glances cast in her direction instead of at silly Polly! The insidious green worm of jealousy coiled around her heart.

Belle put her cool hands to her flushed cheeks. *Why am I mooning over this wastrel? He cares nothing for me except for the reward Papa will give him.* But her soul rejected this easy rationalization.

She untied her gown, pulled it over her head, then laid it across the chair. If Mark had been her lover, he would have merely dropped her clothing on the floor. What was Mark like as a lover anyway? Despite his hot pursuit of all Kat's serving maids, Belle had only caught him twice in the very act itself—both times with the shameless Polly. Belle snorted. What a wanton nursemaid she had been! Belle could have fallen down the well for all Polly cared as she wriggled and giggled under Mark.

Would I wriggle and giggle like that? Despite Belle's highest hopes, she had never experienced such joyful abandon in Cuthbert's embrace. Poor man! He did try to please her but he had had the passion of a wet fish and the endurance of a firefly. Belle had hoped that with time and practice things would get better in the bedchamber—but they hadn't. Then her young, fumbling husband had sickened and died.

A suffocating sensation tightened her throat. *I shall never be truly loved as Papa loves Kat.* Sitting down next to Mark, she lifted one of his hands and fitted her palm against his larger one. What would it be like to hold hands while they walked in the riverside meadow on a golden summer's day? She laced her fingers though his, palms pressed close together and intertwined as lovers entwined around each other. Her yearning for that intimacy swelled within her breast.

His hard calluses scraped against her soft skin—calluses from years of wielding a sword. Belle studied Mark's forearm. She had noticed that he often rubbed it while he talked with her. She laid her hand over the site of the ancient injury. In her memory, she heard again that chilling crack when his bone broke; heard his scream of pain. Belle shuddered at the recollection.

That bright April day had been so full of promise. She had just turned thirteen and was eager to test the new womanly powers that stirred within her. Without a thought of any dire consequences, she deliberately beguiled Mark and led him into Bodiam's apple orchard. Delicate pink blossoms showered down on them as she climbed one of the trees, knowing that Mark followed close behind her. Sitting on a thick bough high over the lush green grass, she tempted and teased him until Mark leaned forward to claim a kiss.

Over his shoulder, she saw Papa coming toward them. If he caught sight of Mark's bold move, the young man would certainly pay a painful price. In a panic, Belle did the first thing that popped into her head. She pushed her would-be suitor off the limb. For once, Mark's cat-like reflexes failed him. Instead of landing solidly on his feet, he stumbled, then fell heavily on his left arm, his sword arm. His look of pain and betrayal was one that had haunted her nightmares ever since.

Brandon was at Mark's side in a flash. For one of the few times in Belle's life, her father had placed the blame squarely where it belonged—on her shoulders. While Mark writhed in his agony, Brandon banished his daughter to her chamber. Vowing not to show her distress, she had marched back to the castle with her head held high and her eyes dry.

Only in the depths of her pillow did Belle weep her remorse for Mark's pain and the loss of the fragile bond that had stretched between them for so short a time. She had wanted to go to Mark's bedside to explain what had happened, but she didn't dare risk Papa's further displeasure; he might send her back to France. She ought to have written Mark a note but no words of apology seemed adequate. By the time Kat allowed her downstairs again, Mark had already gone back to his parents' home to mend.

He never returned to the Cavendish household. A year later under Brandon's sponsorship, King Henry knighted Mark and sent him immediately to Ireland. Belle never expected to see him again. Over the years, she had tried to forget the horrible incident. Now it poured back into her mind with every detail in clear relief.

"I am so very sorry, Marcus," she whispered in the darkness. She leaned over and brushed his lips with hers.

"Mmm," he hummed in his sleep. His mouth twitched.

A daring idea presented itself. *Just this once, I'll do it.* Belle knew she would never get another opportunity to sleep next to him without a stitch of clothing on her. Mark would never be her lover, she knew, but for the remainder of this night she would lie next to him—and pretend. Belle kicked off her house slippers, then peeled down her wool stockings. She pulled back the bedcovers on her side, then drew her shift over her head. The cold air encouraged her into the bed. She pulled the sheet and blankets up to her chin, then turned toward Mark, who still lay fully dressed on top of the coverlet.

"Good night...my love," she whispered in his ear before she laid her head on his shoulder. Even through the bedclothes, his body warmed her.

Mark snored softly.

A pewter half light filtered through the window and the rain still pattered against the thick panes of hand-blown glass when Mark opened his eyes. He yawned. In a half-drowsy state, he wondered why he was still dressed in last evening's clothes. He stretched out his arms—and soundly thumped the woman sleeping beside him.

"Hell's bells!" she groaned. "What's amiss?"

Mark rubbed the sleep out of his eyes. "Tis dawn," he began, glancing over to Belle. "You were supposed to—" He broke off in mid-sentence as he stared at her naked shoulders with growing shock. "God's teeth!" he bellowed. He leaped out of the bed still staring at her as if he had never seen her before in his life. "What are you doing there?"

Belle swept her tousled hair out of her eyes. The coverlet slipped a notch lower. "What do you think I would be doing?" she retorted with a trace of sarcasm.

The blood pounded against his temples. "Are you...naked under that?" She couldn't be! His heartbeat quickened at the speculation.

Belle pulled herself a little more out of the protection of the bedding and lay back against her pillow. The covers slipped further down to reveal a hint of the shadow between her breasts. Mark's breath came out in short gasps.

She folded her hands over her stomach. "Of course. What did you expect?" she replied.

God save me! Mark backed farther away from the bed and nearly stepped into the cooling ashes of last night's fire. *What did I do to her?* "Wha...what happened?"

Belle's pink lips puckered with annoyance. "Methought

you would awake happier than this. After all, I gave you what you most desired.''

"Sdeath!" Why couldn't he remember what had transpired? "I swear upon my honor—"

Lifting one eyebrow, she cocked her head. "Tis a fine thing to talk of your honor...afterward!''

Mark's stomach heaved. Sweat broke out on his brow. ''Belle, forgive me! I must have drunk too much wine at supper. I didn't know what I was doing.''

Belle twirled a lock of her hair. The cover dropped to reveal the tops of her creamy breasts. "Methinks tis a little late to tell me that now.'' She shrugged. A pink nipple winked at him for a split second. "I expected you to be at least grateful for what I did for you.''

Mark's knees turned to jelly; his loins lit up. "Sweet Jesu, Belle, I didn't mean to hurt you. I would never do that to you. I didn't mean to...did I take you? That is, did we go...uh...beyond...?''

He stopped his gibbering when he spied a sparkle of mischief in her eyes. Blast the minx! He strode to the bedside and glared down at her. "Exactly what did you give me that I so desired?''

Her lips curved into a wicked smile. "A good night's sleep, of course! What else could you possibly want so late at night?''

Humiliation and anger followed closely on the heels of his relief. Mark planted his hands on his hips and glowered at her. "Thank you for a most interesting crack of dawn, Belladonna! Forgive me if I stop groveling at your feet.''

His cheeks burned, his throat burned—and his arousal burned. He searched for his boots and when he found them at the foot of the bed, he snatched them up and started for the door.

"Tut, tut, Marcus," said the little witch. "You were

always such a poor sport. Prithee, is the idea of making love to me really that loathsome to you?''

He stopped in his tracks. Pivoting on his heel, he glared at her. A mistake! With a mocking challenge in her blue eyes, she flipped down the covers baring herself to the waist. Arching her back, she lifted her firm ripe breasts for his inspection.

He moaned under his breath. With her hair in fetching disarray and her eyes half-closed, Belle looked fit to be ravished. His desire for her set every nerve in his body on edge. With the greatest reluctance, he turned his back on the tempting sight. He gripped his boots until his knuckles turned white. His lungs screamed for air. ''If you were an eager nursemaid, or a wanton tavern wench or a frisky Irish lass in a barnloft, I would not hesitate for a moment but to take you at your word.''

Mark leaned his forehead against the window panes and sought balm for his heat from the cold glass. ''If you were a bored matron at court or a worldly-wise courtesan, I would strip off my clothes and join you for a merry romp.'' He paused to gather his strength and wits. Her nipples turned a dusky pink and their nubbins hardened in the cold air.

He drew in a deep breath, ''But of all the women in this wide world, you are the only one I would never bed!'' He mopped his streaming face. ''And for pity's sweet sake, cover yourself before you…uh…catch cold.''

Belle's expression turned thunderous. ''I see,'' she spat. ''I am not good enough for you because I am a bastard.'' She yanked the coverlet up to her chin.

Mark closed his eyes for a moment. ''Nay, tis the very opposite.'' He glanced at her. His flaming passion cooled to something more gentle. ''Because you are a Cavendish, a member of the family that I hold dearer than any other.

I would die rather than bring dishonor upon any one of you.''

Belle blinked at him, rubbed the side of her nose but said nothing.

''Your family made me one of their own. Lady Alicia nursed me through fevers and homesickness. The Earl plopped me on the back of a fat pony and took me on my first hunt just as if I had been one of his own sons. Your Uncle Guy taught me to read and write in both English and Latin while his patient lady wife made speaking French as natural to me as my mother tongue. And your father?'' Mark's chest swelled with pride.

''There is no greater knight in this realm than Sir Brandon Cavendish and I count it a supreme honor to have been schooled in the arts of chivalry and warfare by him. In return, I have struggled all these years to obey the only vow that he ever placed upon me.''

Belle moistened her lips. ''What was that?'' she asked in a faint voice.

Mark swallowed with difficulty before he continued. ''When your father brought you home to Wolf Hall, he made me swear on his sword that I would always and forever honor, protect and cherish you. And I have tried my damnedest to do just that in spite of all your tricks.''

Belle turned white. She cleared her throat. ''Cherish?'' she whispered.

''Just so,'' Mark snapped. ''And that means I will not rape, seduce, or meddle with your virtue. You, LaBelle, are forbidden fruit to me. Have I made myself clear?''

She flashed him a look of disdain. ''Marvelously much! In that case, go! You have tarried too long in my virtuous bower.'' She slid further under the covers.

Tucking his boots under his arm, Mark unlocked the door. Before he lifted the latch, he glanced back over his shoulder. "By the way, *chou-chou,* in case you wondered, you have a lovely pair of titties." He skittered out the door before her flung pillow hit its target.

Once in the icy gallery, he released a long, audible sigh of relief. Without bothering to put on his boots, he padded down the mid-tower stairs. Leaving his boots on the dry bottom step, Mark strode out into the courtyard and lifted his fevered face to the cooling rain. He stood motionless, allowing himself to be soaked to the skin before he retrieved his shoes and splashed across the courtyard to his own bed in the south wing. To his surprise, Kitt awaited him with a hostile expression.

"'Tis nearly dawn," the boy chided. "Where have you been with your boots in your hand and why soaking wet?"

Mark snatched up his shaving towel and dried his dripping hair. "Heaven defend me from Cavendishes!" he groaned. He needed more sleep.

Kitt folded his arms across the chest of his nightshirt. His mild blue eyes flared with his family's quick temper. "Have you...used my sister in a wanton fashion?" His chin quivered with his anger.

Mark sat on a stool and unbuttoned his sleeveless overcoat. "On my honor as a consecrated knight, I have not touched Belle in any manner whatsoever, though if you will pardon me for saying it, she desperately needs a good spanking." He balled up the sodden coat and tossed it across the chamber.

Kitt's rigid posture relaxed a little. "Then what *were* you doing?"

Mark untied the laces at his wrists and neck of his linen shirt. "Catching up on my sleep, if you must know, but, Kitt—" He gave the boy a stern look. "Learn this most important lesson: if you intend to live a long and healthy life, *never* ask anyone, man or woman, exactly how and where they passed the night. A great deal of blood has been spilled over that simple question.''

Kitt studied his bare toes while he digested this piece of wisdom. Mark pulled down his breeches and hose, then kicked them into a heap. With a prayer of thanksgiving under his breath, he crawled between the cool sheets of his bed.

Kitt glanced at the piles of damp clothing with disgust. "You are going to sleep now? Methought you just said—''

Mark yawned widely. "I need my strength to push Mistress Griselda through another dancing lesson—unless you would care to do it for me.''

Kitt made a face. "I am content to play the music. You can keep Mistress Griselda all to yourself.''

Mark punched his pillow into the shape he preferred. "Methought as much. Wake me in time to dress for dinner. And, Kitt?''

His little squire replied with a quizzical look.

"Pray tell me, do you know how to carve up vegetables?''

Kitt gaped at him. "Tis work for a kitchen scullion.''

Mark grinned. "Not any more.''

Chapter Fifteen

By an unspoken mutual agreement, Mark and Belle avoided each other as much as possible over the next few days. Mark left Kitt to attend to his sister's needs, and Jobe continued to shadow her on her increasingly bolder jaunts throughout the castle. Mark made it a point not to speak directly to her, not to look into those bewitching sapphire eyes and, most of all, never to be alone with her. Belle had no idea how close to the precipice she had pushed his fortitude. The sooner he concluded this madness, the happier Mark would be.

As All Hallows Eve drew closer, activities around Bodiam, both innocent and haunting, accelerated in frenzy. Mark functioned on less than five hours of sleep each night and the strain of maintaining his pose as Griselda's ardent suitor frayed him to the quick. His deluded lady-love played the wanton jade during the daylight hours, but she fled to the safety of her bedchamber immediately after supper, for which he was most thankful.

Through the combined efforts of Kitt, Jobe and now Belle, Bodiam's restless "ghost" haunted the daytime as well as the night hours. During the past week, many of the castle's staff had left Mortimer's employment despite the raise in wages that the desperate man offered. The phantom hoofbeats, the midnight drumming, the mysterious beestings, the snuffed candles, the rearrangement of furnishings, the missing tools and the eerie howling all combined to send the bravest running for the gate.

In between teaching the galliard to the clod-footed Griselda and avoiding Mortimer's prying questions, Mark spent part of each day riding to and from Montjoy's cottage. In spite of his grumbling and dire warnings, the ancient steward had risen to the occasion in admirable fashion. Montjoy had gathered a number of Belle's former servants into Mark's scheme, and the loyal retainers were more than willing to do whatever was necessary to rid Bodiam of its present occupants.

The long-awaited package from Sir Andrew Ford finally arrived several days before the feast. Mark whistled when he unwrapped the oilskin coverings.

"Hoy day, my friends," he addressed Jobe, Kitt, Montjoy and the curious Ivy, "Andrew has outdone himself this time." A thick packet of instructions explaining the properties of each mysterious cylinder accompanied the trove of fireworks.

Kitt's eyes glowed as he read aloud over Mark's shoulder. "Six White Waterfalls, seven Whistling Rockets, six Catherine Wheels...wonders indeed! Twill be grander than any Twelfth Night in my memory."

"And in mine," concurred Mark. He squinted at the handwriting on the largest creation of the lot. "It merely says *une grand finale* and I am instructed to light it at the very end."

Kitt shivered with excitement. "I cannot wait."

Mark cast him a sidelong glance and made a mental note to hide the fireworks from the boy until All Hallows Eve.

The temptation to test one would be too great for Kitt—as Mark knew from his own experience.

Twenty-two years earlier, he had ''tested'' one of the pyrotechnics reserved for the final day's events at the Field of Cloth of Gold. As a result, a large green dragon had exploded in the sky during the most solemn moment of an outdoor mass celebrated by the legendary Cardinal Wolsey in the presence of the Kings of France and England. Five thousand noblemen and their ladies screamed in two languages. Brandon later said it had been the most entertaining moment of the entire fortnight.

''Let us light a small one now,'' Kitt pleaded. ''To see if it works.''

Mark frowned at him. ''In due time, squire, and until then, you are bound by your oath to me not to touch them.''

Kitt snorted his disappointment. ''Aye, I will do as you say, but tis a hard thing you ask.''

Jobe's dark eyes took on a faraway look that Mark associated with the man's abilities to predict the future. ''Tis but the first of many hard things you will be asked to perform, young Kitt.'' he intoned. ''Do not fail this test of your manhood.''

The lad's eyes grew rounder. He sat up straighter. ''I will not fail,'' he promised in a serious tone.

Mortimer rubbed his bloodshot eyes, then laid his head down amidst the papers and ledgers on his desk. God's teeth, he needed sleep. Even better, he needed to leave Bodiam as soon as possible. Each day this past week had been worse than the one preceding it.

Already his steward and many of the household servants had abandoned him. Only two grooms remained in the stables to care for the horses. Today the cook had come whining to Mortimer that he could not possibly prepare all the food that Mistress Griselda required for her feast with only himself, two scullions and the lackwit potboy. Furthermore, did Master Mortimer know that the kitchen floor had been covered with a coating of flour this morning and that the prints of a large *horse* had been tracked through the mess?

A chill went down Mortimer's spine at this news. Under his desktop, he crossed his fingers and whispered an old incantation against witchcraft. He too had been visited by the vengeful ghost. Large blots of ink covered the pages of his domestic accounts and the name *Belle* was scrawled in charcoal on his hearthstone. Last night, when he had sought the sanctuary of his bed, he discovered that a half-dozen muddy toads also shared his sheets. And every midnight brought more of that infernal drumming. The men-at-arms flatly refused to stand watch on the walls after dark. Instead, they huddled like frightened sheep in the guardroom.

A tiny voice of reason nagged at him to abandon the wretched place. Bodiam's ghosties grew bolder. Let Lord Hayward cope with the twin problems of the castle and Griselda. The rogue appeared to be unaffected by the supernatural manifestations. Mortimer already had a fortune to cheer him. The rents from the estate land brought in a tidy sum that would keep him in claret and mistresses for the rest of his life. But the vision of the fabulous brooch bewitched his reason.

He practically drooled just thinking of that stupefying ruby with its lustrous pearl companion. His fingers itched to caress the jewels as other men itched to fondle a beautiful woman. Why settle for a mere cheese-and-bread existence when roast ox beckoned? With that treasure in his possession, Mortimer could move up in the world—become a gentleman with a riverside manor house full of large glass windows. Chests filled with clothes made of rich materials, twelve courses of delicious food every day at dinner and all the willing women a man could enjoy would be his for the asking. With a jewel like that brooch, he could buy himself a title and a place at court. Such ambitions were possible ever since old King Henry had grown short of cash.

Mortimer rubbed his eyes again, then sat back in his chair. He drummed his fingers on the tabletop, keeping time with the rain that spattered in the courtyard outside his window. Where in the devil's name was that brooch?

The Cavendish family must have been moonstruck to have ever given such a prize to their common-bred by-blow. The chit had no idea of the worth of the bauble she had worn so proudly on her wedding day. Mortimer's heart had skipped a beat the first time he saw the ruby flash its crimson fire in the sun as the bride walked across the court-yard to join Cuthbert before the chapel door. All through the wedding feast, Mortimer could not tear his gaze from the gems.

Neither could Cuthbert. It was then that Mortimer first realized how inconvenient his woolly-headed brother was. Thanks to Cuthbert's stupid whining over the jewel, Belle had hidden it away to spite him. When Mortimer had ar-rived at Bodiam to help Cuthbert out of this world, the deuced brooch was still hidden.

Mortimer pushed himself away from his desk and wan-dered out into the hall where Griselda and Mark directed two of the remaining lackeys where to hang the plaited corn dollies that would decorate the long chamber for the feast. Wrinkling his nose with distaste, Mortimer stalked past the couple with only a curt nod by way of greeting.

This folly had already cost him a half-year's earnings

and Griselda seemed to think there was no bottom to his coffers. Those feathered monstrosities that had arrived yesterday from a Venetian mask-maker in London had drained his pockets of ready cash. Hideous fripperies! Mortimer vowed that he would not wear one on All Hallows Eve no matter how much Griselda whined. God's nightshirt! He would be glad to see the back of her.

Mortimer stamped down the three steps that led toward the east wing. He paused on the landing and studied the two doors that stood at right angles in front of him. The door to the left led to the withdrawing room and the stairs to the master bedroom above it. The door to the right entered the southeast drum tower where more family bedchambers were located.

Absently rubbing his hands together, Mortimer thought back to Cuthbert's wedding night nearly two years ago. As custom dictated, Belle had slipped away to prepare for the ceremonial bedding in the master bedroom. When she had quit the hall, she still wore the brooch, but by the time the wedding guests had brought Cuthbert up to join her, the wench was waiting in her shift in the huge canopied bed—and the jewel had completely disappeared from view. In full hearing of the assembly, Cuthbert had asked her what she had done with it, but Belle had only laughed at him. What an idiot that boy had been! At that point, the guests had left the chamber, and no one, not even Belle's silly maid, Ivy, had seen the jewel since.

So what had she done with it in the twenty minutes she was out of Mortimer's sight?

His two workmen claimed that they had torn up every paving stone in the cellar under the withdrawing chamber. In any event, the ghost had terrified them from further digging, no matter how much Mortimer bribed them. He pushed open the door to the withdrawing chamber—and uttered a curse.

The long table that weighed over a hundred pounds lay upside down. Only someone of exceptional strength could have done that—or the ghost. Icy fear twisted his innards. The hairs on the back of his neck prickled. Mortimer cast a quick glance around the ornate oak-paneled room. He stroked his bristled chin. Perchance there was a hidden cache behind one of the carvings on the wall.

Looking over his shoulder again and muttering a prayer for protection from the evil eye, Mortimer crossed to the nearest panel and ran his fingers slowly along the wood. A splinter wedged itself under his fingernail. The sudden pain brought tears to his eyes and a vile oath to his lips. Before he could move to the next part of the wall, something brushed against the back of his legs.

Mortimer froze on the spot. He squeezed his eyes shut and prayed aloud, stumbling over the words in his haste to get them all out in time. Something stroked his knees. Opening one eye a crack, he looked down.

Belle's obnoxious cat watched him with an unnerving stare. Mortimer raised his foot to give it a kick. The cat immediately swelled itself up to twice its already large size. It flattened its ears, spat and humped its back, bristling its tail like a brush. With a hideous yowl, the beast sprang at Mortimer's leg and sank all its claws and teeth into his calf.

Alternately howling and cursing, Mortimer danced around the room trying to shake off his snarling attacker. At last, the creature let go and leapt out the window that opened into the courtyard. Blood from a dozen punctures trickled down Mortimer's new Italian hose. Sucking his injured finger and limping back to his bedchamber, he abandoned his search for the time being. Once Griselda's fiasco was over and their guests safely in their own homes, he vowed he would strip off every piece of wood from the withdrawing chamber's stone walls. The Cavendish jewel would be his!

Kitt looked up from polishing Mark's boots. His master quietly latched the door behind him, then dropped a heavy, bulging sack at Kitt's feet.

"What's that?" the boy asked with a wary look at Mark's twinkling eyes.

"Turnips—compliments of Montjoy," Mark replied.

Kitt prodded the sack with his toe. "Whyfor?"

In answer, Mark hunkered down, untied the strings at its neck and pulled out one of the bulbous purple-and-white vegetables. "For you!"

Obviously lack of sleep had finally snapped Mark's wits. "I had rather be bowled to death by turnips than eat one," Kitt announced. "In short, I loathe them."

Mark paid no attention to his squire. Instead, he pulled out his eating knife and sliced off the top of the specimen he held.

"I especially loathe them raw," the boy added with a sinking heart.

Mark said nothing but hollowed out the insides.

"Are you well, my lord?" Kitt asked anxiously. Sweet Saint Anne! How could he possibly manage the All Hallows Eve haunting on his own if Mark fell ill at this stage of the game? "Shall I fetch you a cup of wine?"

Mark grinned as he knocked bits of the vegetable onto the floor. "Wine will be most gratefully consumed in a moment, my boy, but first attend to this lesson. Observe how I have prepared this delightful root."

Kitt decided not to agitate Mark's sudden madness any more than necessary. At the earliest possible moment, he would seek out Jobe for advice. In the meantime, he nodded and watched what would happened next.

Mark made an incision through the outside skin of the turnip. "The first time I saw this in Ireland it made my hair stand on end. Twill be most effective at our feast." He cut out two triangles and a jagged, sawtoothed curve under them. "What do you think?" He balanced his creation on the tips of his fingers.

Kitt pulled on his earlobe. "It does not look very frightening to me, Mark. Would you like your wine now?"

Mark held up one finger. "Hold, Kitt, and observe."

He handed the turnip to the boy, then fetched his bedside candle. With a quick stroke of his knife, he lopped an inch off the bottom. Then he chiseled around the wick until he freed enough of it from the wax to light it. Mark reclaimed the turnip and dropped the candle end neatly into its hollow center. Then he lit it with an ember from the hearth's fire.

Yelping, the boy nearly fell off his stool. In the flash of an instant, it appeared that Mark held a shrunken glowing head in his hand.

Mark chuckled. "A pretty piece of trickery, isn't it?"

Kitt gulped. "Aye, tis that indeed." Once his first shock of surprise receded, he saw the immediate possibilities. "I cannot wait to frighten my cousins with one of those." He eyed the bag at his feet. "How many turnips did you say you have here?"

Mark blew out the candle and shrugged. "Fifty pounds or so. Montjoy was not specific. Very well, Kitt, go to." He pointed to the sack. "You have much to accomplish betwixt now and All Hallows Eve."

Kitt pursed his lips. "Me? I am to carve these…whatevers?"

Mark chuckled. "A useful skill to add to your growing

heap of knowledge. And the Irish children call them jack-o'-lanterns.''

Grumbling to himself, Kitt pulled a turnip from the sack. "Methinks my lady mother would not approve of this.''

Mark merely waved at him as he went out the door. Then he stuck his head back inside. "And hide them in the privy alcove when you are finished. By the way, save the innards for Jobe. He is very fond of roasted turnips mashed with butter.''

Kitt said nothing but sliced off the top of the vegetable with a vicious whack.

Belle hated to admit it, but she sorely missed Mark's company at night, though she understood why he kept his distance. He was perfectly polite with her when in the company of Kitt and Jobe, but he always left her little snuggery before the others did. No more slow kisses—not even a peck on the cheek—to cheer her into slumber. *Stewed in my own juices.*

Instead of brooding over Mark's noticeable withdrawal, Belle threw her considerable energies into turning Mortimer's life upside down. As the days went by, she scrawled her name in every conceivable spot he would see. Mortimer found the word *Belle* on a piece of paper inserted among his account ledgers, across his pillow in mud, on his looking glass in wax, and most disturbing of all, on his trencher in the blood of a chicken. This last incident sent him flying from the hall to the nearest privy where he disgorged his dinner.

Belle wasted no pity on her brother-in-law. Instead she took a grim satisfaction in observing the slow disintegration of his health. Turnabout was fair play. Black circles ringed his eyes and his protracted lack of sleep ate into the sharpness of his mind. As he stumbled around the cas-

tle's galleries and chambers, he constantly glanced over
his shoulder. Oftentimes he mumbled under his breath and
increasingly crossed himself. His complexion turned a
pasty white and his already spare frame grew sparer. Yet,
for all his suffering, Mortimer refused to leave Bodiam as
so many of his minions had already done. His monumental
greed for Belle's brooch outweighed his gnawing fears.

The only thing that kept Griselda from collapsing into
a permanent state of hysterics was her infatuation with
Mark and the hope that her All Hallows Eve revels would
dispel the evil spirits that haunted the ancient stone building. Like her unseen sister-in-law, Griselda threw herself
into her preparations for the feast. Poor Mark literally
danced to her tune.

On the day before the festivities, Belle and her constant
shadow, Jobe, watched the final galliard lesson from behind one of the withdrawing room's panels. When she
couldn't stand the sight of Griselda's fawning over Mark
any longer, Belle slipped away, followed by the giant African. They didn't speak until they were once again in her
room.

"Mark is such a churlish dissembler!" she railed at
Jobe, pacing back and forth. "Did you see how he smiled
at Griselda when she trod on his foot for the third time?
And all those compliments he paid to her? Tis a wonder
his tongue doesn't cleave to the roof of his mouth with all
that sickening treacle."

Jobe chuckled. "He does it for you, little mistress," he
remarked.

Belle dismissed that ridiculous idea. "He does it for the
reward my father offered." She curled her lip. "Did you
notice Griselda when she came down to dinner today? She
looked like a painted maypole. And Mark? That knavish

lout told her that she was as beautiful as a rose. He dines and sups on deceit.''

Jobe only smiled. ''For you, *bella cara*.''

Belle leveled her gaze at him. ''Why are you so loyal to that rogue? Are you his slave?''

Drawing his dark brows together in an affronted frown, he struck his massive chest with his fist. ''Jobe is his own man!''

Taken aback by his sudden vehemence, Belle said, ''I pray your forgiveness, good Jobe. I meant no offense.''

He nodded. ''None taken, little mistress.'' He gazed out the narrow window at the muddy river that wound through the rain-soaked fields.

''When I was fourteen summers, I was captured by warriors from a rival tribe and sold to the Portuguese whose slave ships lurked along Africa's coasts like hungry jackals. In turn, they sold me to an Irish chieftain who used my skills as a fighter against his enemies.'' Jobe paused and grinned. ''Iain O'Rourke had many enemies among his own countrymen as well as the English. The sport was very good.''

Glancing at the double bandolier of daggers that Jobe always wore, Belle shuddered. She preferred not to ponder the nature of Jobe's sport among the brawling Irish. ''Since Mark is English, was he your enemy?''

Jobe nodded. ''At first. O'Rourke captured him and would have killed him on the spot, but Mark challenged him to a game of cards.''

''Surely you jest!'' Belle gasped.

Jobe shook his head. ''My dagger lay across his throat.''

Belle sank into the chair. ''So O'Rourke accepted the challenge?''

The African's dark eyes twinkled. ''He could not resist a final insult. They played far into the night. O'Rourke lost everything he owned to Mark—including me. In his anger, the Irishman ordered me to kill Mark.'' He shrugged. ''But how could I since I now belonged to him?''

Belle hugged herself. ''How did you escape?''

He lifted a brow. ''We ran. It took the Irish by surprise for they had drunk too much of their poteen and were befuddled in their wits. We outdistanced them but were stopped by a river. I cannot swim.''

''Marcus can. When I was very young, he taught me in some of the coldest cow ponds in Northumberland.'' She shivered at the memory. ''Methinks he chose only cold windy days for my lessons on purpose. But go on with your tale.''

''We did not swim but waded into the water. Mark found some hollow reeds along the shoreline. He cut them to make breathing pipes. Just as O'Rourke and his men crashed through the underbrush after us, we slipped under the water and pretended we were merely reeds.''

Belle wrinkled her nose. ''Just like Mark to think of trickery!''

Jobe regarded her with a serious expression on his broad face. ''It saved our lives. Since then I have been his man.''

Confused, she asked, ''But not as his slave?''

''Nay. I climbed out of that river free once more. Mark had saved my life. In my country, a life deserves a life. I gave him my vow to remain at his side until I can save his.''

''Then you will return to your homeland?''

''Exactly so.'' He folded his arms across his chest.

Belle mulled over his story. ''Mark says that you can foretell the future.''

He inclined his head. ''I see things in the land of shadows.''

Belle didn't understand what he meant by that but she

decided not to inquire. Instead she asked, "Can you see my future, Jobe?"

He stared at her—no, *through* her—for several heart-stopping moments. "You will find yourself when you stop running away from yourself," he intoned. "And that day will bring you much happiness and sadness at the same time."

"How so?" she breathed.

He shrugged. "I know not how or when or why—only that my words are true."

Jobe's prediction gave Belle much food for thought during the remainder of the afternoon. As she sewed on the cheesecloth gown she intended to wear the following night, his words re-echoed in her mind. She agreed that she had spent her life running, but she had always thought she was in pursuit of something—affection, approval, acceptance. Never did she think she was being pursued, especially by herself.

Yet once she pondered the idea, she found it to be uncomfortably true. How could Jobe have guessed something that she herself didn't know? He had met her less than a fortnight ago. Belle threaded her needle but paused before she returned to her costume.

A flood of childhood memories tumbled over one another in her mind. How she had teased, tormented and hoodwinked the patient, loving members of her family. How she had always insisted on having her own way—even when she was wrong. How she had never cried in the face of her transgressions no matter how hurtful they had been to others, nor had she ever apologized for anything she had done. Apologies and tears were signs of weakness, and Belle knew that she could never be weak. After all, she sprang from a family that was known for its strength especially against the encroaching Scots.

Above all else, the one person whose affection, approval and acceptance she had most wanted—and had never got—was Mark.

The other night's piece of tomfoolery effectively dashed that hope once and for all. He wanted nothing more to do with her. Or did he?

Belle put down her needle, drew up her knees under her chin and stared into her fire. Mark's anguished expression when he had told her that he had vowed to protect and cherish her spoke directly to her heart—especially that word *cherish.*

She chewed on her lower lip. If tomorrow night's haunting effectively frightened Mortimer to abandon Bodiam, she would once again get what she wanted—her home back in her hands. Mark would wave a jaunty good-bye to her as he, Kitt and Jobe rode out of her gates and returned to her father to claim the reward that Mark had so justly earned. Belle would have her castle and the Cavendish jewel, but that victory already tasted hollow in her mouth. How quiet life would be then! She would miss the excitement Mark generated wherever he went.

She would miss the excitement he kindled in her heart. *I love him,* she realized with sudden fearful clarity. *All these years I have loved that pernicious rascal, and in a few more days he will be out of my life—this time forever.* She clenched her jaw to stifle the sob in her throat.

Belle girded herself with a new resolve. Nothing before had ever stopped her once she put her mind to a problem. Nothing would now. All she had to do was to convince Mark that she loved him.

How difficult could that be?

The rain returned that night, plunging Mark into gloom. How could his precious fireworks ignite if it poured like this tomorrow evening? Yawning, he counted the minutes until he could give himself up to a good night's sleep. Tomorrow promised to be an extremely long day.

Kitt and Jobe shimmered with pent-up excitement that overflowed the minute Mark joined them in Belle's room. Dexter lay curled on Belle's pillow. Mark's nose itched. *Another reason why I should only linger here a few minutes.* He gazed at Belle who sat demurely by the fire—too demurely. She looked feverish.

Mark adopted a lighthearted tone to cover his fears for her health. "How now, Belle? Has that fat cat of yours caught your tongue?"

She gave him a tight little smile that held none of the fire he expected. "Dexter has supped well enough tonight. Griselda has already laid out saucers of cream on the hearths in the east wing," she replied.

In the dancing firelight, her eyes glowed with some indefinable emotion. His mind floundered as he tried to fathom what ailed her when she should be dancing a jig.

Mark deposited the oilskin package of pyrotechnics in the privy alcove furthermost from the fire, then knelt by her chair. "What ails you, Belle?"

She shook her head. "Nothing. Nerves mayhap."

"You?" He laughed at the absurd idea. "You've never had a nerve in your body."

Jobe paused in his conversation with Kitt. "There is a first time for everything, *meu amigo*," he said to Mark, though he gave Belle a meaningful glance.

Mark felt a sneeze coming on. He pinched his nose and prayed the ticklish feeling would pass. Drat that furry beast! Mark hurried through his final instructions before his eyes watered.

"Tomorrow, Belle and Jobe should keep well out of sight. Griselda expects her extra help to arrive at eight in the morning. Montjoy is sending a number of your former servants, Belle, and we must not run the risk of disclosure now. Remember, they still believe you are dead.''

She nodded but said nothing. Mark frowned, then continued in a rush. "Kitt, after supper has been cleared from the tables in the hall, make sure that none of the wall sconces are lit. Keep the sides of the hall in deep shadow.''

Anticipation sparkled in his eyes. "And that is when I set the jack-o'-lanterns in their niches?''

Belle looked up with mild surprise. "What are they?'' she asked.

Kitt puffed out his chest. "Wait and see, Belle. I promise twill give you a fright.''

Another sneeze threatened. Mark held his nose. "Jobe, as soon as darkness sets in, tie your rowboat under the hall's great window. I will make sure the window latch is unlocked. Then retrieve the fireworks and distribute them as we have discussed. Belle, don't be gadding about the gallery. You must be here to let Jobe inside.''

She tossed her head with a spark of her usual defiance. "I know my part, Mark. I am more anxious than all of you for this putrid slime to be gone from my house.''

Mark sneezed. After wiping his nose with his handkerchief, he continued. "I will make myself conspicuous all day so that neither one of the Fletchers will suspect that mischief is afoot. And, everyone, remember the most important thing.'' He looked at each one of the conspirators in turn. "No one must begin their part before my signal.''

Kitt chortled. "When the fire in the hearth explodes! I long to see that.''

"So do I,'' Mark said under his breath. He hoped that Andrew's wonderful concoctions would perform on cue.

Jobe stood and stretched his huge frame. "Is that all, *meu amigo?*''

Mark also rose. "Aye, there's nothing left to do now but pray."

The African strode to the door. "Then I am for my bed in the garret. Come, Kitt." He motioned to the boy.

Kitt kissed Belle on her cheek. "May the angels protect you," he said, then added. "All will go well tomorrow. You shall see anon."

Belle rose and hugged him. Brother and sister were almost equal in height. "And may the angels ride on your shoulder, Kitt."

Jobe ducked out through her door followed by the boy. Mark stifled another sneeze before he said, "Well, this is it, Belle. God willing, the next time I see you, Mortimer Fletcher will be running halfway to Hawkhurst and you will once again be the mistress of Bodiam Castle."

Belle took his hand between hers. She lifted her face to him. The firelight enhanced the glow of her natural beauty. Her eyes turned to a deeper blue and her gaze bathed him with warmth. She moistened her lips with the tip of her pink tongue.

"Stay with me tonight, Marcus."

Chapter Sixteen

Mark drew in a deep breath. Belle held hers, afraid he would turn her down and walk away. It would serve her right if he did after all the years of abuse she had heaped on him. She tightened her grip on his hand as she stared up at him.

Mark returned her gaze; his dark eyes filled with bewilderment and something else that Belle could not identify, but it gave her encouragement to press her advantage.

"Lie with me tonight, Marcus," she begged.

His jaw muscles twitched before he replied, "I am not in the mood for another one of your artful jests, Belle. I must go."

He remained rooted to the spot.

She drew closer to him. How handsome he had grown! The firelight softened the chiseled planes of his face and turned his brown eyes into pools of liquid richness. His male presence stirred her deepest yearnings. She longed to slip her arms around his neck and lay her head on his broad shoulder.

"'Tis no jest tonight. Take me to bed and be my love," she whispered. In all her years of daring, this moment was her boldest venture yet.

He covered her cold hands with his warm one. "You know why I cannot," he murmured.

Belle's heart skipped a beat. She placed his hand over her breast covered only by the thin muslin of her shift. "Twas a vow you made when we were children," she replied with a tremor in her voice. "Now we are past our majority. I have been wed and widowed. You are a man of much experience. We both know the ways of the world."

Mark's expression changed, softening into the one she recalled from times gone by. It was the same look he had had when he'd found her after she had wandered away from a family picnic and gotten lost on the moor. The same one he'd worn when he had rescued her from an unfriendly dog she had encountered at a village fair. The same one he had had when he'd read her stories of heroic knights while she lay fretful with a sprained ankle after another one of her misadventures. Why hadn't she recognized his affection then?

Mark stroked her cheek with a touch infinite in its tenderness. "Your father sent me to rescue you, not debauch you."

She leaned into his caress. "You promised to cherish me, Mark. Cherish me now."

He groaned under his breath. "Oh, sweet Belle, you have always been my downfall."

Remembering the apple tree, she smiled. "Twill be a softer landing this time, I promise. Please, Mark?"

She stood on tiptoe, closed her eyes and offered her lips to him. *I have set my life upon this one throw of love's dice. I will accept the hazard of my toss.*

The moment seemed to hang in time, then with a low growl, Mark sweep her into the circle of his embrace.

"God forgive my weakness, Belle. I cherish you with all my heart."

His mouth sought hers with fearful urgency. When their lips met and parted for each other, Belle felt she had found a safe harbor at long last. She wound her arms around his neck. As their kiss deepened, Mark crushed her to his chest. They kissed until they ran out of breath.

She clung to him, tears of joy welling up in her eyes. Mark whispered her name and many silly endearments in between the soft kisses that he rained on her cheeks, her moist eyelids, her nose, her earlobes and in the hollow of her throat.

"You are shivering, *ma petite chou-chou,*" he murmured; his breath fanned her neck.

"Aye," she whispered in his hair, "but tis not with cold." She clung to him since all strength had left her legs. Her skin sang with his touch while her mind spun like a rainbow-hued whirligig.

"Then to bed," he replied, lifting her in his arms.

"Warm me," she answered.

Mark chuckled low in his throat. "Tis my heartfelt intention, my sweet, and tomorrow take the hindmost."

He set her down in the center of the coverlet. Then he narrowed his eyes. His voice suddenly changed its tune. "Hang off, ramping cat," he snarled.

Belle shook the love languor from her eyes in time to see Mark turn away from her and head for the door. What puling trick was this to lull her into bed with sweet words only to abandon her? Was this Mark's revenge for his broken arm? A hot retort formed on her tongue, but she quelled it when she heard Dexter's mew of protest as Mark shut the door in the cat's face.

He blew his nose and gave her a rueful smile that made him look even more handsome than before. "Cats should be forever banned from bedchambers,'' he observed. He sat down beside her and undid the first silver button on his doublet. "Now, *chou-chou,* where were we?''

With an inward sigh of relief, Belle laid her head on the pillow recently vacated by Dexter. "Methinks you were about to demonstrate how to keep me warm on a cold wet night.''

Leaning over her, he smoothed away the wisps of golden hair that fell across her eyes. "Just so,'' he replied before he kissed her again.

Hot fire rippled through her veins at his touch. Belle pulled him down on top of her. He slipped his hands around her waist and pressed her hips against his. Through the material of his breeches she felt his hard shaft. She moaned under her breath as his tongue delved deeper into her mouth, foretelling how their bodies would soon entwine each other.

Belle could not get enough of him. She gave her tongue to him and he took it eagerly. Her mouth burned for him, her skin tingled. She arched her back, offering herself to him.

Mark ripped off his doublet, casting it and a few loosened buttons to the floor. His linen shirt followed afterward. His chuckle turned to a gasp when Belle tentatively touched his chest muscles, well-developed after two decades of wielding swords and lances. She traced her fingers along her forearm until she encountered a small hard bump.

"There?'' she breathed. "Is that where you fell?''

"Aye,'' he replied, watching her through half-closed eyes that smoldered with his passion.

She kissed the spot, massaged it, and then kissed it again. "I have wanted to do that for a long time,'' she told him. She swallowed a lump in her throat, "And to beg for your forgiveness.''

He combed through her loose hair with his fingers. "Your apology is a long time in coming," he observed lightly.

She touched his lips with her finger. "Too long," she agreed. "I was banished to my chamber."

He massaged the back of her neck; his fingers worked magic on the knotted muscles there. "Did you forget how to pen a letter?"

She traced his cheekbone, memorizing his face with her fingers. "There were not enough words at my command to express the remorse I felt. Methought I would never see you again."

Mark took her hand and kissed her palm, "Nor I to see you. The circle of fortune has given us both a second chance."

She held out her arms to him. "Then let us not waste a minute more for the night hours flee past us like hares across a field."

"Give me your sweet lips again for I am a starving man," he whispered as he descended once more.

They came together with a whirlwind of emotions too deep to be spoken aloud. Belle did not know when or how Mark removed her shift nor when he shed his boots and hose. Their bodies, gleaming in the low firelight, melded together; hip to hip, knee to knee, breast to chest, lips to lips. He explored every bare inch of her with tender kisses and tantalizing caresses.

When his tongue flicked the hard tip of her nipple, she writhed under him. Fire licked her; pleasure radiated through her. His hands, roughened by weapons, cradled the soft flesh of her breasts with infinite gentleness. She arched her back again, pressing herself hard against him. Her breath came in short gasps of delight at the wondrous pleasure he gave her.

Mark kissed her deeply again and, as he did so, he slid his free hand down past her flat stomach and into the curly thicket that concealed her most secret place. When he stroked her, she bucked under him. His finger circled around her feminine core as she arched and writhed. His torture was exquisite, agonizing and sweet.

Sparks of golden fire flashed behind her closed eyelids. Her body throbbed with the rhythm of his lovemaking. She moaned how wicked he was even as she opened her thighs to receive more of his tantalizing punishment. Taking one of her nipples in his mouth, he suckled her even as he continued to play her as a musician upon a lute.

Belle gripped his shoulders, nipped the smooth skin at the base of his neck and begged him never to stop. He increased his tempo. Whimpering, she felt as if he lifted her above the earth, higher and higher until the sun's rays burnished her. A sudden explosion of fire and ice hurled her beyond the stars and returned her to earth on a golden cloud of warmth and peace.

Mark chuckled in her ear. "Tell me, sweet, did Cuthbert ever pleasure you like this?"

Belle opened her eyes. "Nay," she gasped. "I had no idea of such joy. Please, Marcus, take me to paradise again."

He lowered himself between her open legs. "Let us go together. I promise to be as gentle as I can, but tis been a long time for me."

Belle wrapped her legs around his hips. "Tis been a lifetime of waiting for me."

He slid into her as a sword into its own sheath. Belle welcomed him with kisses and clung to him as if her life depended upon only this moment. Together they ascended to the fiery firmament where they hung for a delicious, heart-stopping instant before the world about them flew apart in a blinding array of lights and colors. With deep soul-felt sighs, they descended once again to open their eyes and greet each other as if they had never before truly met.

Tears, great gushing droplets, rolled down Belle's cheeks. Mark cradled her close to his chest. His beating heart drummed in her ear.

"Did I hurt you, my sweet?" he asked in a husky voice. "I did not mean—"

She placed her fingers over his mouth to still his words. "N-nay, Marcus, I am f-fine." She sobbed all the more.

"Tush, tush, *ma petite chou-chou.* What is it?"

Belle mutely shook her head even as her tears bathed his shoulder. She had no clear idea why she cried, only that it gave her a great sense of release, as if a massive weight had been lifted from her heart. Mark rocked her in his arms and soothed her with soft noises and gentle kisses. As her racking sobs grew quieter, he drew the blankets over their cooling bodies. Belle fell asleep nestled in the comfort of his embrace.

For once she did not dream at all.

Mark awoke slowly, suffused with a sense of well-being. The fire had gone out and the window framed the gray pre-dawn. Light rain pattered on the glass panes. The unwelcome sound brought him back to reality. Today was October thirty-first, All Hallows Eve, and the deuced rain still poured from the heavens.

He gazed down at the woman he held in his arms. A little trail of salt on Belle's cheek was all that remained of her tears. Mark brushed the evidence away with the pad of his thumb. She stirred in her sleep.

Her tears had disturbed him more than he had expected. Women had cried in his arms before. Past experience had taught him not to question the reason, but only to offer the comfort of his shoulder. Belle's tears were a far different matter. She had never cried, not even when he had extracted a three-inch thorn from her leg when she was six or seven. Belle took pride in her hard exterior. Tears were for babes, she once told him. She maintained that she had cried her fill in France.

This morning in the stillness of her sleep, Belle looked softer—and more vulnerable than ever. A wave of fierce protection surged through him. The activities of the coming night would require all the courage that Belle and Mark could muster. He prayed that he would not let her down—especially not now.

He had to leave her, but he was loath to slide away from her side without a sound. Only a churl would take his pleasure then disappear. Mark kissed Belle's forehead.

"Good morrow, *chou-chou*," he whispered in her ear.

She wrinkled her nose. "Tis still night," she replied without opening her eyes.

He kissed her again. Sdeath! He wished he could spend the whole wet day in her warm bed. "Nay, sweetheart. The cock will soon crow."

She snuggled closer to him. "Tis the owl you hear," she mumbled into the pillow.

Mark grinned. Belle had never liked the earliest hours of the day. "I must leave you and prepare for battle," he said, shaking her shoulder. He dropped a kiss on the spot.

"We are not at war," she muttered, throwing the covers over her head.

Mark sighed. "That remains to be seen."

He pulled on his hose, then his shirt. When he turned to step into his breeches he saw that Belle watched him from her nest amid the bedclothes. He winked at her. "Have no fear, *chou-chou*. By this time tomorrow, Mortimer Fletcher will be scurrying back to his lair in London with the brittle Griselda right behind him.''

Pulling herself into a sitting position with the blanket tucked under her arms, Belle rubbed the side of her nose. Her delicate brows creased with worry. ''He may not,'' she said in a flat tone.

Mark sat down beside her and gathered her in his arms. ''Then I will chase him across the drawbridge at the point of my sword.''

Belle studied his face for a moment, then stroked his cheek. ''You always did charge off where angels feared to tread, but not this time, methinks.''

He planted a kiss on the soft skin of her palm. ''Do you doubt my resolve? Look at me. I am as hare-brained as ever.''

Her faint smile held a touch of sadness. ''Nay, tis I who have been the hare-brained one—as usual. I fear I have endangered you as well as my little brother and Jobe because of my hard-headed foolishness. I should have let you carry me away that first night.''

Mark rolled his eyes with mock exasperation. ''*Now* you tell me?''

She caught his hands in hers. ''The time for jesting has passed, Mark. If we fail tonight....'' She swallowed.

He kissed the tip of her nose. ''Screw up your courage, *chou-chou*. We will not fail.''

Belle gripped his hands tighter. ''Nay, Mark, listen to me. If Mortimer refuses to budge, though we surround him with the denizens of hell itself, then let us quit this place and return to my father with all speed.''

Mark whistled under his breath. ''You would give up your home to that onion-eyed rabbit-sucker?''

She caught her lower lip between her teeth before she nodded. ''My selfish whim has put you in danger, mayhap more than we realize. Please, promise me if something goes amiss, do not tarry but fly. We will find another way to win this game." She kissed his hands. "I would not have you harmed on my account. My stubbornness has hurt you enough as it is."

Mark smiled at her; laughter bubbled up in his throat. "I thank you for your concern for my life and limbs, but I am so deep in this tomfoolery now that I have no desire to run—especially not from such a weasel as Mortimer Fletcher. Fear not. All will be well." He eased her back into the pillows. "Methinks you need a wee bit more sleep, sweet slugabed. Then you will feel like your old self."

Still chuckling, he rose and put on his doublet. Then he threw her a kiss. "Heigh ho, sweetheart! As Jobe says, tonight will be most excellent sport. Adieu until we meet after dark." His gaze drank up her love-tousled looks. "Great Jove, Belle! *You* are the true treasure of Bodiam Castle."

"Mark!" She held out her arms to him. "I...that is..."

He gripped the door latch. He had to leave her now or he knew he would be back in her bed in an instant. His loins ached for a rematch. He wrenched open the door. Dexter marched inside with his tail held high. Looking neither left nor right, he crossed the floor and leapt onto the bed. He circled several times before curling himself up next to Belle. Mark glowered at the fat creature.

Enjoy your ease now, cat. The day is coming when you will be out—permanently.

Mark slipped down the west gallery and into the south wing without detection. He considered that a good omen for the day. By the time he reached his own chamber, the damp dawn had broken. Kitt snored on his pallet. With a grin, Mark rumpled the bedclothes on the large four-poster to allay the boy's prying questions. Kitt did not need to know all of his master's nocturnal activities. He stripped off his clothing before awakening his squire.

"Get up and face the new morn!" He yanked the blankets off the boy. "Tis All Hallows Eve! Where are my razor and soap? Where is my hot water? Where is my morning strop of ale to cheer me?"

Kitt stumbled to his feet with a choice oath. Mark cocked his eyebrow. "Hoy day, my lad! If your lady mother ever hears that sweet word on your tongue, you will be eating soap for a month."

Kitt yawned as he struggled into his clothing. Without another word, he slammed out of the room to fetch the required ale and water. Mark laughed. Great Jove! He felt new-made this fine morning. Kneeling beside the clothes trunk, he inspected his wardrobe for the day. His hand chanced to brush against a folded piece of paper. Mark lifted it up to the window for closer inspection. He grimaced when he realized he held his betrothal contract to Griselda, still unsigned. He balled it up and almost hurled it into the cold fireplace when a thought struck him.

Though Mark did not give much credence to Belle's fresh worry, he had to admit she might have a point. They needed a second line of defense if Mortimer proved more obstinate than Mark expected. He considered the paper in his hand. Amended slightly, this document could be the perfect answer. All Mark had to do was sign his name.

Kitt reappeared in a slightly better mood. Mark took a deep drink of the ale, wiped the froth from his lips, then remarked, "We burn daylight."

"Tis barely six o' the clock," the boy observed, stropping Mark's razor on a piece of thick leather.

Mark lathered his face with a small slice of soap. "Just so. Time enough for you to find pen and ink."

Kitt shook out Mark's discarded doublet. "Whyfor? Look you, did you know you are missing two buttons?"

Mark snapped his fingers. "A fig for the buttons! Tis pen and ink I require."

"Where should I find such items at this ungodly hour?"

Mark shaved one cheek before answering. "A good squire uses his wits. Be creative." He shaved his other cheek.

Kitt pursed his lips. "You mean steal them from Master Fletcher's office?"

Mark shot him a reproachful look. "Did I say 'steal'? Would I lead my good squire down the rosy path of wrongdoing?"

Kitt grinned. "Aye, you would."

Mark leaned closer to his looking glass and prepared to shave under his chin. "Don't get caught," he advised.

By the time Kitt returned with the purloined items, Mark had dressed in plain garb. He had much work to do and he had to save his best clothes for the feast tonight. While Kitt busied himself with emptying the water down the privy hole, tidying the beds and brushing their boots, Mark settled on the windowseat. He scratched out several words on Mortimer's contract with the tip of his penknife. Taking a deep breath, he inserted the words that could change his life forever. If nothing else, they would guarantee that Belle's beloved home would always remain hers. When he finished, he waved the paper in the air to dry the ink.

"Kitt, my boy, tis time you and I had a serious talk, man-to-man."

The squire paused in the midst of his chores and grinned. "Tis no matter, Mark. Jobe told me all I need to know."

Mark stopped waving the document. "How now? What did he say, pray tell?"

Kitt attempted to look worldly-wise. "Oh, you know. The things a man must do to pleasure a woman," he replied in an offhand manner. "The little tricks of this and that," he added.

Caught unawares, Mark didn't know whether to laugh or to swear. Lady Kat would die of shock if she knew the full extent of her precious son's education. "By any chance, did you two discuss the morality of the act of love?"

Kitt thought about it for a moment then shrugged. "I cannot recall."

Mark blew out his cheeks. "When time and leisure present themselves, you and I will speak further on this subject. In the meantime, do not practice your new wiles on young Ivy."

Kitt turned bright red to the roots of his golden hair. "I never gave it a thought."

Little liar! Mark cleared his throat. "Tis a legal matter I must discuss with you as you are the only male member of the Cavendish family within a hundred miles."

Kitt squared his slim shoulders and assumed an air of grave attention. "Tis true. I am."

Mark's palms sweated. He wiped them on his breeches before the moisture blotted the paper he held out to the boy. "Read this carefully. If you agree to the terms, then sign it at the bottom and write the word *guardian* after your name."

Mark pretended to inspect his fingernails while Kitt worked his way through the densely written verbiage. He drummed his fingers on the windowsill. He rubbed the back of his neck. He felt like a man awaiting the verdict of a jury.

Tis nothing but a piece of paper and only for use in an extreme emergency. The thought gave him cold comfort.

Kitt's eyes bulged. "You mean this?"

Mark attempted a weak smile. "Every jot and tittle. Tis to insure Belle's future. Will you sign it?"

The boy giggled. "With a right good will." He scrawled *Christopher Cavendish, Guardian* with a flourish across the bottom. Then he returned the quill to Mark.

The feather trembled in Mark's fingers as he dipped the pen into the inkpot. *A mere stroke or two and tis done— tis merely a precaution.* He swallowed hard, then signed and backdated the contract. He blew gently on the wet letters. "Tis done," he said in a weak voice.

When the ink had dried, Mark refolded the paper and held it out to Kitt. "On your honor and your life, I entrust this to your safekeeping. Use it only if and when the situation proves necessary."

"How will I know?"

Mark turned away from him. "Your instincts will tell you."

Kitt straightened himself with a new-found dignity. He took the paper and thrust it deep in the suede pouch that he wore on his belt. "I will wrap it in oilcloth and seal the seams with wax straightway. I will not fail you, my lord," he replied with surprising maturity.

Was I ever that young? Mark wondered.

Chapter Seventeen

Mortimer limped into the great hall and glared balefully at the preparations for the evening's festivities. His leg still hurt from the wretched cat's fangs. His pain and the clammy cold weather put him in a foul humor. In the midst of a flock of temporary servants, Griselda glowed. For the first time in her life, she had the opportunity to command a small army to obey her every whim. Mortimer squinted at the bustling potboys and maids. Where had all these people come from? He ground his teeth. This cleansing of the castle's demons had already cost him a small fortune and Griselda showed no signs of curbing her expenditures now. He pitied Lord Hayward.

Mortimer studied his future brother-in-law. Something about the man disturbed him. Though he knew they had never met, Mortimer thought he had heard his name some time in the past. Perchance Cuthbert had known him during the boy's short tenure amid the glittering nobility of the king's court. Strange, Sir Mark had never mentioned any former knowledge of the Fletchers.

Griselda pretended to wobble at the top of a small ladder and her betrothed obligingly caught her. She screamed her laughter and Hayward smiled in return.

That rogue is too handsome. Why would a titled gentleman seek marriage with the daughter of a wool merchant—particularly one who is a shrew?

That question had nagged Mortimer ever since Sir Mark had arrived out of the clear blue. Something didn't seem to fit, though Mortimer could not put his finger on the cause of his misgivings. No matter, he told himself. The betrothal would be announced tonight and the first banns published on Sunday. Griselda would become Lady Hayward within a month. Then Mortimer recalled that he had not yet received Sir Mark's signed contract. He limped toward the couple.

"La," screeched Griselda, spying her brother. "Here comes a sad-faced shadow. By my troth, Mortimer. Try to smile for once. I am to be a bride after all. That thought should fill you full of joy." She cast a fond glance at the tall man beside her. "Is that not so, my love?"

Sir Mark laughed easily—too easily. "Spoken truly, my sweet-tongued hawthorn-bud."

Mortimer lifted a corner of his mouth in an approximation of a smile. "A word in your ear, my lord," he muttered.

Griselda linked her arm around Hayward's. "What pressing business could you possibly have with my darling Mark when I need his full attention here? Our guests will be upon us before you know it and—"

"Peace, Griselda!" her brother snapped. "'Tis a man's conference I desire and 'twill take less time to accomplish than your protestations against it. Come, my lord." He limped toward his office.

Mark untangled himself from Griselda's clutches and kissed her chapped hand. "I shall return to your side in a twink, you saucy wafer-cake."

Griselda brayed like a jackass before she turned back

to her task. Mortimer rolled his eyes heavenward and prayed that this day would end soon. He hated having all these strangers inside his domain. He slammed his door behind Sir Mark, then eased himself into his chair without offering his noble guest a seat. Sir Mark lounged against the wall by the narrow window that overlooked the moat.

Mortimer made a show of riffling through his papers. "I fear I cannot find the marriage contract that I gave you the other day, my lord. Methinks it must still be in your possession."

Sir Mark whistled his surprise. "Is that so? Methinks I put it on your desk yesterday—or was it the day before? Surely you have not misplaced it?" He eyed the piles of correspondence and accounts on the table. "Have you closely examined all those papers, Master Fletcher? Perchance it has slipped within the leaves of a ledger?"

Mortimer opened his mouth, then shut it again. Best not to ruffle this man's feathers until after he was safely wedded to Griselda. He snatched up the topmost book and flipped through its pages. Nothing. Mark yawned, covering his mouth. Mortimer ruffled through the second book. Again, nothing. This was such a farce. Mortimer was sure Lord Hayward had not returned the document. He shook a third book. A folded sheet fell out.

The nobleman smiled. "Ah, I see you have found it."

Mortimer doubted that. This paper was not as thick nor as well made as the stock he used for his contracts and deeds. He opened it. The words on the page caused him to quake. Written in red ink—or could it be blood?—the ominous message read: "Your sands of time will run out on All Hallows Eve. Prepare to meet your doom. Written by the hand of her whom you have sorely wronged, LaBelle Cavendish."

Lord Hayward pushed himself away from the wall. "What is it, Fletcher? You look pale."

Mortimer mopped his brow with his sleeve. "Tis nothing, only some unfinished business I must attend to. Please return to your lady love, my lord. I desire to be alone."

"As you wish," Sir Mark replied as he left.

With shaking fingers, Mortimer struck a spark from his tinderbox and lit the lone candle on the desk. Then he fed the hell-sent note into its flames.

How he wished this blasted day were yesterday's ashes!

Waiting was the hardest part for Belle. She had never been a patient person and today the hours barely inched toward the twilight hour, despite the comings and goings in her room. First, Kitt arrived bearing her dinner and the small sack of white flour that she needed to create her ghostly pallor. Before Belle could ask him what Mark was doing, the boy scampered out the door mumbling something about his mysterious "jack-o'-lanterns."

In the mid-afternoon Jobe came for the bundle of fireworks. "The rain has stopped," he informed Belle with a broad smile. "The Creator of us all must wish to behold these wonders for himself." He too left in a hurry.

Belle gathered Dexter into her lap. "Everyone is doing something exciting except me," she complained to the sleepy cat. She stroked his thick fur. "I suppose tis still too early to roll you in the fireplace soot. I know you will hate it, but you must be disguised as much as the rest of us. Poor baby." Ignorant of his impending indignity, Dexter purred with his eyes shut.

Belle tried on her robe of cheesecloth. Its train trailed perfectly behind her and the stringy material made her look as if she were dressed in a cobweb—or a decayed winding sheet. She inspected the effect in her small hand mirror. *I shall wear my hair loose and in disarray.* She adjusted the hood and consulted the mirror again.

"It needs something more," she told the cat who now slept on the bed. "Blood dripping from my hands? Nay, twould make the candlestick too slippery. I must not set fire to myself or I will become a true ghost indeed."

She played with the neckline, first pulling it high, then tugging it low enough to expose a scandalous expanse of her breasts. "That might interest Mark." The memory of his tongue on them gave her delicious shivers.

Belle stared into the mirror. What she needed was something colorful and dramatic. Something that would shine out in the darkness of the hall. Something unforgettable. She snapped her fingers as a brilliant idea leaped into her mind. "The very thing, Dexter! Every eye in the place will be riveted on me for sure."

Tingling with excitement, she quickly changed from her costume into a plain brown gown. Wrapping a black woolen shawl around her shoulders, she unlocked the door. "I shall return soon," she told the cat as she slipped out. Pausing behind the tapestry, she listened for any sound that would warn her of another person in the gallery, but there was none. Grinning to herself, she stole down the mid-tower stairs to the courtyard. This would be tricky, but she had to cross the open space to the door of the castle's chapel.

The courtyard was alive with servants rushing to and from the front gate carrying covered baskets toward the kitchens and buttery. The busy scene reminded her of the happier days when Bodiam hummed with activity. Griselda must have ordered food and drink for hundreds of people. Belle chuckled to herself. Mortimer must be swearing rafter-shaking oaths by now. He hated to part with so much as a farthing.

Belle drew her shawl over her head to hide both her face and her brilliant hair. She grabbed an empty bucket from the nearby trough. Taking a deep breath, she hunched her shoulders and made her way purposefully across the yard. No one gave her a second glance.

Please let the door be unlocked. She pushed down on the latch that led unto the chapel's crypt. It opened without a sound. Leaving the bucket by the door, Belle slipped inside. Though only a feeble light came from the solitary barred window on the far side, Belle knew every stone on the floor. She crept up the winding stairs to the chapel proper and paused in the shadow of its arched doorway.

No one prayed on this hectic day. Ever since King Henry had broken with the pope, holy devotions had been sparsely attended. The door that led to the master bedchamber was shut fast. Belle stepped into the vaulted room. The waning afternoon's light through the triple-arched stained-glass window cast pale squares of blue and green on the polished floor. She was halfway to the chancel when the bedroom door latch rattled. She skittered back to the shadowed landing just before Mortimer entered.

The man looked like death itself. His expensive clothing sagged on his thin frame. His gaunt eyes burned with a haunted look. He staggered to the railing before the altar, then dropped heavily to his knees. Though he prayed in silence, Belle saw that his shoulders shook.

Methinks you found my latest note, Mortimer. Your soul is skewered by your greed. If you only knew how close you are to your heart's desire!

Mortimer remained in his humble position for ten more minutes, shivering and shaking all the while. Once or twice he sobbed aloud. Though she was surprised by Mortimer's religious fervor, his abject condition did not move Belle to pity. She was glad that his guilty conscience whipped him raw.

I wonder what he would do if I suddenly jumped out at him?

Though the idea was tempting, Belle resigned herself to wait until dark. Mortimer would need all the blessings of his prayers tonight. Finally, he rose and limped out the door by which he had come. He closed and locked it behind him. Belle waited a few more minutes in case Mortimer felt the need to return, but only silence filled the holy space.

Once more she tiptoed across the floor to the same railing that Mortimer had just left. She swung her legs over the simple barrier between the clergy and laity. Boldly, she ascended the two low steps to the altar itself. She sank down before it.

"Thank you for guarding my family's treasure so well," she whispered, "but methinks the time has come to wear it once again. Bless me, Lord," she added.

Belle lifted the white brocade skirt of the altar cloth. It hid a beautiful cross carved on the front panel. Belle rotated the medallion to the right, revealing a small cache behind it. What a sly fox the builder of Bodiam had been to have consigned his most precious possessions to the protection of holy sanctuary! Belle reached her hand into the opening and pulled out a small packet wrapped in one of her handkerchiefs—the one that she had hidden here on her wedding night.

Resisting the urge to immediately look at the brooch, she replaced the cross and straightened the cloth over it. After whispering another prayer of thanksgiving, Belle retraced her route down the stairs to the crypt. Before she opened the outer door, she stuffed her precious burden deep inside her bodice. Then, pulling her shawl lower over her face, she stepped into the courtyard.

It had grown dark while she had been inside the chapel and the activity in the courtyard had increased. Hunching over her bucket, Belle hobbled her way back to the west wing in the manner of an elderly woman. With her heart beating in the back of her throat, she practically flew up the mid-tower stairs to the second floor. She did not breathe easily until she was safely inside her own room once again. Her elation at her daring made her dizzy.

Belle swooped down on the still-slumbering Dexter. "Look, you slugabed!" she said, shaking him awake. She unwrapped the packet. The blood-red ruby sparkled in her hand. The large pearl shimmered against her skin. "Behold the root of all my happiness and sorrow."

The words caught in her throat. It was exactly Jobe's prediction. Was today the day he had foretold? Belle had awakened with great joy; would she sleep tonight with great sadness? A chill skittered down her spine. She squared her shoulders. Come what may, she would be ready for it.

When Belle admitted Jobe a few hours later, they each stared at the other with wide-eyed amazement. The Cavendish brooch flashed on her bodice. After studying the magnificent jewel for a moment, Jobe nodded his approval.

"Tis a good night to wear it," he remarked.

For her part, Belle was speechless at the sight of him. A long black cape swathed the African from his neck to his ankles. His face drew her immediate fascination. Jobe had found or made a pure white paint and he had applied it lavishly in stripes across his forehead, around his eyes and down the bridge of his nose. Thin white lines snaked down the backs of his large hands and over the tops of his bare feet. Though the night had grown cold, Jobe gave no sign that he felt it. Instead, he positively glowed with excitement.

With his golden earring and shining copper bracelets, Jobe looked like a pagan god come to life.

He grinned at her awe. "Methinks twill be most excellent sport tonight."

Belle swallowed. "Twill be unforgettable."

The crescent moon rode the billows of scattered black clouds. Mark whistled a merry tune as Kitt helped him into his court dress. Tonight he had to look the part of a wealthy lord betrothed to the host's sister. Gold lace edged his small neck ruff and the cuffs of his white lawn shirt. His ivory silk stockings fit snugly over his calves. He stepped into a pair of cinnamon-and-green paned breeches. Little golden bells decorated the points of his laces just above the knee. Kitt buttoned the doublet made of cinnamon-colored satin slashed with ivory silk. Over this, Mark slipped on a sleeveless overcoat of green velvet trimmed with gold. A jaunty flat bonnet also made of green velvet and decorated with a black ostrich feather completed his attire.

Stepping to the center of his chamber, he posed and asked Kitt, "How do I look?"

The boy cocked his head. "You make a fine show. Mistress Griselda will surely swoon."

"Not immediately, I hope," Mark muttered.

He took a small rolled tube of blue paper from his clothes chest and placed it carefully in his pouch. He did not relish carrying a handful of black powder so near to his private parts. He would be glad to get rid of the dangerous package. Then he slipped his long dagger down the inside of his black boot. Mark would have preferred to face this evening with his sword buckled to his side but such a precaution would have attracted unwelcome questions. He smoothed Kitt's collar over the boy's wine-red jerkin.

"Do you carry a weapon?" he asked.

Kitt wet his lips. "Do you think I might need one?"

"I pray that you won't, but a wise man never ventures into the unknown without some defense."

Though the squire grew a little paler, he straightened his shoulders and held his head higher. "My hunting knife?" he asked. "Tis all I have."

Mark sighed inwardly. "Twill do. Wear it belted behind your back where twill not draw attention. And the paper that I gave you this morning?"

Kitt tapped his pouch. "Here, well-wrapped in wax."

Mark clapped him on the shoulder. "Are we ready, squire Bertrum?"

The boy flashed him a grin. "Twill be excellent sport, methinks."

Mark cuffed him lightly on the ear. "Mind you watch for my signal instead of leering at Mistress Ivy's bosom."

He nodded. "Count on me, Mark."

"I do," Mark replied before he opened the door.

Bodiam's great hall abounded with merry guests, all of whom sported Griselda's fanciful masks chosen from several trays that were stationed beside the double arch doorways on the entrance landing. A band of five minstrels, all former Bodiam servants, arrived, carrying not only their instruments wrapped in cloth sacking but also several large bags that Mark knew contained a multitude of dazed bats broom-swept from local barn lofts and church steeples. The young men grinned at each other as they hurried up the curved stairs to the minstrel's gallery high over the hall.

Mark smiled to himself. Montjoy has done his job very well. He looked around for the elderly steward and found him predictably by the fire that roared in the huge hearth. His visage was hidden behind an owlish creation. Ivy, decked with a cascade of ribbons and a silver mask representing the moon, stood by his side. Kitt gave her a little wave. He giggled when she returned it. After donning a purple, green and gold mask, Mark ambled over to Montjoy.

"Well met, old friend," he murmured. "I see you have packed the hall with cohorts. Do they know what to do?"

Montjoy snorted through his brown feathered mask. "Of course! The lads and lasses are as anxious as I am for the Fletchers to be gone from Bodiam."

"Do they know that Belle lives?" Mark whispered.

Montjoy shook his white head. "Nay. Methought twould be better if they reacted naturally when she makes her appearance. How does the sweet child fare?"

Mark thought of last night's pleasures and grinned behind his mask. "She is in most excellent spirits, if you will pardon my pun."

Spying Mark, Griselda squealed with delight and pushed her way through the throng. "Oh my lord! How wondrous pleasing you look tonight!" she shrieked.

Mark swept her a bow. "As you yourself make the goddess Diana green with envy," he replied, concealing a shudder. Griselda's overblown gown reminded him of a gaudy tent at a fair. "By my larkin, your mask maker is a magician indeed. Your designs are—"

"—simply unbelievable," she supplied before he could finish his sentence. "Aye, everyone here has complimented me on them." Leaning closer to Mark, she asked in a none-too-subtle voice, "Where did all these people come from? I had no idea we had so many neighbors."

Mark took her hand and escorted her away from the proximity of the crackling fire. The gunpowder in his pouch made him extremely nervous. "This countryside is blessed with many good folk whom I have come to know on my daily rides," he bantered. "In truth, my gilded nymph, you should ride out in the fresh air more often."

Her pouting lips protruded from under her long-beaked stork's face. "I hate horses," she replied with a snap.

Before Mark could think of a complimentary reply, the kettledrum rolled to announce the first dance of the evening. He bowed to Griselda again. "Shall we foot it and show these country folk a thing or two?"

Griselda snorted with laughter as Mark led her to the far end of the hall where many couples took their places for the Grand Pavane. The musicians struck up their recorder, sackbutt, schwam, viol and drums, filling the hall with the sounds of music. As Mark guided his shambling partner through the stately figures of the dance, his gaze swept the large chamber for Mortimer. He finally spied his quarry making forced small talk with a rotund man who wore a golden grotesque face. Mortimer, dressed entirely in black, was the only person in the hall without a mask. He looked glum and ill at ease. Mark chuckled. *Mortimer is probably counting up in his head every penny this merriment is costing him.*

The long table had been pulled to the exact center of the room. It groaned under the weight of several lighted candelabra and a cornucopia of food and drink. Large apple tarts sent their succulent steam curling toward the vaulted ceiling. Heaps of tempting soul cakes and moist dark gingerbread filled many platters, while large dishes of crowdie, an apple cream sweet, beckoned to the guests. Cabbage pudding and a whole suckling pig, roasted and sliced, made up the heartier fare. The serving boys, Kitt among them, kept the revelers' cups and mugs filled with tart applejack and the more potent sackwine. The music changed to a rowdy galliard and the general din swelled.

So far so good, Mark thought as he twirled Griselda through a lively bransle two hours later. He noticed that the loyal Bodiam retainers drank sparingly while Mortimer's minions and the innocent townspeople whom Montjoy had invited imbibed with abandon. Mortimer's face grew longer and longer as he surveyed his provender disappearing down the throats of a hundred citizens of Hawkhurst. Mark executed a series of quick steps in time with the lively music, then kept the pace while Griselda attempted to follow suit.

Over the heads of the crowd, he saw Kitt and one of Montjoy's lackeys light the little jack-o'-lanterns that sat in the lower scaffolding niches along the walls. Soon several dozen little faces gleamed their ghoulish grins. The guests, who clustered around the brightly lit table and the roaring hearth, took no notice. Mark danced by the great casement that overlooked the moat. Earlier in the day he had unlatched it. After darkness had fallen, he had tied a thick rope around the window's stone center frame. He was relieved to see that his preparations remained undisturbed and the latch still hung free. By now Jobe should be in position at the other end of the rope. The witching hour was about to commence. Mark cast a quick glance at the far end of the hall, now in deep shadow.

Belle, I hope you are in your place and ready.

At the conclusion of the dance, Mark suggested to Griselda that they have something cool to drink. Griselda, her mask askew, nodded between gasps for breath. Mark guided her to the table and signaled Kitt to present her with a brimming cup of applejack.

"Tis time," he whispered in the boy's ear.

Though he pretended that he had not heard Mark, Kitt grinned. While he poured more of the hard cider into Griselda's cup, he complimented her profusely on her dancing skill. *That boy is already a silver-tongued devil!*

Mark sauntered over to the fireplace and nodded to Montjoy. The old fox and Ivy moved to the side for they knew what would happen next. Opening his pouch, Mark took out his handkerchief—and the tube of gunpowder.

He took a final survey of the hall. Both Mortimer and Griselda were in perfect positions for the coming show. Mark's heartbeat accelerated. He took a deep breath then tossed the gunpowder into the flames.

All hell broke loose.

Chapter Eighteen

Fire accompanied by large clouds of gray smoke exploded from the huge fireplace. Hissing, popping and an enormous *bang* rocked the hall. Laughing nervously, a few of the guests assumed that the noise was the announcement of the evening's entertainment. Most, however, screamed with fright.

Kitt leapt into action. Under the cover of the chaos, he extinguished the candelabra on his side of the table. Ivy did the same at the other end. One of Montjoy's henchman, forewarned what to expect, doused the hearth fire with a full bucket of water. Only then did people notice the hoard of devilish jack-o'-lanterns that surrounded the company on all sides.

Griselda's distinctive voice rose above the din. "Mark! Mark! Where are you? I shall swoon."

But not before I am there to catch you, I'll warrant. Mark pushed his way through the crowd until he drew to her side. Griselda all but jumped into his arms. Her icy fingers clawed at his neck.

Before he could say something to quiet her gibbering, the minstrels in their eyrie above the hall unleashed the flocks of panicked bats. Trilling their high-pitched cries, the disoriented creatures crisscrossed above the heads of the crowd. Griselda shrieked all the louder and ducked this way and that. Mark hoped she would faint soon and be done with it.

A lighted torch suddenly appeared in front of the hall's great window. "Look there!" shouted someone in the darkness.

Jobe! Mark pressed forward to see what wonder his friend had promised. Though Jobe had hinted he would perform something impressive, Mark whistled under his breath when he beheld the giant African.

Standing astride the stone windowseat, Jobe held out the torch in front of him so that his captive audience could see him in all his splendor. With his free hand, he tossed back his long cape over his shoulders. Instead of shrieking, the guests sucked in their collective breaths. Except for a leather codpiece strapped around his waist to cover his private parts, Jobe stood completely naked before the shocked throng. His bandoliers of daggers, his bracelets and his earring gleamed against his ebony skin. Most terrifying of all, white lines covered his entire body so that he looked like a great skeleton come to life.

Flashing a white-toothed grin, Jobe threw back his head and uttered his monkey love call. The eerie sound bounced off the walls. Then he broke into a sort of hopping, knees-up dance the likes of which Mark had never seen before. One of the minstrels had kept his wits about him for he took up an accompaniment on the kettledrum. Mark watched his friend's danse macabre with awestruck fascination. Though Jobe often spoke of his southern homeland, Mark had forgotten that in the Congo of Africa men spoke an unknown language, observed barbaric customs and practiced an entirely different religion. Now in the heart of England, Jobe gloried in his own culture.

"'Tis the devil himself!"

Many people, especially the innocent citizens of Hawkhurst, fell to their knees and hid their faces from the sight.
Others made signs against the evil eye. Without uttering a
sound, Griselda collapsed in a heap of garish satin skirts
before Mark realized that she had truly fainted. With a final
whoop, Jobe tossed the torch into the moat. He wrapped
his cape around his body and appeared to vanish, though
Mark knew he had slipped out the window, down the rope
and into the waiting rowboat.

Mark hefted Griselda in his arms and looked for one of
Montjoy's men to carry the woman out of the hall. Though
he had no love for the shrew, he did not want her to be
trampled when Ivy and the other chamber maids of Bodiam started their prearranged stampede toward the courtyard. Spying one of the grooms standing next to Montjoy,
Mark handed over Griselda's limp form to his less-than-
tender mercies.

"Don't drop her in the moat," he cautioned the grinning
man. "Just make sure she gets safely on the far side on
the drawbridge."

"Aye, my lord," replied the groom. He slung the unconscious woman over his wide shoulder as if she were a
sack of flour, but he did not move lest he miss the rest of
the spectacle.

Mark looked for Mortimer and found the man still standing in the same spot as before. Illuminated by the dim light
of the jack-o'-lanterns, the once-preening lord of the manor
moved his lips with either prayers or curses.

Now for the final act of our play. Mark searched the
deep shadows at the far end of the hall where he expected
Belle to make her ghostly appearance. Instead, a horse's
hoofbeats pounded in the courtyard.

Moving as one, the company turned toward the lighted

entrance of the hall where torches still burned on the landing. Iron horseshoes clattered against the cobblestones at the base of the low wide stairs. Then a dark horse and rider stood silhouetted in the arched doorway.

Mark blinked. What new piece of trickery was this? He glanced around the hall for Montjoy but could not locate the old gentleman. The rider spurred his great steed into the hall. People scattered to the left and right as the black horse pranced with arched neck down the length of the chamber. The rider was clad entirely in an old-fashioned suit of black chain mail. Over this he wore a sable surcoat that bore an unusual coat of arms: a golden roundel pierced by three black triangles and a dancette line that zigzagged across the bottom. A festoon of green leaves nestled around the roundel's base.

The knight's fourteenth-century closed helm hid his face. Gold and black silken streamers fluttered from the wreath that encircled the steel brow. A heavy two-handed broadsword hung from the man's belt. His left arm supported a black shield decorated with his heraldic device while he held a sharpened lance in his right hand. A black and gold mantle covered the war-horse's flanks and red-orange sparks flew when his hooves scraped the hall's paving stones.

That can't possibly be Montjoy!

Kitt appeared at Mark's side with a broad grin on his face. "He makes a grand sight, doesn't he?" he breathed.

Mark cast a sidelong glance at his squire. "You know him?"

The boy nodded, though he did not take his eyes off the mysterious knight. "I cannot recall his name. Indeed, I had forgotten all about him until this minute. He used to play with me here when I was quite young. I haven't seen him since we moved to Wolf Hall to take care of Grandpappa."

He cocked his head, as the rider halted at the far end of the hall. "I don't remember him looking so fierce. He has a kind face with white hair and a mustache."

An elderly family retainer put out to pasture? Mark wondered. Montjoy must have contacted the old boy to join in the frolic. Mark applauded the man's strength. The huge stallion looked ready to bolt.

As if the knight read Mark's thoughts, he spurred his steed. The horse rose on its hind legs with sparks flying from its hooves. Then he plunged at full tilt back down the hall toward the assembly. Everyone pressed themselves against the walls. The knight saluted Mark as he swept past him. A moment later he shot through the doorway. The hoofbeats quickly receded into the night.

Everyone broke into more nervous laughter as they compared the marvels they had witnessed. Many called for torches. Women begged to be taken home. People bumped into each other as they stumbled about in the darkness. No one could locate a tinderbox or a hot coal.

The beam from a single candle blazed at the far end of the hall. A large black cat, swelled to twice its size with anger at his sooty indignity, stalked across the floor and dashed out of sight. Growing quiet again, the guests eagerly waited to behold the next wonder.

Mark heaved a sigh of relief. *Tis Belle—finally.*

A pale wraith walked down the center of the floor, leaving a trail of white dust behind her. Belle had sprinkled herself with too much flour, Mark judged. As she drew nearer, she removed her cowl and held the candle closer to her face. A blood-red ruby flashed on the base of her neck.

The Cavendish jewel! Nice touch!

"Tis Mistress Belle!" cried Will, staring at her with a

mixture of joy and awe on his face. "Methought ye were dead."

"Tis her spirit come back to torment us," wailed Ivy, sounding truly alarmed for the first time. "Mother of God, protect us!" Without waiting for the signal, the girl dashed toward the archway.

Her cry galvanized everyone else. As Montjoy had predicted, the sight of the deceased mistress of Bodiam was enough to turn the strongest man's blood to ice. The company fled the hall like wolf-hounded sheep. Their shrieks and screams echoed around the courtyard as the crowd thundered through the gates and across the drawbridge. Within a few minutes, not a soul remained in the great chamber except Belle, Mark, Kitt—and Mortimer.

At last shaken from his glazed stupor, the pale host of the ill-fated feast clutched his throat and croaked, "Begone, spirit of hell!"

Belle pointed her finger dramatically at him. "I will take you there with me."

Mark clenched his fists. *Run, you whoreson villain!*

Instead, Mortimer's face assumed an alarming expression that hinted at obsessive madness. "My brooch!" His eyes burned. He clawed the air in front of him. "Give it to me!" He hopped up and down. "Tis mine! I've earned it! Give it to me!"

Though taken aback by his behavior, Belle stood her ground. "Repent your wickedness, Mortimer," she continued her rehearsed speech. "Confess the wrongs you have done to me."

Instead of turning tail as expected, Mortimer lunged and grabbed her arm.

She's overstepped her part! Mark drew his dagger from his boot.

When he realized that he held a living woman and not

a vengeful ghost Mortimer's expression changed. "Slut!" He shook her. Flour dust filled the air. "You still live, but not for long!" He reached to snatch the brooch from Belle's gown.

"The jig is up!" Mark shouted to Kitt as he ran toward Belle.

She shoved her candle against Mortimer's cheek. The flame licked his skin and then went out. Howling with pain, Mortimer dropped her arm and clutched his face. Mark caught Belle's hand.

"Our revels are ended," he shouted to her. "Kitt, let's away! Sorry about the mess," he added to Mortimer over his shoulder.

Belle bunched her frayed costume in her free hand and gripped Mark tighter. The three of them dashed for the archway.

Behind them, Mortimer shouted, "Guards! You dogs! After them!"

Mark had no time to wonder if any of Mortimer's men still remained inside the castle. He pulled Belle down the steps into the courtyard. Kitt, his long legs pumping hard, raced beside them. The gateway yawned open on the far side of the deserted quadrangle. Mark looked over his shoulder and his heart skipped a beat.

"Hell's bells!" he muttered when several men-at arms clattered down the mid-tower stairs and took up the pursuit.

"Thieves!" Mortimer shouted. "Shoot them! Kill them!"

An arrow sang over their heads.

"God's mercy!" shouted Belle, glancing behind her.

More arrows rained down from the east wing battlements where two lone guards raised their bows. The portcullis over the gateway shuddered, groaned and squealed, then fell with a massive crash, barring their escape. Mark ducked as an arrow missed his shoulder by inches.

"God's teeth!" Kitt moaned. "We're doomed!"

Belle pulled Mark toward the left side of the yard. "This way!"

She raced for the west mid-tower. Mark didn't bother to ask what she was doing. If anyone knew how to smuggle them out of Bodiam, it was Belle. Kitt swore under his breath but followed blindly after them.

Once inside the tower, Mark bolted the door. "Where to now?"

Belle pointed at the spiral stairs. "Up!"

"Are you—?" Mark began but Belle raced ahead of him. Kitt scampered behind her. Shaking his head, Mark followed.

Belle paused only long enough to bolt the gallery doors on the second floor landing before continuing her ascent. Following the two Cavendishes, Mark tried to formulate a reasonable plan of defense. Sooner or later, they were going to run out of stairs.

By the time Mark reached the garret on the third floor, Belle and Kitt were already inside the bare room. Two stories below, the outer door splintered under Mortimer's assault.

"Lock the door," she panted.

After sliding home the bolt, Mark turned to her. Never had Belle looked so beautiful as she did at this moment. Cheeks pink with excitement, her breasts heaved against the thin fabric of her costume and her eyes glowed with cobalt fire.

Mark motioned the brother and sister to the far wall. "Stay back. I'll cut them down as they enter. There can't be too many of those puling minions left." He prayed that there weren't. He couldn't let the Cavendishes know how truly terrified he was—not for himself, but for their sakes as well as for their parents.

Belle glared at him. "This way, you jolthead! I do not intend to wait here for Mortimer!" She led them into the privy alcove and lifted the cracked wooden seat.

"In there!" she pointed at the black hole. "Quick!"

Mark gaped at the privy shaft and then at her. "You're moonstruck!"

Belle ripped away the trailing material of her costume. "It hasn't been used in ages," she replied, kicking off her shoes. "I used to do this all the time. How do you think I got outside after dark?"

Kitt puckered his lips. "Where does it go?"

"Into the moat," she replied. "'Tis the only shaft that ends at the waterline instead of below it. Well, don't just stand there, you flea-brains! Jump in! Hurry," she added. The guards' voices echoed in the stairwell.

Mark shuddered. "'Tis a sixty foot drop."

"More or less," Belle agreed. She grabbed him by his shoulders. "Trust me, Mark. I know what I'm doing. This chute was built as an escape route hundreds of years ago. 'Tis wider than the others."

Gauging the diameter of the hole, Mark knew his shoulders were too broad. But Belle and Kitt were as slim as the wily fourteenth century fox who had constructed such an unusual exit. It might work—it had to. "Kitt, do it! That is my express command, squire," he ordered when the boy looked ready to balk.

With a grimace, Kitt gingerly lowered himself down the shaft. "Sdeath, Belle! What a foul odor!" He lifted his arms over his head and literally disappeared from view.

Mark held his breath for what seemed like eternity. Then he heard a faint splash.

Belle grinned at him. "See? Tis child's play. Come on!"

Mark pulled her to his chest in a fierce embrace. "You go, I'll follow after." He sugared his lie with a smile.

She cocked her eyebrow. "Is that a threat or a promise?"

Mark gave her a lopsided grin. She had the heart of a lion. "Both," he replied. "Kiss me—for luck."

"For luck," she whispered, wrapping her arms around his neck.

The kiss was not long enough for Mark to show her how much she meant to him. He needed a lifetime to do that. He had less than a minute.

Someone pounded on the chamber door.

He broke away from her. "Quickly!" he urged. "And give my regards to your parents," he added as he helped her into the filthy hole.

She looked up at him. "You're not coming, are you?"

The outer door shuddered under heavy blows.

He held her by the wrists. "Later, *chou-chou,* I have some business here to finish." He lowered her down. "I love you," he added at the last moment. He might not get another chance to tell her.

"I know." She smiled at him, tossed him a kiss, and dropped out of sight.

Mark listened for the splash. When he heard it, he relaxed. Let Mortimer do his damnedest now; Belle was safely away from his clutches. He strolled into the chamber and leaned against the wall with one leg crossed over the other in a nonchalant pose. He used his dagger to clean his nails while he watched the thick door buckle and splinter asunder.

Four guards fell inside, with Mortimer frothing at the mouth behind them.

"Good evening, gentlemen," Mark greeted them with a cocky grin. "Is anything amiss?"

"Seize him!" Mortimer screamed. "And do not be gentle."

Gripping handfuls of grass, Belle pulled herself up the moat's slippery bank. By the faint moonlight, she saw her brother lying on his back panting like a landed trout. The chill air raised goosebumps on her skin.

"Kitt?" she whispered, "we must get to Montjoy quickly."

He rolled over and pulled himself to his knees. "Wait for Mark," he gasped.

Belle swallowed back a sob that rose in her throat. "He's not coming."

"God's nightshirt!" Kitt sputtered, staggering to his feet. "We've got to go back and save him."

Belle pulled him down into the tall weeds. "Not now, and keep your voice down. Mortimer may have his men on the west wall by now." She clenched her teeth to curb her chattering from the cold. "We will free Mark, do not fear for that, little brother. Let's find some warmth. We will be no good to him if we freeze to death now."

The boy nodded. Keeping low to the ground, the two raced for the trees that marked the boundary of the home park. Once within the safety of the wood, they straightened up and circled around to the front of the castle.

It was over six weeks since Belle had last been outside the walls of her beloved home. How cold and deserted Bodiam looked now—as if its very heart had stopped beating. *Stay alive, sweet Marcus! I'll come for you, I swear.*

Nearby, a bird whistled in the dark. Kitt's head snapped up, then he answered with a similar call. "'Tis Jobe," he told his sister. "He taught me how to sound like one of the birds from his homeland."

"G-good," she shivered.

The African stepped from behind a tree. "Did you fly from the walls?" he asked. "*Diabo!* You are wet." He whipped off his enormous cape and wrapped it around both of them. In the time since he had vanished from the great hall, he had washed off his paint and was now dressed in a civilized fashion.

"Where is Mark?" he asked, as they skirted along the forest's edge.

Belle nodded toward the dark castle. "Still in there," she said with a catch in her voice. "He was too big to fit through my escape hole." She grasped Jobe's hand. "Our plans went all awry, didn't they?"

He put his arm around her. "Not so, little mistress. No one who was in the great chamber will ever forget this night. As I lay in the dark, I heard them shout to one another as they hurried down the road. You have created a legend that will live for many years to come."

Belle sighed. "If I have lost Mark, twill all be for nothing. He is worth more to me than that heap of stones or a priceless jewel." She touched the brooch that was still pinned to her ragged garment.

Jobe squeezed her shoulder. "You have become a very wise woman this night."

She glared at him. "What good is wisdom if it comes too late?"

Jobe stared at the castle. "Mark is safe enough. Tis not yet his time."

Hope swelled in her breast. She shook Jobe. "Truly? He will not die?"

Jobe chuckled. "We all die, mistress, but not tonight. And everything is not yet over. Come, you will see."

Belle started to ask him what he meant, but she knew enough of Jobe to realize that he never explained his cryptic answers until he was ready. Huddling close to Kitt under the cape, she stumbled after the giant man. Much to her surprise, Montjoy waited for them in the driver's seat of a small pony cart filled with hay.

"How did you know?" Belle asked, snuggling gratefully into the sweet-smelling load. Kitt curled up next to her.

Montjoy sniffed in his usual fashion. "This black wizard of yours told me to bring the cart and wait. I am sure that he gleans his knowledge from unholy sources but tis prudent not to ask." He draped a dry blanket over the Cavendish siblings.

Instead of leading the pony down the road, Jobe sat cross-legged and faced Bodiam. "Soon now."

As he spoke, a small pinpoint of light shot up into the sky and exploded red stars over the silent castle. Suddenly, a sparkling silver waterfall poured from the hideous mouths of all the gargoyle rainspouts in the northeast drum tower. The three other drum towers guarding the castle's corners erupted with similar firefalls.

Kitt's eyes glowed. "Uncle Andrew's fireworks! I had forgotten about them. But who is doing it?"

Jobe tapped the side of his nose with his forefinger. "Four bright lads who have spent the whole day hiding in the stable loft."

Despite being chilled to the bone, Belle couldn't help but admire the sight of Bodiam Castle clothed in silver. The moat's dark waters reflected the light. "Mortimer will kill those boys if he catches them."

Jobe shook his head. "They will not be captured. I showed them some of your secret passages. Mortimer will think he has more rats within his walls."

"What secret passages?" snapped Kitt.

Belle frowned at him. She didn't care to reveal all her secrets to him. "I found them ages ago. If you are a clever boy, you'll find them too someday." *If we ever return to Bodiam.*

As the firefalls died out, whirligigs of colored lights spun along the battlements. The fire starters were indeed clever for they kept several jumps ahead of the confused guards. Shouts inside the castle floated over the still waters of the moat.

"Tis too bad that the townspeople missed this show," Belle remarked to Montjoy. "Uncle Andrew has outdone himself."

The old steward chuckled. "There are more of us hiding in these woods than you think, my dear," he replied. "Many of your good friends knew of the fireworks and once I had convinced them that you were not a ghost, they stayed to watch."

I wonder if Mark can see it. Belle closed her eyes for a moment and sent a prayer for his safety winging to heaven.

Shrill whistling rockets suddenly ascended from the four cardinal points. They arced high over the castle and exploded into gold and red stars.

"Tis true, Jobe," Kitt breathed with wonder as he watched the sparks cascade down from the sky. "You once told me there would be a devil darkness and a night of brilliant stars."

"Just so," Jobe replied.

The castle grew still again. "Is that the lot?" Belle asked.

"One more, though where it will come from not even I can guess. Wait and watch."

Belle peered into the night, not knowing what to expect. They waited, listening to the confused guards shout to each other along the battlements. The stable boys lay very low. Then, from the southern mid tower another rocket shot into the sky. Belle heard a small *pop* followed by several more. Suddenly an enormous silver wolf's head hung directly over the castle. Its eyes spun with red pinwheels and a large red tongue spewed red stars down into the courtyard.

Tears pricked Belle's eyes when she beheld the Cavendish family's wolf badge. Kitt jumped up, rocking the cart.

"Huzzah!" he shouted waving both hands in the air. Then he threw back his head and shouted the family war cry for the first time in his young life. "A Cavendish! A Cavendish to me!"

Belle glowed with pride and determination. "Nothing will stop us, Marcus. You'll see!"

Chapter Nineteen

Mark spent the remainder of that memorable night curled up at the dry end of Bodiam's foul oubliette located deep under the northwest tower. He pulled his knees closer to his chest and listened to little rodent feet skittering across the dank stone floor. He hated rats, especially now when he couldn't see them. One dropped onto his arm. With an oath, he flipped the creature in the general direction of the tiny cell's flooded end. At least Belle and Kitt were safe, he consoled himself.

He touched his tongue to the split on his lip. Before Mortimer's men had dragged him down to this hellhole, they had beaten him practically senseless while Mortimer stood by exhorting them to strike harder. The man was more barbaric than Jobe could ever be.

Another rat ran over his foot. Mark kicked at it. It didn't matter that he had no light to see by. His eyes were swollen shut from the heavy-handed louts who had taken their pleasure pounding him into a pulp. He rubbed the old break on his arm. It throbbed from warding off the blows that had rained down on him.

An enormous furry rat pushed itself against him. Jesu! This one felt as large as Belle's cat. Then it mewed.

"Dexter?" he mumbled. His jaw ached with the effort.

With a snarl, the cat launched itself at an unseen enemy. A rat squealed its death throes. Dexter returned to Mark's side.

"Good boy," he said through his bruised lips. He tentatively petted his protector. "How did you get in here?" he asked.

The cat purred against him. Mark continued to stroke his thick fur. If the cat found a way in, there might be promise of a way out—if only Mark could see.

Dexter stiffened, snarled, then launched himself at another rodent. When he had dispatched the attacker, he returned once more to Mark's side.

"You are the prince of cats," he praised. His nose had been so pushed out of shape that he couldn't sneeze even if he wanted to. In any event, he infinitely preferred Dexter's company to being eaten alive by the rats.

After several more defensive actions by the cat, the scuffling ceased altogether. As the hours crawled by, Mark's joints stiffened from the cold and the punishment he had endured. He shivered. Dexter crawled into the space between his chest and his thighs. The cat's warmth brought him a tiny measure of comfort.

"Now I see why Belle loved you so much," he remarked as Dexter curled up against him. "You are truly a friend in need."

Mark put his head down in the crook of his elbow and prayed for sleep. He needed all his wits about him when next the guards came for him.

If they ever came for him.

The groaning of the rusted hinges on the trap door above his head woke Mark. The lantern light hurt his slitted eyes. With little ceremony and many curses, Fowler and his men hauled Mark out of his confinement. His cramped muscles refused to sustain his weight. The guards dragged him up the stairs to the courtyard. Dexter trotted behind them.

The rain had returned during the night. Mark lifted his battered face to its healing drops and stuck out his tongue to slake his burning thirst. Five horses stood saddled in the courtyard, including Artemis. Hunched inside the protection of an oilskin cloak, Mortimer glowered down at his prisoner.

The churl looks as if he has had as vile a night as I have.

"Good morrow, Fletcher," Mark croaked. "Did you sleep well?"

Mortimer ignored his jibe. "Bind his hands!" he barked to Fowler.

As if I had the strength to fight or run!

With a cold glint in his eye, Fowler wrapped a thick rope around Mark's wrists and pulled the knots tight enough to hamper circulation. Mark gritted his teeth but said nothing. *I will remember your smiling face, villainous knave. You will rue this day, I swear.*

Then two of the guards hoisted Mark onto his horse. He clung to the pommel while his numb feet searched for the stirrups. Before he could seat himself squarely into the saddle, Mortimer gave a signal and they rode out through the open gateway. Mark did not bother to cast a backward glance as Bodiam receded behind him. The castle was only a hollow shell; its life extinguished by the villain who rode ahead of him.

Instead, Mark squinted at the woods on either side of the road. The rain turned everything into a blur of brown and orange. Just then, a bird's shrill whistle rose above the raindrops' patter. Mark cracked his lips in a semblance of a smile. Somewhere among the trees, Jobe followed them. Mark wondered what action his friend would take.

Must be ready.

At the crossroads, the company turned away from Hawkhurst and rode steadily toward the seacoast. *Mortimer must be taking me to Rye, either to jail me or to put me out in the Channel in a leaking boat.*

Mark's head throbbed from lack of food and his injuries. It took all the strength he could muster to stay upright on his horse. Twas a good thing that Belle could not see him now, he thought, as Mortimer relentlessly pounded down the road ahead of him. Mark was not the picture of a heroic knight.

Every so often throughout the remainder of that wet miserable journey, Mark heard Jobe's whistle. At least, his friend had the prudence not to attempt a rescue against such well-armed odds. By the time the party drew up in front of Rye's town hall, Mark was near to falling from his mount. He laid his head on Artemis's neck while Mortimer went inside the building to vent his grievances into the nearest bailiff's unsuspecting ear. Mark did not care what happened next as long as he could sleep and eat. His guards looked longingly down the cobbled street at the cheery sign of the Mermaid Inn.

After a tedious delay Mortimer emerged from the building and signaled for Mark to be brought inside. The guards pulled him out of his saddle and dragged him up the steps. At least he was now out of the rain. The bailiff, portly with his own importance, cast a piggish eye at Mark.

"Take him down," he instructed several other men who hovered by the door.

I wonder what lies Mortimer has told them.

The bailiff looked like the type of rogue who lined his ample pockets with bribes. Mark comforted himself with the thin hope that his friends would soon sort out his current plight. The guards dragged him down a set of stone steps and tossed him into a foul cell that reeked of urine. At least it had a small window, though stoutly barred and open to nature's whims. Later a minion brought him a bowl of watery gruel, a crust of stale bread and an armful of clean straw. When Mark attempted to question his keeper, he discovered that the man was deaf and dumb.

Warmed by the scant fare, Mark collapsed on his straw and fell into a deep, healing sleep.

His first visitor arrived the following morning; but it wasn't Montjoy or Belle as he had hoped but Lady Katherine Cavendish, Sir Brandon's wife. Though taken by surprise, Mark struggled to his feet and gave her a pale imitation of a bow. With his best clothes now torn and filthy, his face battered and unshaven, and having had no opportunity to clean himself, his appearance deeply embarrassed him.

"My lady," he said hoarsely. "Tis good of you to come. Forgive my—"

Lady Kat shook her head at his apologies. "No need for forgiveness, Mark. Sit down before you fall down."

The keeper appeared behind her carrying a load of bags and baskets. He dropped them in a heap, then scurried off to find a stool for the noblewoman. Lady Kat waited until they were alone once again before she resumed the conversation. She tucked her skirts closely around her feet then gave Mark a warm smile.

"Well, my boy, you seem to have landed yourself in a deep pickle barrel this time."

Mark returned her smile though it hurt his swollen lips. "Just so, my lady. Tell me that I am not dreaming. Why aren't you at Wolf Hall? How fares Belle? Is she safe? And Kitt?"

"All in good time, Mark." Lady Kat pointed to one of the canvas bags. "In there are some blankets. Wrap yourself up this minute. I will not have you freeze to death while we talk.''

Mark mumbled his grateful thanks as his stiff fingers untied the bag. He drew out a clean thick woolen blanket and draped it around his shoulders. Now I know exactly how Belle felt when I first saw her, he thought ruefully. ''And Belle?'' he asked again. ''Nothing is ill if she is well.''

Lady Kat arched her brow. ''Tis very gallant of you to say that considering where you are. Belle is in London staying with Francis's old tutor at the Inns of Court. She is getting you a lawyer. You are going to need one.''

Mark hid his disappointment. He wanted desperately to see Belle and yet for his vanity's sake, he was glad that she was not here. ''What are the charges against me?''

Lady Kat drew in a quick breath of astonishment. ''Sweet Saint Anne! Did no one tell you?''

He pulled the blanket tighter around his shoulders, reveling in its warmth. ''Nay, my lady. My gaoler's tongue is tied up and I have seen no one else till now.''

Lady Kat gave her shoulders a little shake. ''Master Fletcher is indeed a nasty piece of work. As I understand it, he has brought suit against you for breach of contract, fraud and disturbing the peace.''

Mark shrugged. ''All false and can be easily proved in my favor. Can you arrange bail for me, my lady? I will pay you back in full measure.''

She gave him a sweet sad look. ''Ah, dear Mark, if I only could! But there is one other charge that is the most dire. Fletcher swears that you have stolen some personal property of his worth over a thousand pounds.''

Mark gaped at her. ''Surely he jests!''

She shook her head.

He slumped against the cold plaster wall. ''Tis a hanging offense," he muttered. "But what property? I have nothing to my name now but what is on my back."

"I know not, nor could Brandon discover the particulars though he shouted a great deal at that ass of a constable."

Mark lifted his brows. "My lord is here? But his hip—"

"Is mending well," Lady Kat replied. "And your predicament is the perfect tonic for his spirits. He wanted to challenge Mortimer Fletcher in personal combat. Fortunately, I talked him out of it. Brandon still depends upon his crutches."

Mark grinned. "I would like to have seen Mortimer's face if my lord had indeed sent his challenge. Twould be worth all my bruises."

Lady Kat handed him a small basket. "You have a most loyal friend in your African. He told us of your mistreatment. Here are some salves and ointments made especially for you by Mistress Owens. Also bandages and some poppy juice to ease your pain."

Mark pressed his lips together for a moment until he had his raw emotions under control. "Please convey my most profound thanks to that wonderful woman. By my soul, Lady Kat, tis good to know that I have friends in this cold world."

Her eyes sparkled with a liquid brightness. "You are loved far more than you can imagine." She cleared her throat. "And if you look out of your window, you will spy Jobe in the alley across the way. He has watched over you ever since he informed us of your capture."

Mark set the basket aside. He would make good use of its contents later when Lady Kat was gone. *Bless you, noble African!* He swallowed the lump in his throat. "Then you are not too angry...about Kitt?" he ventured to ask.

The boy's mother rolled her eyes. "That scamp should be hung by his heels for the anxious moments he has given me this past month, but to tell you the truth, I am full of amazement when I see him. All of a sudden, my little boy is more grown up. He and Brandon had a long conference together.'' She snorted. ''Not for a woman's ears, they told me, though I soon learned the whole tale of your adventures. Brandon does nothing but puff out his chest with pride in his son. He, that is we, would count it an honor if you would keep Kitt as your squire.''

''Before or after they hang me?'' Mark asked, only half in jest. Mortimer's calumny troubled his spirits.

Lady Kat shook her head. ''Tush, you will live to break many more hearts.''

He looked down at his hands. ''There is only one heart I want now,'' he whispered. *And the flighty chit has gone to London. Once more she leaves me without a word of comfort.* Aloud he asked, ''Have you now returned to Bodiam, my lady? I fear we left it in great disarray.''

A dark frown crept over her beautiful face. ''Nay, we lodge outside Rye at the home of dear friends. Alas, Bodiam is still plagued with that maggot Fletcher. As he is legally Belle's brother-in-law tis his right, especially since Belle is still thought to be dead. Oh! I could cut that man up in pieces inch by inch when I think of the pain his loathsome letter almost caused us. That man's heart is a chunk of ice.''

Mark whistled through his teeth. ''He has more perseverance than I suspected.'' He cleared his throat. ''Tell me, does Kitt still have a paper that I gave to him?''

Lady Kat nodded. ''Aye, though he did not say what it was.''

Good lad! Mark swallowed. ''Please tell him that I said to give it to you and my lord. Please, my lady, think kindly of me when you read its contents. In truth, I want nothing for myself. Tis only for Belle's sake. I wrote it only to protect her property from that churl. When this episode is past and Bodiam Castle is once more in her sweet care, tear up the document. I will be content.''

"You have aroused my curiosity, Mark," she said. "What does this interesting piece of paper say?"

Mark avoided her eyes. "Twould be best if you read it through first, rather than hear of it from my mouth. My brains are so scrambled at the moment that I can barely think straight. I have not eaten a real meal in two days."

The lady struck her brow. "Sweet angels! You are not the only one with a muddled mind. I have clean forgotten to give you this." She pushed the largest basket toward him. "Tis a wealth of provender from practically every household in Hawkhurst. Tis food enough to last a week."

Mark clutched at it and whipped off the top. His mouth watered when he beheld the array of wrapped bundles. "Your pardon, my lady," he said, tearing open the nearest one. "I am famished." He sank his teeth into the plump leg of a cold roast chicken. Paradise on earth!

Lady Kat chuckled. She handed him several fat wine-skins. "Take these for your thirst. And that bag contains clean clothing for you. I fear we were not allowed to bring in a razor but Kitt will visit you anon and will shave you." She winked at him. "Tis amazing what miracles occur whenever a bit of gold crosses an outstretched palm."

Mark swallowed his food. "I am in your debt, sweet lady."

She shook her head. "Nay, Mark, Brandon and I are forever in yours. You have not only returned our children to us, but they are now better than they were before."

Mortimer limped into the empty great hall of Bodiam and surveyed the shambles of his domain. In the pale cold light of the November morning, the remains of the All

Hallows Eve feast rotted on the tables. Crouching in the midst of the broken crockery and scattered food, that damnable cat ate his fill. No servant had lingered to clear away the mess since that horrible night a week ago. All had deserted Mortimer save for a few men-at-arms who skulked in the gate house. Only one aspect of the entire debacle cheered Mortimer—Griselda had fled back to their father's home in London. At last, Mortimer was spared her glass-shattering voice morning, noon and night.

He gnawed the inside of his cheek. How had his brilliant future turned so quickly to ashes? True, he still held the castle, but its possession was a hollow victory. While he was in Rye, the bailiff had reminded him that the taxes on the estate were past due. The sum of eight hundred pounds had staggered him. He knew that the holding was large but his quest for the fabulous jewel had blinded him to the details of day-to-day management. Now he not only had lost the brooch that he had expected would fulfill his vaulting ambition, but the overdue taxes would pauper him.

All because of that chit and her swaggering paramour. The instant he had seen them together that ghastly night, Mortimer remembered exactly who Sir Mark Hayward was. Belle had mentioned his name several times after Cuthbert died. Mortimer ground his back teeth. How stupid he had been to miscalculate Lord Cavendish's affection! Because the vixen had been born on the wrong side of the blanket, Mortimer had presumed Sir Brandon would be glad to shed her as soon as possible. He should have known that Belle's renowned father would not sit idly by while he snatched away her jointure. Of course Sir Brandon would send his most trustworthy man—his former squire.

A chill wind blew through the hall. Mortimer wrapped his dressing gown tighter around his thin body. He could not muster up the energy to light a fire in the yawning fireplace. Why bother? His own room was warm enough. He swore at the cat.

A tiny voice in the back of his mind suggested that he abandon the castle with its staggering debt and return to the old comforts of London. He still owned a share in his father's profitable wool business, though the expenses he had incurred at Bodiam had eaten sharply into his assets. Forget the Cavendishes and their blasted jewel. But his mouth watered when he recalled how that enormous ruby had glinted in the firelight that night. Once again he saw the luster of the huge teardrop pearl in his mind's eye. He clenched his fists until his nails drew blood on his palms.

The brooch was his by right. He would have it yet. His day in the court of justice would end in triumph. As a canny business man, he had pursued an active interest in the law. He had more knowledge of legal twists and turns than the country bumpkins of Rye. In two weeks, the Quarter Sessions would meet and Mortimer intended to be ready. He would win his plea with ease.

Let Mistress LaBelle weep anew to see her scheming lover swing from the gallows tree. The very thought cheered Mortimer.

Belle latched her chamber door, then leaned against it as if she sought the oak's strength from its panels. For the past two weeks she had spent every waking moment reading ponderous tomes of the law under the guidance of old Doctor Bellario, her half-brother's tutor from Oxford. Her head ached from her studies. Tonight, the doctor pronounced himself well satisfied with her progress. Tomorrow she would ride down to Rye and the day after...

She swallowed at the thought. Of all the wild schemes she had ever concocted, this one was the most bold—and the most important one in her life. She must not fail. Pushing herself away from the door, she crossed to the small dressing table that Doctor Bellario's housekeeper had hastily set up for her when Belle had first arrived on the famous lawyer's doorstep. She placed her lighted taper close to the square looking glass. Then she drew a large pair of scissors from her apron pocket. The silver metal gleamed in the candle light.

Belle sat down on the stool before her glass and stared at the pale face in the mirror. They say that the ancient gods honor great sacrifices with sweet incense. Mark had sacrificed his precious freedom for her and would perhaps lose his life as well if she were not clever enough. This small sacrifice of hers was nothing in comparison to his. Barely worth a grain of frankincense. Yet how she trembled at the thought of what she was about to do.

She lifted her chin. LaBelle Marie was a Cavendish through and through. Cavendishes feared nothing. She removed her simple coif and unplaited her hair. It shimmered in her fingers. Belle had always been proud of her shining glory. *Too proud! Twill teach me much needed humility. Besides…twill grow again.*

She brushed out her long tresses, enjoying the feel of her hair as the bristles pulled through its golden wealth. Her lower lip trembled. She bit it. *None of that! Just do it!*

Selecting a lock over her ear, she picked up the scissors. The blades looked sharp and hungry, reminding her of an impatient crane ready to snap up an unsuspecting minnow. She drew in a deep breath. *Don't be such a goose. You have done far more frightening things in your checkered past. What is a snip or two?*

Guided by her reflection, she slid one blade along her cheek until it disappeared behind the curtain of her hair.

The steel was cold against her flushed skin. Do it now! She squeezed her fingers together. The long tress parted from her head just above her ear. Belle gazed at the mass of golden threads in her hands. *Tis begun. There is no turning back now.*

She allowed her shorn locks to flutter to the floor. An hour later, a sea of spun gold surrounded her stool. The candle burned low in its brass socket. Leaning closer to the mirror, Belle trimmed her bangs. She blew away the tiny snippets from her mouth and nose. Then she sat back and regarded her new appearance.

The face of a young man stared at her. The bodice of a woman's gown appeared ridiculous on such a youth. Belle grinned. *By my larkin, I look like Kitt.* And not much older than he. She made a face at herself, then retrieved a castoff lock from the floor. She held it under her nose. A mustache would definitely suit her better, especially since she intended to portray a young doctor of the law.

Belle fluffed her short hair with her fingers. Her head suddenly felt very light and free. She stood and backed away from the dressing table so that she could catch more of her reflection. With her fists planted on her hips, she struck a wide-stance pose.

Methinks I will make a right pretty fellow. I will wear my dagger with as brave a grace as Francis and speak in a low voice. I will tell of a thousand bragging tricks that I have played against sweet innocent maids. Oh, I shall be the most strutting of all the preening peacocks in England!

And, if my manly attire does not offend the Lord God, I will win the freedom of my only true love.

Chapter Twenty

The fortnight had done healing wonders to Mark's body, but his mind grew more uneasy with each passing day. No word—not one scribbled note from Belle. Though Kitt and his mother visited him often, they professed to know nothing of her except that she was still in London and that she enjoyed excellent health. On the morning of his trial, Kitt appeared in his cell with a new set of clothing in suitably muted colors of buff and brown.

"What news of the world?" Mark asked while the boy carefully shaved his bruised face under the eagle eye of the deaf mute keeper.

Kitt wiped the razor clean of lather. "The courthouse was filling to the rafters when I came down here." He furrowed his brow. "I hope that Papa has saved me a good seat."

Mark rolled his eyes. "Are you so anxious to witness my downfall?" he asked after Kitt shaved under his chin.

The boy patted Mark's face with a bit of toweling. "Nay, you will win, I am sure."

Mark eyed himself in a sliver of looking glass. Not too many nicks this time. Kitt's skill as a barber had much improved. "Has my blessed lawyer appeared yet?" he asked as casually as he could. He dared not reveal to the lad how nervous he was. Mark hated the idea that some stranger would fight his most important battle for him while he was forced to stand by in silence.

Kitt shrugged. ''I have not seen nor heard of his arrival, but there are many strangers in the courtroom. I am sure he will not let you down.''

Mark wet his lips. ''And Belle? Will she be there?''

Kitt shrugged again. ''I do not know. Mama has said nothing about her to me—and I *did* ask her.''

Mark turned away from him. ''I thank you for that, Kitt. You are a good squire—the best a knight could ever have.''

''Truly?'' He asked in awe.

Mark flashed him a brave smile over his shoulder. ''Cross my heart and hope to spit,'' he replied.

Two sour-faced guards appeared at the grilled door. ''Tis time,'' one of them growled. He rattled a pair of rusted handcuffs connected with a length of chain.

Mark nodded. Then he clasped Kitt in a fierce bear hug that caught the boy by surprise. ''Take good care of yourself,'' he said in a husky undertone. ''And tell that wild sister of yours that I love her.''

Kitt gulped. ''Aye, my lord,'' he mumbled.

Mark adjusted a fold of his short cape. If this was to be his last day on earth, he intended to look his best. He squared his shoulders and stepped between the guards. They fastened the irons on his wrists, then led him up the winding stair to the second floor. Mark heard the roar of the crowd long before he entered the prisoner's box. He held up his head with pride. Only his eyes moved as he scanned the audience for any friendly faces.

Most of the leading citizens of Hawkhurst had come. Montjoy looked old and gray beside a solemn Ivy. Mark's heart leapt when he spied Sir Brandon and Lady Kat seated in the center of the gallery next to the Lord Mayor of Rye bedecked in his golden chain of office. Jobe, shrouded and hooded in his long black cloak, sat directly behind the noble couple. Kitt wiggled his way through the press of people to join his parents. He sent Mark an encouraging wave. Brandon's expression suddenly turned thunderous.

Mark followed the line of his mentor's gaze and nearly swore out loud. A young man with fashionable close-cropped hair and a golden mustache conferred with several officials. The newcomer handed them a thick letter sealed with red wax. Then he looked directly at Mark. His brilliant blue eyes widened when he beheld the fading bruises of Mortimer's beating still visible on Mark's face.

God's teeth, tis Belle!

What had she done to her beautiful hair? Mark cast another quick glance at Brandon. He was as surprised to see her as Mark was. Mark clamped his jaws together. What hare-brained folly was this? If Belle's true gender was discovered, she would certainly suffer for it. Old King Henry may have rejected Rome's authority, but the new bishops of England still clung to their old-fashioned views when it came to women masquerading as men.

Belle hitched up her long black robe and stalked across the floor with a purposeful stride. At least, she didn't mince her steps like a woman.

"Good day, my lord," she greeted Mark in a deep voice. She would not look him in the eye. "I am Doctor Bartholomew from London. I have been engaged to speak in your defense."

It was on the tip of Mark's tongue to ask her what the hell she thought she was doing, but he stopped himself in time. If Belle intended to play her role even to him, he would make good use of her own game.

He bowed his head. "Good day, Doctor, I thank you for your pains on my behalf, but I fear I cannot pay you for your services."

She fiddled with the tassels of her neck ties. "No payment is necessary. When I win your case, I will be well satisfied and that is my reward." She turned to go.

Mark caught her arm. "Nay, good Doctor, I am a man of honor, though it is currently in tatters. I pray you, take this ring of mine for your fee. Tis the only thing of value I have to offer you except my heart and that I have already given to a fair lass."

She shot him a quick sidelong glance before she asked, "And do you love this most fortunate woman?"

Despite the seriousness of his situation, Mark smiled. "With every fiber of my wretched being. For her sake, not mine, please take this ring." He pulled off his gold signet ring from his little finger and held it out to her.

Belle stared at it, then nodded. "For the lady's sake, I will accept it," she replied in a gruff tone. She slid the band over her left ring finger. "Be of good cheer, my lord. Tonight you will be with your love once more."

Mark pressed his lips together before he replied. "For her sake and mine, I pray that you are right."

A black gowned bailiff struck the floorboards three times with his thick staff, then intoned, "Oyez, oyez, oyez! All rise. This court is now in session. The honorable Justice Matthew Barnes and the honorable Justice William Noble presiding. All those who have business with this court come to the bar. To the rest, be seated and be silent."

Everyone sat except Mark. As the accused, he was not granted the privilege of a stool. Squaring his shoulders, he gripped the edge of his box. Belle took her place at the table in front of him. She opened her leather case and laid out an impressive number of papers in front of her. On the other side of the chamber, the crowd parted to allow the plaintiff to step forward. Mortimer Fletcher, dressed in a rich black brocade doublet and a white frilled collar, advanced to the railing before the two somber justices.

Mortimer inclined his head in a show of respect. "Honorable lords, I am Master Mortimer Fletcher, a wool merchant late of London and now residing at Bodiam Castle. I seek justice and fair restitution to the fullest measure of the law."

Someone hissed from the packed gallery. Mark wondered if it was Kitt but was afraid to look. The bailiff rapped his staff.

"Read the charges," commanded Justice Noble.

The bailiff unscrolled a document. "That upon the thirty-first of October of this year, Sir Mark Hayward did purposefully and with intent to defraud present himself as a suitor to Master Mortimer Fletcher's sister, Mistress Griselda Fletcher of London; that the said Lord Hayward did willfully and with cruel intent break his spousal contract with the said Mistress Fletcher; and that the said Lord Hayward did maliciously and with full intent wreak substantial damage upon the household and furnishings of Master Fletcher in excess of eighty shillings. Finally, that the said Lord Hayward did abscond with and deprive Master Fletcher of a rare jeweled brooch worth in excess of a thousand pounds."

The crowd gasped at the enormous sum. Mark dug his nails into the wood of his box. So the Cavendish jewel was the crux of the matter! He should have known that Mortimer could not let it go.

Justice Barnes turned toward Mark. "How does the prisoner plead?"

Before Mark could reply, Belle rose. "Not guilty on all counts, my lord justice."

The court buzzed with her sudden appearance. Leaning over their high desks, the two justices stared down at Belle. Standing her ground, she returned their look.

"Who speaks for the prisoner?" bellowed Justice Barnes. "Come forward and be recognized by this court."

Belle stepped around the table and approached the bench. "I am Doctor Nicholas Bartholomew from the Inns of Court in London. I bring a letter from Doctor Richard Bellario whose reputation I am sure precedes him, even here in Rye."

Mark sucked in his breath through his teeth. *Don't get too arrogant, Belle.*

The justices nodded. Justice Noble signaled for the letter. After receiving it from the bailiff, he looped a pair of spectacles over his ears, and read aloud, " 'To the Justices of the Peace at Rye, greetings. At the request of the Earl of Thornbury, I have undertaken the defense of one Sir Mark Hayward. A recent illness has unfortunately left me too weak to travel. In my stead, I beg your worthies to accept Doctor Nicholas Bartholomew. I have acquainted him with the points of this controversy between Master Mortimer Fletcher and Sir Mark Hayward. After a great deal of study of the matter, I have furnished him with my opinions. I beseech you, let not his lack of years be an impediment in your reverend estimation of his qualities. In truth, I have never known so young a body with so old a head. I commend him to your gracious acceptance. Written by the hand of Doctor R. Bellario, London.' "

The judges conferred with each other, then Justice Noble proclaimed, "This court is pleased and honored to welcome Doctor Bartholomew to its bar."

Before the introduction of Mark's lawyer, Mortimer had looked the picture of supreme confidence. Now his complexion turned chalky. He pulled a white linen handkerchief from his sleeve and mopped his brow. Brandon Cavendish reclined against his high-backed chair, crossed his arms over his chest and smiled at the flustered man. Mark tried to relax but failed. Belle's bold deceit could crumble at any moment.

Justice Noble turned to the plaintiff. "Master Fletcher, do you swear before Almighty God that the testimony you are about to give this court is the truth, the whole truth and nothing but the truth whatsoever?"

"Aye," Mortimer snapped. He glared daggers at Mark.

"Kiss the holy book as a sign of your oath," the justice continued, motioning to the bailiff.

After kissing the Bible, Mortimer assumed the expression of the injured party. "Honorable lords," he began in a reedy voice. He cleared his throat, and continued, "I beg for justice under the law. That man, Mark Hayward who calls himself a gentleman, came to my manor at Bodiam Castle masquerading as a suitor for my poor beloved sister, Griselda."

Mark curled his lip. *Hogwash! You loathe her.*

Mortimer hurried on. "There are many witnesses among my servants who will attest to this farce. Hayward and I drew up a marriage contract by which he would stand to gain a sizable portion of the Bodiam estate. The villain sought to defraud me of my property by his counterfeit betrothal. Furthermore, he broke the contract and left my poor sister in a state of near collapse."

Justice Barnes turned to Belle. "What says the prisoner to these first and second charges?"

Belle stood tall in her lawyer's robes. "Not guilty, my lords. I beg the court's indulgence, but before we discuss the matter of Sir Mark's alleged betrothal, may we first examine the plaintiff's claim to the estate of Bodiam? Tis Doctor Bellario's opinion as well as my own that the crux of all the charges hinges upon the exact ownership of this property.''

Mortimer's shoulder's slumped at this. Mark grinned to himself. Good for you, Belle. Stab him in his greedy heart. He drew his first easy breath since the proceedings began.

Mortimer pulled himself together and snapped, ''Methought the question of my ownership of Bodiam Castle and its estates was a foregone conclusion, my lords.''

Justice Barnes steepled his long fingers. ''Pray explain yourself for the enlightenment of the court,'' he replied in a silky tone.

Ha! Justice is not as blind as I feared. The good judges have already scented out that polecat.

Mortimer rubbed his hands together in a distracted manner. ''Tis quite simple. My dear younger brother was Master Cuthbert Fletcher, late of London. Two years ago this Christmastide, he married the natural daughter of Sir Brandon Cavendish of Northumberland.''

Though her expression remained steady, Belle flinched at the words ''natural daughter.'' Mark wished he could leap over the railing and rip Mortimer's sneering tongue from his mouth.

Gathering strength as he continued, Mortimer elaborated his testimony. ''Thanks to the generosity of her father, Mistress LaBelle Cavendish brought Bodiam Castle and all its estates to my brother as her marriage portion. Specifically among the goods and furnishings was a ruby brooch of great value. In June of this year, my brother fell ill of a fever. He died shortly after my sister and I arrived at Bodiam.''

Mark fixed him in his glare. *Did you have a hand in Cuthbert's sudden demise, knave?*

Mortimer rambled on. ''My sister-in-law was much saddened by her young husband's untimely death. Indeed, her grief so unhinged her mind that she fell into a melancholy madness. As her most loving brother-in-law, I took it upon myself to administer Cuthbert's estates until Mistress LaBelle had regained her wits." He lifted his hands palms upward. "Alas, twas not to be. I regret to say that Mistress LaBelle took her own life on the twenty-second of this past October."

The spectators murmured among themselves. The Cavendish family remained impassive, though Brandon's eyes flashed an ominous fire. Belle pressed her lips together but did not stir. Mark wondered what thoughts ran through her head.

Mortimer cleared his throat and waited for the chamber to grow quiet again. Then he concluded, "As your honors well know, under the law established by our late King Henry VII—may God rest his soul—the goods, chattels and properties that a woman possesses become her husband's upon marriage. My brother died without a will and without issue. As I am his next of kin and since his deranged wife is also now deceased, Bodiam Castle and all it entails rightly belong to me," he ended on a note of triumph.

Turning to Belle, Justice Barnes asked, "The case of ownership seems clear enough, Doctor. Is there any particular point you wish to examine?"

Belle rose with a dignified air. "All of it, my lords, from top to bottom."

Again a murmur rose among the spectators. The bailiff rapped for silence. A whisper of a smile flitted across Brandon's face as he watched his daughter move to the center of the floor. Mark's heartbeat pounded against his chest. How young Belle looked! He should be the one defending her rights, not the other way around.

"Proceed," intoned Justice Barnes. He propped his

hand under his chin and assumed an attitude of strict attention.

"Tis true that Mistress Cavendish brought a great wealth to her marriage with Master Cuthbert, but the castle of Bodiam and all the goods, chattel and furnishings within it were hers by right of jointure, not dowry. They were hers to keep for her lifetime. This specific point was written into the spousal contract signed by Cuthbert Fletcher, his father Master Engelbert Fletcher and by Sir Brandon Cavendish in November of the year 1540."

She crossed to her table, shuffled among her papers, then held up a heavy piece of parchment. "I have here Sir Brandon's copy of this contract, duly signed and witnessed. Sir Brandon is present in court and can attest to its validity."

She passed the document to the bailiff who conveyed it to the justices. While they scanned the contract, Mortimer wiped his face several times with his handkerchief. Mark raised an eyebrow at his accuser. *How do you like turning on your own spit?*

Justice Barnes addressed the chamber. "Tis legal and binding in all respects, Doctor, but since the woman in question is dead, Master Fletcher's claim remains valid."

Belle's expression turned feline. "I crave your gracious permission to question Master Fletcher as to the particulars of Mistress Cavendish's demise."

The chamber grew deathly still. No one dared to cough or sneeze. Public description of a suicide was a rare thing. The crowd held its collective breath.

Justice Noble nodded. "You may proceed, Doctor."

Mortimer blanched but did not move. He wrung his hands as if he washed blood from them.

Belle bowed to the judges then asked the plaintiff, "Can you describe the circumstances of Mistress Cavendish's confinement?"

Mortimer's eyes bulged from his pasty face. "I did not say she was confined."

Belle cocked her head. "How now? I have taken depositions from several of your servants that you kept Mistress Cavendish locked within the garret of one of Bodiam's towers. How say you to this?"

Mortimer attempted to shrug. "Do you refer to Will Allen, a potboy? My lords, the scullion is a lackwit and has been so since birth. His mind is that of a six-year-old child. His evidence is not substantial."

Belle nodded, "That is true, but there are others who have also sworn to the ill-keeping of Mistress Cavendish—several former guards, your cook, a stable boy who spied her at the window of her prison—and Christopher Cavendish, LaBelle's own brother who saw her in her most pitiful state."

Kitt stood up and leaned far out over the gallery railing. "'Tis true, my lord justices. My sweet sister was kept in that cold room without a fire or blanket to warm her, nor did she have food to give her strength. This I saw with my own eyes."

The chamber rocked with outrage. Kat gasped and leaned against Brandon, who looked eager to pounce on Mortimer and kill him where he stood. The judges stared aghast at the plaintiff. The bailiff beat his staff on the floor for some minutes before order was finally restored.

Justice Barnes pointed to Kitt. "You are the deceased's brother, Christopher?"

Kitt squared his shoulders. "I am, and my good parents here beside me will attest to my claim."

Justice Barnes shifted in his seat. "Your noble parents are well-known in this shire, Master Cavendish, however you are tender in years and do not yet know your own mind."

The Cavendish temper colored the boy's complexion though he kept his voice steady. ''I am eleven-and-one-half years old, my lords. I am long past the prescribed age of reason and am near to the coming of my manhood. Unlike poor Will Allen, I possess all my wits.''

Belle retrieved another paper from her table. ''I have one further deposition, my lords. Mistress Griselda Fletcher—''

''What?'' Mortimer exploded. ''What pernicious lie is this?''

''Signed by her own hand,'' Belle continued, ''and witnessed in the presence of the High Constable of London whose seal is here affixed.''

Mark whistled under his breath. *I understand now why you were so busy in London, chou-chou.*

Belle handed the paper to the bailiff who passed it to the judges. ''Mistress Griselda states that her brother kept Mistress Cavendish locked away for over a month and would allow no visitations.''

Mortimer's face contorted. ''In truth, my sister-in-law was mad, I tell you. Of course I kept her locked up. Tis a tried and true remedy to effect a cure for lunacy. Ask any physician.''

''Describe how Mistress Cavendish died,'' Belle requested. ''Please tell the court in explicit detail.''

Mark hid his smile behind his hand. How would Mortimer explain a heap of ashes and duck bones?

The plaintiff visibly shivered. ''Twas a ghastly sight, my lords, and not fit for those members of the weaker sex to hear,'' he gabbled.

''Tell us, Master Fletcher. Justice and truth demand it if you wish to prove your claim,'' Belle added with a certain gleeful snap.

Mortimer looked ready to faint. He coughed several

times then replied, "Twas the devil's own doing. When I came to visit her, I found that her body had shriveled to dust and tiny bones."

A number of the spectators unthinkingly crossed themselves, though the new Church of England forbade such customs.

Belle glowered at the perspiring man. "And what did you do with the...remains?"

He narrowed his eyes. "What any Christian would do in such a circumstance, I sealed up that hideous chamber."

Belle returned her attention to the justices. "Tis a grim tale, my lords, and one suitable for telling around a fire at night, but I fear tis not the truth."

Mortimer clutched the bar for support. "How dare you question me, you puling waterfly! You are barely out of the schoolroom."

Belle ignored his outburst. Instead, she continued to address the judges. "Master Fletcher's testimony is false from beginning to end, my lords, for the woman in question, Mistress LaBelle Cavendish, still lives!"

Chapter Twenty-One

The chamber erupted in a frenzy of wonderment as the spectators in the crowded benches voiced their shock, horror and disbelief to their nearest neighbors. Belle cast a look out one of the chamber's long windows and saw that a large mob had gathered in the street before the courthouse. By nightfall, the events of this most unusual trial would be discussed around every hearthside in the shire. Good!

Even the judges paled. Justice Barnes gripped his notes. "How now, Doctor Bartholomew? Can this statement be proved?"

Belle lifted her voice. "Aye, your honor, it can." She extracted yet another paper from her pile and waved it before the intrigued crowd. "Here is Mistress Belle's deposition written in her own hand in the presence of Dr. Bellario, the Chief Constable of London and several magistrates. She charges that Master Fletcher did attempt to steal away her jointure and when she would not yield to his demands, he imprisoned and starved her."

The bailiff handed the paper to the judges. While they read it carefully, Belle glanced over her shoulder at Mark.

Very slowly he winked at her. Anger whipped through her. *Blast and fogs, he knows who I am!*

Refusing to acknowledge his salutation, she looked up to her parents. Kitt grinned back at her. *Am I that transparent? Pray to God that Mortimer does not catch wind of my disguise.*

Justice Barnes searched the gallery for Sir Brandon Cavendish. "My lord?" he called. "Have you seen your daughter alive since the report of her death?"

Brandon hoisted himself to his feet. Kitt put his arm around his waist to support his father. Belle swelled with pride at the sight of them together.

"Aye, my lord justice, I have," Brandon's voice reverberated around the courtroom. "Last week in London. I saw her as plainly as I see Doctor Bartholomew there. Belle is alive and well, no thanks to that…that piece of perfidy!" He pointed to Mortimer.

Though visibly shaken by the unexpected turn of the proceedings, Mortimer refused to yield his case. "My lords!" he shouted over the din. The chamber immediately grew silent.

"My lords, I rejoice in this good news, but you can see for yourselves how I was hoodwinked by that woman and by her partner in crime, Lord Hayward. I have been wrongly and cruelly abused by these two. Tis no wonder I have been unwell. In truth, I have barely slept a wink since the fateful night when I found those gruesome bones. I still maintain that I am the sole owner of Bodiam and all its contents."

"By what right?" asked Justice Barnes.

Mortimer gripped the railing in front of him. "By my rights as Mistress LaBelle's brother-in-law. Though she lives, you have witnessed how she has abused me and my poor sister. The woman is not perfect in her wits. All of her life she has delighted in tricks and counterfeits designed to drive everyone around her to distraction. There are no end of witnesses who can vouch that truth. How can such a light-headed female possibly administer such a large estate as Bodiam? Besides, she has obviously abandoned the castle now, leaving me in sole possession.''

While the two judges conferred, Belle shivered under her heavy black robe. *Zounds, my childish follies will undo me yet!* She shot a quick glance at Mark. He leaned toward her and beckoned. *Now what?* She stepped up to his box.

Bending down, he whispered in her ear. ''Return to the matter of the betrothal contract.''

Belle gritted her teeth. ''So that my downfall will be complete?'' she snarled.

He had the nerve to chuckle. ''Tis not you who stands here accused of a felony, but me. Or had you forgotten that fact?''

''Nay,'' she snapped. ''I am trying to save your miserable neck.''

''Trust me, *chou-chou*,'' he whispered. ''As I trust you.''

Despite the serious circumstances, Belle's body tingled at the seductive tone in his voice. His warm breath fanned her cheek causing her blood to surge through her.

''You blush, lawyer,'' Mortimer remarked with a sneer. ''Methinks you are out of your depth.''

Belle bit her tongue while she controlled her fury. She chose her words with care. ''If I blush, Master Fletcher, tis to witness such an example of rapacious greed as yours. You have an ambitious eye. No man nor woman's pie is free from your grasping fingers.''

A number of spectators guffawed.

Justice Barnes frowned at the breach of decorum. ''We declare that Master Fletcher has proved his point. We declare him to be the rightful owner of the disputed property.''

Belle gritted her teeth. *Over my very dead body!*

"The contract!" Mark whispered behind her.

Belle gulped a deep breath. "Very well, my lords. Then let us consider the charges concerning Mistress Griselda's broken betrothal.''

Mortimer waved his handkerchief. "Minor charges, my lords. Let us instead consider the theft of the ruby brooch—my brooch.''

"Don't let him change the subject!" Mark whispered loudly as he leaned half out of his box. His guards jerked him back.

Under the cover of her long sleeves, Belle balled her hands into fists. "I fully intend to address the matter of the ruby, my lords, but first let us clear the docket concerning the breach of contract.'' She held her breath.

Justice Barnes nodded. "Proceed, Doctor Bartholomew, but be quick about it. We burn daylight with this bickering.''

Belle straightened her posture. "Exactly so, my lords. Master Fletcher, you said earlier that Lord Hayward came to Bodiam Castle posing as a suitor for your sister's hand?''

Mortimer lifted a corner of his mouth in a sneer. "He did. He wooed Griselda with sweet words and a great deal of off-key singing. She was instantly smitten. She has the mind of a sheep, your honor.''

Belle nodded. "Indeed, so I have been told.'' She riffled through her papers until she found the stack she sought. "My lords, I pray your patience. I have here more depositions from members of Master Fletcher's retinue at Bodiam. These witnesses—'' She waved the documents at the judges. "Swear that Master Fletcher was most anxious to rid himself of his sister, Mistress Griselda, whom the witnesses say he cordially hated. These witnesses, including the steward of Bodiam and the chamberlain, swear that Master Fletcher *presumed* that Lord Hayward had come a-wooing.''

Belle handed the papers to the bailiff. ''In actual fact, Lord Hayward had come to Bodiam at the request of Sir Brandon Cavendish to seek out the whereabouts of Sir Brandon's daughter. You will find that Sir Brandon's deposition is duly signed and sworn.''

Justice Noble fixed Mortimer in his stare. ''Did Lord Hayward *say* in exact words that he had come a-wooing Mistress Fletcher?''

Mortimer stuck out his chin. ''Aye, he did so and in full hearing of many of my retainers.''

Belle hunched under the verbal blow. How could she defend Mark's actions when his own words had already condemned him? A vision of the hangman's noose swung before her eyes.

Mark leaned forward in his box. ''Most worthy justices, may I speak?''

Belle frowned at him but Mark ignored her. Did the fool intend to thrust his own head into the deadly loop?

The justices conferred, then agreed.

''Tis true, I did come to Bodiam to woo Mistress Fletcher,'' he began, ''but *not* Mistress Griselda. I came to woo the Widow Fletcher—Mistress *LaBelle.*''

Belle opened her mouth but no sound came out.

Mark continued. ''When I arrived at Bodiam, I quickly discovered that Mistress Belle was under lock and key by order of Master Fletcher, as we have already heard.''

Justice Barnes waved his hand. ''Go to! Do not waste the court's time.''

Belle's ears burned. *What foul piece of tomfoolery is this?*

Mark cleared his throat. "When I discovered this dire situation, tis true that I played at wooing Mistress Griselda, but only until I had the opportunity to seek out Belle and to free her from Fletcher's tyranny. I had no intention to injure Mistress Griselda. The ashes and duckling bones were my own invention, and not LaBelle's."

Mortimer squirmed at the mention of duck bones. Belle lifted a brow. *Methinks I spy a guilty conscience, but he will never confess to it.*

A smile ruffled Mark's mouth. "The truth of the matter is that I did indeed sign a betrothal contract, but not with Master Fletcher. My contract was with the Cavendish family whom I have known and loved all my life. In short, my lords, I arrived at Bodiam Castle in early October to claim both my bride and her marriage portion."

Belle collapsed on her bench. Her head buzzed. *Please God, don't let me faint now.* She bit the inside of her cheek.

Mark looked down at her. "I fear I have taken my lawyer by surprise, your honor. I had no opportunity to acquaint him with this matter."

Belle gnashed her teeth as rage gnawed at her heart. *I will hang you myself, you traitorous dog!* So she was the rich wife Mark had bragged about, and it was Bodiam's lush fields that had been promised to him, not the acreage in Northumberland. *Oh, Papa, how could you do this to me!*

Mortimer's confident demeanor slipped askew. "Do you have this spousal contract? I demand to see it!"

"Here, my lords!" Kitt stood on his bench so that all the spectators could see him. "I am Lord Hayward's squire and I hold the document for him." He jumped down and leaned over the gallery railing. He dropped a packet into the bailiff's waiting hands.

Belle moaned under her breath. *You, too, Kitt? Is there no one left in this world who has not betrayed me?* Would she never be the mistress of her own life, but always at the beck and call of some man?

The judges slit open the waxy envelope and studied the contract. Belle gathered her robe around her, pushed herself off her bench and stalked over to her client.

"You have not won me if that's what you think," she snarled in an undertone.

Leaning down, Mark whispered. "Tis not you I want to win, but Bodiam."

A red blur clouded her vision. "Of course! I should have known!"

"Nay," the handsome viper protested. "Tis not for me but for—"

"Silence the prisoner!" bellowed Justice Noble.

Once more the guards yanked Mark away from her. He mouthed something to her but she could not decipher it, nor did she care to. She had believed too many lies from those honey-sweet lips of his.

Belle addressed the court. "Your gracious pardon, my lords. Twill not happen again, I assure you. May I beg your indulgence and see this contract for myself?"

The bailiff passed the document to her. Her heart grew heavy as lead when she read the words that bound her and her possessions over to Sir Mark Hayward. She swallowed an oath at Kitt's looping signature across the bottom. The oath changed to a muffled sob when she noticed her father's firm countersignature. Sold like a horse!

Belle returned the document to the bailiff. She had a good mind to walk out of this courtroom right now and leave Mark to his fate. Let them hang him. Then she would be free at last.

To do what? Sit in her cold, dark castle nursing her injured pride while his too-handsome body rotted away in some graveyard? Let the wretch live, but he would have to muddle through life without her.

The splatter of heavy raindrops against the thick glass windows broke her musings. She shook her head to banish any tender thoughts of him that still clung there. Justice Barnes cast a stern eye on the prisoner.

"Under your most solemn oath, do you swear that Mistress LaBelle knows of this betrothal?"

Mark's mouth twisted. "Aye, she most certainly does."

Belle glared at him. *Hedgepig!*

"And," the justice continued, "does Mistress LaBelle wear your ring of promise?"

Mark nodded. "She does indeed this very minute, your honor."

His golden ring seared Belle's finger. *Maltworm!*

Justice Barnes's grim features softened. "And have you exchanged a kiss with Mistress LaBelle to seal this agreement?"

Mark grinned. "We have indeed, your honor. Many sweet ones."

Belle's lips burned. *Thieving weasel!*

The judges again conferred in whispers. The crowded courtroom squirmed in their seats. None of them could remember such a fascinating afternoon. Mortimer mopped his face with his wrinkled handkerchief. Mark hissed for Belle's attention. She refused to glance his way.

Justice Barnes nodded to the bailiff, who rapped his staff for silence. "'Tis the opinion of this court that the estate of Bodiam Castle with its furnishings, chattel and in-come—including the aforementioned ruby brooch—belongs to Sir Mark Hayward lawfully betrothed to Mistress LaBelle Cavendish Fletcher. Furthermore, this court judges that Lord Hayward has been wrongfully and shamefully accused of diverse crimes by Master Mortimer Fletcher. Therefore, we find for the defendant. Not guilty of all charges!''

Kitt and Brandon broke into lusty cheers. The spectators stamped and hooted. Mortimer shook the railing in front of him and screamed, "Tis another plot to wrest my fortune from me!''

Justice Barnes gave him a cold look. "Do not try our patience any longer, Master Fletcher. Go back to London and consider yourself a most fortunate man. If you dare return to Sussex or ever harass Sir Mark Hayward in any manner, this court will take a serious interest in the exact nature of your late brother's death.''

Mortimer looked as if he would faint.

As soon as his guards unlocked the fetters on Mark's wrists, he pointed to Fletcher.

"I thank you, my lords, for your just verdict. Mortimer Fletcher, I give you one day and a night to vacate my house at Bodiam,'' he shouted.

The crowd cheered again.

Belle fumed. *His house already! I'll make him rue that pretty speech!*

Without further ado, the justices descended from their bench and disappeared behind closed doors. Mortimer pushed his way out of the chamber. Pandemonium erupted on all sides as the citizens of Hawkhurst and Rye jostled each other in their haste to congratulate the victor and his lawyer. Belle jammed her papers back into her case. The sooner she could flee this den, the happier she would be. She would return to London and there sort out what she intended to do with the rest of her life.

"Doctor Bartholomew!" Mark called over the heads of his admirers. "A word in private, I beg you."

Belle ignored his continued entreaties. She snatched up her case, lowered her head and elbowed her way through the mob of well-wishers. At all costs, she had to avoid not only Mark, but also her father, Kat and that wretched little brother of hers. Get out of this building, doff the confining gown in the stable where she had quartered her hired horse and be off to London. The devil take the weather! She would ride all night.

Mark caught her at the top of the stairway. "Bel... Bartholomew! A word!"

Belle twisted in his grasp. "I have nothing more to say to you."

He chuckled. "Good! Just listen for I have much to say to you."

He dragged her into an arched doorway. Jobe appeared from nowhere and stood in front of them, effectively blocking not only her escape but also the scrutiny of curious eavesdroppers. Belle twisted off his ring.

"Here!" She pressed it into his hand. "Take back your ring. I wish I could take back all those kisses as well."

Mark's dark eyes blazed. "For once in your life will you shut your mouth and open your ears? I signed that agreement for you, not for my personal gain. You told me you wanted Bodiam to be yours above all else in this world. So be it! Now you have got it, including that deuced ruby brooch. I want none of it."

She snorted. "Ha! Pigs fly in legions around chimney pots!"

He shook her shoulders. "Will you listen? That contract was given to me by Fletcher, not your father. I changed some of the wording as a safeguard to your property. If you take the time to study the document, you will see that

I changed the date to a month earlier. Kitt agreed to sign it of his own free will."

She curled her lip. "My poor little brother! You have already infected his brain with your lying tricks. My congratulations."

Mark's face hardened. "If you were truly a man I would challenge you for that remark. Unplug your ears, Belle. I love you!"

Those last words stabbed her heart. Of all the lies he had ever told her, this one was the very worst. Without thinking, she slapped him. "Go tell that to your mistress, you knave. She might believe you. I never will. You could have spared me that final perfidy. You are too cruel by half."

He released her. His face drained of all its color. "And you have no woman's heart under that lawyer's robe. Everything must be your way or no way. Your stubbornness will never let you see what is right in front of your nose. Very well. I have done with you. A clean break, Belle, for I will not let your sword pierce me again. I have suffered enough injuries for your sake already."

He clapped his hand on Jobe's shoulder. "Let us be gone, my friend. There is nothing more for us here."

"The horses await us in the stable across the square," Jobe told him.

Mark nodded, then he ducked under his friend's outstretched arm and clattered down the stairs.

Mark's sudden departure took Belle by surprise. Before she could stop him or shout to him, Jobe backed her against the paneled door.

The African's dark eyes glinted. "Did you enjoy that, Belle?"

She swallowed but refused to give way to the veiled

threat in his voice. "Aye, I relished it! Mark has no rights over me. I will not be bought and sold like a cow."

He gave her a smile without warmth. "In my homeland, a woman would consider herself most fortunate indeed if a man paid five cows for her. In your case, I might offer a goat."

Her lower lip trembled. "How very fortunate for both of us that we are not in Africa!"

"On the other hand, Mark has sacrificed everything for you." Jobe pushed his face closer to hers. "Everything. He owns nothing now but the borrowed clothing he wears, his exceedingly faithful horse—and sour memories of you."

Belle felt chilled. "I gave him back his ring. And he now has Bodiam's wealth to fill his pockets."

Jobe shook his head. "And still you do not hear what has been said to you. Mark told your parents and your brother as well as me that he does not want your pile of stones for himself—only for you. He was willing to sacrifice his freedom—even his very life to see that you got your dearest wish."

Icy fingers closed around her heart. "Papa...Papa gave him land near Wolf Hall. Mark has that."

Jobe bared his teeth. "While he sat in his cold cell, he gave back all that had been promised him by your esteemed parents. He said that his honor would not allow him to accept their generous fee since he had handled the affair so badly. I repeat—he has nothing!"

"Where will he go?" she asked in a small voice.

His eyes narrowed. "Far away from England. We will seek adventures in the wide world, enjoy good times, share much wine and many women."

Nay! her heart shouted. "Do you see this future in your land of shadows?"

Jobe's gaze pierced through her. "I know it to be true."

She tossed her head. "Mark is English. He will come home as he did before."

"But not to you," the African rumbled. "You knew him when he was a callow youth and followed your bidding like a puppy. I know him as the man he has become. He will never reappear in your life." Jobe straightened up and pulled his hood over his head. "I once told you that you would find happiness when you stopped running from yourself. Tis too bad that you are afraid, for you have tossed your happiness away like a child's broken toy. May your pride keep you warm—alone."

Pride? Alone? Memories of Mark crowded into her mind, clamoring for her attention. How he had teased her, taught her, protected her, fought with her, fought for her—and most of all, how he had loved her! He couldn't leave her now. Bodiam was nothing without Mark to share it.

Dear God, what have I done? Bunching her robe in her fists, Belle dashed ahead of Jobe and plunged down the stairs. Tears burned her eyelids. She pushed open the heavy door to the square.

The rain poured down in sheets. Shielding her eyes, she searched for Mark. There! Across the way in the semi-shelter of a narrow alley, he sat hunched over his saddle, holding the reins of Jobe's mount. While he waited, he rubbed his forearm—exactly the place where she had broken it so many years ago.

"Mark!" she shouted over the deluge. She raced across the street, slipping on the wet cobblestones. "Marcus," she said when she reached his side. She took hold of Artemis's bridle. She wouldn't let Mark ride out of her life.

He gave her a cool look. "What did you do with Jobe? Push him down the stairs?"

Belle wanted to say how sorry she was. She wanted to

thank him for everything he had done for her. To tell him how much she had loved him since she was a young child. Instead, she blurted out, "I want my ring back."

Mark wiped the rain out of his face. "Could you please repeat that?"

Swallowing, she gripped the bridle tighter. "I said I want my ring back—please, Marcus," she added. "I...I love you."

He threw his head back and laughed in her face.

The rain hid the tears that streamed down her cheeks. "I'm sorry I have been such a dolt. That I didn't listen to you. I'm sorry! I really am! Didn't you hear me? I said I love you. What the hell are you laughing at?"

Still chortling, he dismounted. "Your mustache is melting off," he said, draping his cape over her shoulders.

Belle touched her upper lip and caught the bedraggled thing before it fell to the ground. "Great Jove!" she mumbled ducking her head. "I am undone."

Mark pulled her closer to him. "I know a good lawyer if you need one," he murmured in her ear.

She glanced up. His eyes had softened into the look she had grown to love. "Then may I have my ring back? I swear I will never part with it again."

Mark cocked his brow in the most endearing fashion. "Hold, lawyer! Will my ring be received as a token of a promise to marry?"

Belle's teeth chattered. "Aye, and the sooner the better before we both die from a chill."

He pulled the circlet of gold from his little finger. "The season of Advent comes upon us quickly. If the banns are published tomorrow, we could be married in a week. If not, we must wait until Christmastide."

She held out her left hand, fingers spread wide apart. "You know I have no patience, especially when it comes to waiting for Christmas,'' she replied. ''Don't tease me so, Marcus.''

He tapped her wet nose. ''One thing more—do you also promise to be married in your shift? I will have no man say that I took you only for your wealth.''

She nodded. ''Agreed, as long as we don't get married out of doors in the middle of a snowstorm. Sweet Saint Anne, I am wet to the skin now!''

Mark slid his ring over her finger. ''Then tis a match. I would kiss you to seal our bargain but we have already attracted some attention. I don't want the good people of Rye to think that I have an unholy interest in young men.''

Belle grinned at him. What a roguish devil he was! ''Then take me home—to Bodiam.''

He lifted her into his saddle, and then mounted behind her. Jobe crossed the street and took up his reins. ''I see that we are now three,'' he remarked.

Reaching over, Belle touched his arm. ''Thank you, Jobe. I am forever in your debt.''

Mark saluted him. ''Whatever you did, my friend, you saved my life.''

Jobe flashed his broad smile. ''Exactly so!''

Mark kneed Artemis into a walk. ''I have just thought of something, my sweet,'' he said in Belle's ear.

''What?'' she asked, shivering in earnest.

''When you marry me, you will attain your heart's desire.''

She glanced over her shoulder. ''Your love?''

He chuckled. ''That as well, but I was speaking of something else. You will finally become a true lady—Lady Hayward.''

''Oh!'' Belle had never before considered that pleasing aspect. ''Twill seem very strange. You will have to teach me how to be one.''

Mark chuckled then he whispered into her ear. "I will be happy to give you the first lesson just as soon as we can find an accommodating inn and I can get you out of those wet clothes. Truly, *ma petite chou-chou,* you are far too desirable to remain a boy!"

Epilogue

November's icy rains ceased just long enough to bless Mark and Belle's nuptials with sunshine. Three days before the beginning of the Advent penitential season, the happy couple pledged their lives together in a simple but heartfelt ceremony in Bodiam's chapel. Walking slowly but without the aid of his crutches, Sir Brandon Cavendish gave away his only daughter to the one man he had always hoped she would marry. Lady Kat wept with joyful abandon. Montjoy drank a great deal of spiced wine so that Jobe had to carry him home. Stormy weather prevented Belle's half-brother Francis from crossing the Channel in time but he promised to fete the newlyweds at Christmastide when he returned from his studies in Paris.

The bride, as promised, wore only her shift, an exquisite garment of ivory linen, trimmed with lace and many colorful love knots fashioned by Ivy with a good deal of help—and hindrance—from Kitt. The legendary Cavendish brooch sparkled from Belle's bodice, but Mark had eyes only for her.

"One day our own daughter will wear it when she marries some knavish fellow," Mark told Belle much later that night when he unpinned the ruby.

Belle snuggled against her new husband. "But we don't have a daughter—yet."

"Tush, *chou-chou.*" He kissed her lips, lingering there for a delicious moment. "All things will come in good time." He drew the bed curtains tight around them to keep out the chill of the November night and to keep in the warmth of their love.

Long after midnight an elderly white-haired knight dressed in black chain mail with a black surcoat stepped silently through the stone wall near the master chamber. His spurs scraped against the floor.

"Good evening, grandfather," Jobe said, moving out of the shadows.

The knight looked at him with an expression of gentle amazement. "You can see me, Jobe?" he asked in a pleasant voice.

The African nodded. "I have observed you ever since we first came to Bodiam."

"And do you know who I am?" the knight inquired.

Jobe's grin flashed in the darkness. "Aye, venerable one. You are the builder of this keep and now its guardian spirit."

"Very good, my son," the knight agreed. "You do indeed possess the Sight."

"So my esteemed father told me," he replied. "You made a grand show when you rode your fine horse through the hall on All Hallows Eve."

The knight chuckled. "You think so? Twas the best I could do for Belle. She was always one of my favorite children."

Jobe moved closer to the ghost. "Twas you who taught her Bodiam's secrets and its hiding places?"

The knight wiggled his white mustache. "Not all my

secrets, but most of them. I was sorry when she grew older, though Kitt was good company until his parents moved north.'' He knotted his brows. ''Francis was a different kettle of fish altogether. Far too studious for his own good. He didn't believe in me, so naturally, he never saw me.''

Jobe chuckled. ''Take good cheer, grandfather, soon this old castle will ring again with the shouts of little ones.''

''Does your Sight tell you this, my son?''

''Indeed,'' Jobe replied.

The knight smiled. ''Then you have made a very old man very happy. But I see you are dressed for traveling. Whither away?''

Jobe slung his pack over his shoulder. ''This English weather chills my blood and the call of my homeland grows louder in my ears. My work here is finished. I am off to warmer climes to seek new adventures.''

The knight lifted his hand in a blessing. ''God go with you, my son.''

Jobe flashed him another grin. ''He always has so far, grandfather.'' Saluting the knight, the giant African slipped down the stairs to the courtyard where his horse pawed the ground with impatience.

The knight glided along the gallery to the alcove outside the bridal chamber. Kitt, stuffed full of gingerbread, sugared almonds, tansy cakes and wine, slumbered on his truckle bed. The knight adjusted the blanket that had slipped off the boy.

''Good evening, Dexter,'' he addressed the cat who lay curled on a pillow beside Kitt's head. ''Have you been behaving yourself as usual?''

Dexter mewed, then licked his long whiskers.

''As I thought—too many sweetmeats. Twill catch up with you one day, my friend. Sleep well.''

The cat shut his golden eyes and laid his chin on Kitt's shoulder.

The knight passed through the door to the inner chamber and hovered outside the drawn curtains of the nuptial bed. The bride and her groom slept entwined in each other's arms. The knight blessed them.

"Tis good to have you home," he said though he knew they could only hear him in their dreams. "I look forward to meeting your children."

* * * * *

Afterword

Lord and Lady Hayward enjoyed a happy married life. They had two sons, John and Thomas. Sir John Hayward married, at an early age, to a pretty maid of honor in the court of the young Queen Elizabeth. In due time, Sir John inherited Bodiam Castle with its resident ghost. His marriage, though happy, proved to be childless. The couple died together during the plague year of 1578. At that point, Bodiam Castle passed out of the Hayward family.

Sir Thomas Hayward became a valued servant of Queen Elizabeth. He too was blessed with a happy though brief marriage to a distant French cousin of Belle's Aunt Celeste Cavendish. In 1567, Thomas's young wife died during childbirth but the infant survived. The Queen graciously stood as the baby's godparent. Thereafter she took a great interest in the motherless child of her favored courtier. Thomas's daughter was named Elizabeth after her godmother and she grew up to become a charming young woman.

The story of Lady Elizabeth Hayward and her most unusual romance is recounted in *FOOL'S PARADISE*. Lady Elizabeth married her own true love in November 1586.

A year later, she proudly wore her grandmother's heir-loom—the famous Cavendish ruby and pearl brooch—when her husband was created the Earl of Fawkland.

And thereby hangs my tale.